FORGET ME NOT

THE JASON EDWARDS FBI CHRONICLES: DANGEROUS SECRETS SUSPENSE BOOK 3

RACHELLE J. CHRISTENSEN

PEACHWOOD
press

PRAISE FOR JASON EDWARDS FBI CHRONICLES

Praise for *Forget What You've Seen*

"Fans of award-winning author Rachelle Christensen will be standing in line for her latest release. With tension, action, danger, and definite hints of romance, this book represents everything we love to read."

—Tristi Pinkston, author of the Secret Sisters Mysteries

"Rachelle Christensen does it again! This book is a real page-turner with a resourceful protagonist you'll root for."

—Heather Justesen, author of *Family by Design*

Praise for *Forget What You've Heard*

"I was captivated by it from the very beginning of this high intensity thriller, until the very end. She writes with a passion and love of words that blows me out of the water. I honestly had to finish the novel all in one night, because I knew I'd never sleep if I didn't!"

--Jenni James, *author of Northanger Alibi*

"A gripping plot that revs its engines on page one, accelerates with each new chapter, and doesn't come to a stop until you close the book at its satisfying conclusion."

—ToriAnn Perkey, *editor*

"A fun, fast read! It gripped me right from the first scene and pulled me along for the ride all the way to the end!"

—Heather Justesen, author of "The Ball's in Her Court"

"Here's the exact way to turn an improbable plot into a rollicking suspense novel, full of surprises and twists, and wonderful

characterizations... Christensen keeps you on the edge of your seat."

-- Jeff Needle, book reviewer from AML

"An exciting debut novel that took me by surprise both for the quality of writing and for firmly capturing my interest in the first chapter. This is a romantic suspense novel with the emphasis on suspense and first time novelist, Christensen handles it like a pro."

--Jennie Hansen, *Meridian Magazine*, author of *If I Should Die*

ALSO BY RACHELLE J. CHRISTENSEN

Claire's Christmas Dance

Nonfiction:

What Every 6th Grader Needs to Know: 10 Secrets to Connect
Moms & Daughters

Lost Children: Coping with Miscarriage

Forget Me Not

Thrills for the Heart

FOR A LIMITED TIME

Sign up for Rachelle's
VIP Mailing List
to get your *FREE* book.

Get started here:
www.rachellechristensen.com

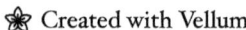

DEDICATION

To my mother, Andrea: I couldn't ask for a better mother, champion, friend, or supporter than you. You have always believed in me without a doubt and your belief has fueled the fires of my dreams. I love you more than every drop of water in the Snake River. Thank you.

NOTE TO READER

Dear Reader,

This book was originally published under the title, *River Whispers*, which won the Rone Award for Mystery! I have revised and edited this book and updated the cover to reflect those changes. I'm thrilled to include this book in the Jason Edwards FBI Chronicles as a companion novel. I think you'll like finding Jason's connection to this story. I hope you'll love the mystery that lies beneath the current in *Forget Me Not*.

Thank you for joining me on this writing journey. I hope you enjoy this book!

Rachelle

CHAPTER ONE

IN THE QUIET before Jack Bentley opened his eyes that morning, he thought he heard Gina humming. He groaned and
rolled over, cracking an eyelid at the empty side of his bed.
She wasn't there, no matter that he could have sworn he felt
her near him. Jack had never understood how much you could
miss someone until he lost her.

The sunlight slanting through the wooden blinds reflected
off the glass beads of Gina's necklace. They hung there
silently on the peg by her dresser, four necklaces, like some
sort of new age decoration for their bedroom. Jack had given
two of them to Gina for Christmas—their last one together.
He reached out with a trembling hand. A thin coating of dust
had settled on top of the blue beads. He picked them up—
they felt cool in his hands. Rubbing the dust off with the hem
of his shirt, Jack thought about putting the jewelry away. The
clothes in the closet, the purse hanging by the door, her
shower gel and bath salts. They had always been there, and
now she wasn't.

He heard a creak from Hallie's bed and glanced at his doorway as he put the necklace back on the peg. Taking in a deep breath, he moved to the one thing that kept the seams of his life from splitting wide open. His five-year-old daughter stood yawning in the doorway of her bedroom. Pink painted toenails curled into the carpet as she stretched her arms toward him.

"Mornin', Sweetheart." He picked her up and she wrapped her arms around his neck. "Did you sleep well?"

She nodded against his neck. For a moment, he wondered if he shouldn't go today. Maybe if he stayed home, he could take a day for Hallie to try to help her, but how could he help her do what he couldn't? He was tied up in knots inside from missing so much work, something completely against his nature. Worry nagged at him that he wouldn't be able to provide for Hallie. And another worry that his construction work wouldn't be enough to fill the holes in his heart.

Jack pressed his nose into his daughter's brown curls. They matched his own light brown hair, but he wondered if her hair would go darker, like Gina's, as she grew. He swallowed that thought and inhaled slowly. "Hmm, smells like a little monster in here. Should we brush it out?"

Hallie laughed—a low throaty laugh like Gina's—and Jack forced himself to smile at his daughter. "Ready to go to Grandma's today?"

Hallie nodded again. Jack set her down in the bathroom. "Hurry and get ready and I bet Grandma will have breakfast for us, okay?"

The corners of her mouth turned up slightly and she skipped into the bathroom.

Jack went through the motions of getting ready; trying to ignore the tightness in his chest every time he thought about what he would do today. The road he would travel. He hooked the belt buckle on his Wranglers and slipped on his cowboy boots. The faded brown leather needed a good polish. Gina had always reminded him of things like that before. He sucked in a breath, pursing his lips and cursing his memories —every one outlined with pain.

Hallie was quiet as usual as he loaded her into the cab of his blue Ford pickup, but no—it wasn't usual, not like Hallie had been. It was the new normal and he hated how it had stolen her little-girl grins. The silence was deafening and yet he carried it with him everywhere. Even in a crowded place, he felt the absence of Gina—her silence consumed him. Her silence wrapped Hallie in a blanket of numbness so she didn't have to face each day without her mother.

Jack drove for six minutes and pulled in front of Helen's house next to the mailbox with Rasmussen printed in blue vinyl letters. The N on the Rasmussen name was peeling and Gina would have found a way to fix it. Gina and her mother had always been close, so it was natural for Jack and Gina to find a home nearby. The distance seemed to lessen after Gina's death. Jack and Helen's grief met somewhere in the middle, neither able to overcome the sorrow of the woman they loved.

Hallie loved her grandma. Sometimes in Grandma's company the silence would break and Hallie would speak. Jack longed for his daughter to recover—to be that smiling, giggling, chatterbox he loved so much.

He knocked twice on the rickety screen door and let himself in. "Good morning," he called toward the sounds of the kitchen.

"You're just in time for pancakes. Come and pull up a chair." Helen wiped her hands on the red and white ruffled apron Gina had sewn for her.

Hallie wrapped her arms around Helen's legs and Jack

swallowed the memories bubbling from the pit of his empty stomach. "You know, I'm a bit behind, so I'll let you two eat that stack of pancakes, right Hallie?" He winked, and she climbed up in the chair and picked up her fork.

Helen laughed. "At least take one of my blueberry muffins and a banana." She grabbed a napkin and handed him the food.

"Thank you." Jack squeezed her hand. He kissed the top of Hallie's head. "Be a good girl for Grandma."

She nodded and Jack waved as he headed for the door. Helen followed him. "Don't worry. Hallie will be just fine."

Jack hesitated. "That's what the doctors keep telling me. They say she'll talk in her own time, but I do worry."

"I know, and that's normal." Helen smoothed out the ruffles on her apron again and tucked a strand of dark hair streaked with white behind her ear. "It's four months today, isn't it?" The tears gathered in her eyes as she asked the question she already knew the answer to. "I miss her so much."

"Me too." Jack tried not to think about how Gina had the same blue eyes as her mother. "I don't know what we'd do without you."

"I could say the same," Helen whispered.

Helen put her arms around Jack's middle and hugged him. His mother-in-law was just over five feet tall, so he always felt like a giant, leaning his six-foot-one frame over for a hug. "I'll try not to be too late," he said.

"Don't worry," Helen murmured, releasing him and patting his arm. "We'll be fine."

Jack nodded and hurried out to his truck. His eyes burned; and the broken edges of his heart seemed especially sharp today. He tried to do one of the relaxing breathing cycles his pastor had taught him, but he winced as the anguish tightened his lungs.

On the freeway toward Idaho Falls, his eyes flicked toward the low-hanging gray clouds in the distance. He set the cruise control and drove in silence, his lips moving in a wordless prayer—the same petition he sent up to the heavens every day. *Please, Lord, help me get through this day.*

He left the Snake River behind him for now, but it would crisscross over fields and sagebrush to eventually catch up with him again on his drive. Growing up in Heyburn, Idaho, Gina and Jack had spent their summers swimming in the Snake. Whether it was the actual river or one of dozens of irrigation canals spawning from the mammoth waterway, he'd never feared it. Jack Sr. owned a small fishing boat and one of Gina's favorite memories was when Jack had taken her out on a date and the motor had failed in the middle of Lake Walcott. Jack swam nearly a half-mile towards shore before he was able to flag someone down to help them.

The memories overtook the pain, and for a moment he was so immersed in them he didn't realize how quickly the bridge was approaching. This was the first time he'd attempted the commute since the accident. As a partner in a large construction firm, it was expected that much of his work was spread across the different sites he managed. He'd been fortunate to rely on others and do most of his work from home over the past few months, but there were several things that needed his personal attention and time this month. One of those was the progress of the side-by-side potato cellars going in on the Whitman farms. Each cellar was roughly the size of a football field and would be filled with potatoes stacked nearly twenty feet high. The construction check on the mammoth cellars couldn't be neglected. And so with gut-wrenching anxiety he was headed down the same path that he'd made hundreds of times over the past ten years. His regular schedule included a day trip to the Idaho

5

Falls area once a week, a two-hour commute from his home in Heyburn. He visited clients, interviewed contractors and usually took someone to lunch before checking construction sites and the progress they were supposed to be making.

Jack hadn't planned on stopping, but just before he reached the bend in the road that connected to the bridge, he saw a flash of yellow—someone standing near the edge of the river. The tires squealed as he slammed on his brakes and pulled to the side of the road.

It was Gina. She wore the same clothes she had on when they pulled her from the river. But it was just his mind playing tricks on him, wasn't it? He looked toward the water and saw her yellow blouse, the one with the silver buttons. She was barefoot, wearing tan capris, her hair dripping wet. Gina looked out toward the river as if searching for something.

Jack jumped from the truck and ran toward her, climbing over the railing on the freeway. He'd longed for a chance to see her, just one more time. She was there in front of him. All he wanted to do was hold her. Jack stumbled and looked down to find sure footing. When he looked back up, she was gone. The pain of losing her hit him full force and he slumped to the ground. Gina was gone. Jack knew that, but he couldn't resist looking for her. He rubbed at his eyes with the palms of his hands. An eighteen wheeler rumbled by, the smell of exhaust lingering in the air for a moment before Jack's nostrils filled with the familiar odor of moss tangled along the riverbank. He struggled to breathe, his mind circling around what must have been a grief-induced hallucination.

He sat there, his chest heaving, forcing down the hot ball of tears working its way up his throat when a memory assaulted him. A tiny bundle with blue booties and dark hair nestled against Gina's breast. His son. It was Easton who always brought the tears to Jack's eyes. His son, his little miracle, fit so perfectly in Gina's arms.

After Hallie was born, Gina yearned for another baby, but after trying for three years, the doctors told her the endometriosis had overtaken one ovary, and the other fallopian tube was nearly blocked by scar tissue. They recommended a hysterectomy when they detected endometrial tissue on her kidneys. Gina begged for another chance. She went through another round of laparoscopic surgeries to clear out the endometriosis and went on a strict diet. A year later, she still wasn't pregnant. Jack had done his best to console her, and Gina kept up smiles for Hallie, but he could see her pain.

They put away the crib and sold the other baby items. The following month, Gina surprised him with a brightly wrapped present that held three positive pregnancy tests. Easton was born eight months later, healthy, and sporting a few fat rolls at nine pounds, five ounces, and twenty-one inches long. He'd never seen Gina so happy. She loved her family, but it wasn't complete without Easton.

Jack buried his face in his hands as the horrible sensation of loss washed over him. For a moment he thought about heading back home, but then he heard something. Lifting his head, he saw the branches of the Russian olive tree drifting lazily in a breeze. It wasn't the wind. The traffic zoomed on behind him, but that wasn't the sound he searched for. He wasn't even sure he'd heard it, maybe he'd just felt it. He stopped and shook his head. What was wrong with him? One of his friends had told him how crazy she'd felt when her husband died. Jack wondered if he'd finally cracked.

Jack.

The hair on the back of his neck stood up and gooseflesh

scattered down his arms. Crazy or not, it was Gina's voice. He had longed to hear her voice again, prayed for even a chance to dream of her, but there had been nothing. He stood, brushing the dirt from his pants and stared at the water churning twenty-five feet away. Each step brought him closer to the scene of the accident. He walked carefully toward the edge of the river, lost in tortured memories.

May fourteenth was not a typical day for a rainstorm in the Idaho desert, but four months ago they'd received an inch of rain in two hours. Gina had been on her way to meet him for lunch; an unexpected errand had brought her along the same path as his commute and so they'd planned a date. Hallie was at preschool. Seven-month-old Easton was asleep in the back seat, buckled into his car seat snug and warm.

The police officer had told Jack that Gina's silver Camry was approaching the bridge when a pickup crossed the median and T-boned her. The force, matched with the freeway speeds, pushed Gina's car into a roll off the road and into the raging waters of the Snake River.

"No, I can't do this today," Jack mumbled. He scrubbed at his eyes and took a ragged breath. His clients would understand, but it'd be hard on Toby. Toby Harmon was the owner of the construction firm and he'd covered for Jack since Gina and Easton's death. Maybe Jack should try again next week. He turned to walk back toward his truck, uncertain as to what had just happened.

His mind felt foggy, buzzing with energy when a memory overcame him. He shook his head, but the images were vibrant and clear. Gina rocked Easton in the recliner, cuddling him, humming a melody that vibrated against the crown of his head. Easton sighed in his sleep, his perfect mouth sucking at his fist. Jack's senses were jumbled but then he realized the memory wasn't his, it was Gina's. An overpowering feeling of love blocked out any noise from traffic, the rushing river, the whisper of wind. The only sense Jack had was of Gina's love for Easton.

He's alive.

CHAPTER TWO

"WHAT? GINA?" Jack spun around, searching frantically for the source of her voice. His heart ached while at the same time love filtered through his body.

I'm here.

This time Jack closed his eyes. *Gina?* He asked in his mind.

Easton is alive.

"No, Gina. He's—he's dead," Jack spoke aloud and slumped to the ground. A dirt clod loosened and bumped into the water's edge. Jack bowed his head against his knees and gritted his teeth. For the thousandth time he asked, "Why couldn't it have been me? Hallie needs her mother. And Easton."

A memory from Gina invaded his mind, and it was so forceful that he gasped. It was the middle of the night and Easton was about four months old and being fussy. Jack walked the floors humming and patting Easton's back. A fire engine had roared past their house, sirens wailing and Easton had started crying again. It had taken Jack another forty-five minutes to settle him down. Gina had found Jack sleeping in the recliner with Easton sleeping peacefully on his chest.

He's alive and you must find him.

Jack felt sick to his stomach. He didn't understand what was happening. Was he really hearing Gina? And if so, then why wasn't Easton with her?

He remembered how his friend Vincent, a County Sheriff in Idaho Falls, had explained their findings as well as their questions about the accident.

The driver's side door had been smashed in from the collision, pinning Gina inside. As the car sunk into the frigid waters, the current moved it toward the western bank of the river. What had baffled police was the missing car seat. When they pulled Gina's body from the wreckage, they fully expected to find Easton. Instead, they found only the base of his car seat still buckled in the middle of the back seat.

Search and Rescue didn't recover Easton's body, but they did find his car seat tangled in the bushes about a half mile downstream. The top part of the harness was still buckled together. No one could figure out how the car seat had made it out of the vehicle, but they guessed that Easton's body had slipped out of the restraints because the leg harness wasn't buckled together.

None of it made sense to Jack, his wife drowning in her car—an excellent swimmer trapped in a metal grave. His baby boy floating somewhere in the river, finally settling to the bottom of the tangles of moss growing on the riverbed. But the car seat made the least sense of all. Gina was the most conscientious mother he knew. She *always* buckled the kids in; even to go the four blocks to Hallie's preschool. Those car seats were a pain in the neck, but Gina was religious about her children's safety. So what had happened that rainy day in May?

Find Easton.

Jack turned in a full circle, surveying the area. He was alone. "Gina," he whispered. Then he cleared his throat and spoke louder, "Easton drowned on May fourteenth. We couldn't find his body. I'm sorry honey, but he's not here." He listened and then began walking up the riverbank.

Suddenly everything was still. Jack turned around. The leaves hung silently on the branches, even the river seemed to slow to a whisper. For a moment, he thought he heard one sound in the silence: Gina was crying.

When a gust of wind blew sand in his eyes, Jack hurried back to his truck. He looked toward the river for a few more moments and then pulled back onto the freeway. It was already eight-thirty; he'd be late for his nine o'clock appointment. For the hundredth time, he wondered if he should just turn around and go home.

Instead Jack pushed the voice activation button on his console. "Call Alex."

"Hey, Jack," Alex answered on the first ring, his voice chipper. "Looking forward to seeing you today."

"Yeah, I'm running a little behind. Can we push our meeting back thirty minutes?"

"Sure thing. That works. I'm running to another meeting now."

"Thanks man."

Jack's mind churned like the river water and he sped up, increasing the distance between him and the serpentine course of the water. The image of Gina standing by the river burned in his mind and he struggled to shift his focus to something, anything to free his thoughts from that mournful cry he'd heard.

His next counseling appointment wasn't until Friday. He'd cancelled the last two, hating the way he felt so vulnerable in front of Dr. Radkin. But she'd been patient with him, continually encouraging him to come for the sake of Hallie. Maybe he should see if she had an earlier appointment. Jack clenched his jaw and turned on the radio.

He thought of his friend, Jason Edwards, the FBI agent who lived in Utah who had come up on his own time to search the area looking for signs of what might have happened to Easton. Jason hadn't been satisfied with the outcome of the investigation. He had even wondered about foul play, and especially didn't accept Easton's missing body. But after a week of searching, even Jason had considered the tragic turn of events and offered his condolences. "I wish it wasn't the case," he had said as he patted Jack on the back, "but sometimes nothing makes sense."

What would Jason say if Jack called to tell him about seeing Gina by the river? Jack shook his head and focused on the road. Only twenty more minutes until he could get out of his truck and put the morning behind him. He checked his reflection in the rearview mirror—hopefully his dark brown eyes would hide the turmoil inside.

Alex Whitman met him at the door of Whitman Farming Enterprises—a huge business running nearly three hundred thousand acres of farmland. His light brown hair was trimmed short and he had a pair of sunglasses on top of his head. He and Alex had been friends before they worked together and their business association had added another layer to their friendship that Jack appreciated. "I'm glad you could make it in today, Jack."

Jack nodded and shook Alex's outstretched hand. "Me, too," he forced himself to say. Alex didn't ask how Jack was doing; he'd done plenty of that over the phone for the past four months. Instead, he rubbed his hand along the stubble on his chin, a nervous gesture Jack recognized.

"Stan has been worrying like crazy about the cellars, but we're going to make it, right?"

Jack nodded. "I know it's been hard working with the delay and I apologize because it is my fault, but my team has been great. You're in good hands."

"That's what I've been trying to tell Stan." Alex wasn't even thirty and had been working for his uncle Stan for over a decade already. He worked alongside his brothers and cousins to increase production of potatoes and grain in the Snake River Valley. Jack had been working with Whitman farms for the past six years as they continually expanded their operations. He liked the Whitmans. Their down to earth nature made them easy to work with, and they always sent him home with a box of potatoes in the fall.

"The presentation for the Idaho Potato Council is coming up and Raymond wants to make sure the north cellar will be ready for a tour," Alex said.

"I spoke with the foreman and he said that shouldn't be a problem as long as they're finished with the ductwork," Jack replied.

Jack went over the timeline for completion of the potato cellar and talked about future plans with Alex for the next thirty minutes. After Jack double-checked the progress on the cellar, he walked with Alex out to the potato packing plant. They'd finished up construction on that project two years before.

There was a brisk wind, and Jack inhaled, noting the lingering scent of freshly tilled soil. The harvest season had been Gina's favorite time of year. His face tightened and he took another breath. October would be upon him before he knew it, and he didn't feel ready to face the memories of autumn without Gina.

Alex looked over at him with an anxious expression. "Jack, I hope you'll forgive me for giving out advice, but it just won't leave me alone."

Jack braced himself. "Okay."

"How do I say this?" Alex rubbed a hand over his face. "Maybe I shouldn't."

"Just say it, man," Jack replied. "I can handle it."

"Well, it's weird but it just keeps bothering me, so I guess I'll tell you." Alex paused outside the door to the packing plant. "You can have your grief, but don't hold on to it too tight. You can have love in your life again."

"Really? Four months out and this is the advice you're giving?" Jack bit his lip before he could say more.

"I know, I know," Alex held up his hands. "Believe me, if I felt like I had a choice I wouldn't say anything, but I'm worried for you. You look like you're holding onto that pain for all you're worth."

"Maybe because I don't have anything else to hold onto." Jack clenched his hands into tight fists.

"Counseling is good and all, but it can't release the stranglehold this has on you." Alex looked him in the eyes and shook his head.

Jack could see that Alex really cared about him. Alex had always been a good friend, and this advice was coming from his heart, however misdirected. It was like what Dr. Radkin had told him, "People just don't know what to say. They're hurting too, so they often say something that makes them feel better instead of the person mourning. People don't like it when the world doesn't make sense so they try to find some justification and make the grieving person swallow it."

Jack remembered her counsel with a tightening in his

shoulders, but when he glanced at Alex, he relaxed. His friend looked like he was in pain as he clasped and unclasped his hands.

"I guess I felt like I should tell you because if you keep your eyes shut tight, always cringing when someone looks your way, you might miss something important." Alex hesitated, he looked so young and suddenly Jack felt old. "I shouldn't have said anything," he muttered.

Jack patted Alex on the back. "No worries. You can always be honest with me."

Alex studied Jack's face and then smiled. "Let's go get those spuds."

Jack thought about what Alex had said for several miles on his drive to the next construction site. Was he missing something important? He still didn't know what to make of his episode by the river earlier—having a conversation of sorts with his dead wife. It would be nice if he could blame it on medication, but when Dr. Radkin had offered antidepressants he'd refused. Everything he was feeling—hearing—in his brain was his own brand of crazy. He'd wished for a second chance to talk to Gina so many times that now his mind was granting the request for him. But if he was being truthful, that didn't make sense either. It had been so real.

He chewed on his thumbnail as he drove, worrying out the situation in his mind. If he cut out the crazy notions and just reviewed what he *thought* had happened earlier, then maybe he *had* seen something. Gina had been standing by the riverbank. The way the ends of her hair curled up when it was wet reminded him of the many times he'd watched her twisting the strands as she read her favorite mystery novels. She had been leaning forward on the balls of her feet, looking out toward the river, and then before he'd stumbled she had turned to look at him. The way her eyes had widened in recognition—the crystal blue color pulling him forward—it all seemed like a dream now. But he was wide awake.

Jack let his mind open to the dark corridor where he kept his anguished feelings blocked. He hadn't properly grieved for his son—it was too overwhelming. He figured most people felt the same, because they usually talked about Gina with tears in their eyes, but they choked on the words they wanted to say about Easton. Babies aren't supposed to drown, and they aren't supposed to die. Easton should have been approaching his first birthday, ready to gobble down some cake while treating everyone to his contagious giggles.

A pain shot through Jack's middle. This was why he didn't let himself venture into that dark part of his mind. How would he ever have enough strength to deal with the death of his wife and son? The pain colored every part of his world and it shamed him that he didn't know how to help Hallie deal with it either. Five years old was too young to carry the burden that she kept strapped tightly to her heart. At first she'd asked about Easton constantly, "Why isn't he sleeping with Mommy?"

Her little mind had accepted that Mommy was asleep and would never wake up from her pretty silk bed. Hallie had watched the coffin carried to the gravesite, still asking, "Where is Easton?" Then she stopped asking, nearly stopped talking altogether. For the past five weeks, she'd said less than a hundred words. The silence permeated the house.

Jack recalled Gina's voice, urgent in his mind this morning. *Easton is alive. You must find him.*

If only she were right.

CHAPTER THREE

EMILY GRAY PULLED her blonde hair into a ponytail and splashed her face with cool water. Last night's dream still clung to the edges of her consciousness and she found herself thinking about Gina again. She missed her best friend, her old college roommate, the girl who could make anyone smile. Gina had been happy in her life. It wasn't fair that she was gone. At the funeral, Gina's husband had been torn up, unable to really carry on much of a conversation, and Emily's heart went out to him. She'd always viewed him as ruggedly handsome, strong, and capable, but on that day he'd seemed a shell of his former self.

Last week Emily had seen Jack and Hallie walking into the grocery store in Burley and she thought he looked better, but the endearing smile he'd always worn was missing. But then Jack had boosted Hallie up into his arms and a flicker of a smile had appeared. Jack was always so sweet with Hallie—a good father who was probably doing his best to hold the pieces of his life together. Emily shook her head. Why was she thinking about Gina's husband? He was kind and good-looking, but definitely off-limits right now when he was still coping with the loss of his wife.

Turning back to the dresser she had been painting, Emily struggled to focus on the details of roses she had painted on the knobs. Jack had brought Gina red and white roses once when they were dating. Emily squeezed her eyes shut and groaned. She knew the reason Jack kept coming to mind, but she wasn't ready to admit it yet. If she could just forget the dream and Gina's request, she could go on with her day. She rolled her shoulders back and picked up her paintbrush.

Jack made it through the rest of his checkpoints on the construction sites and even met with a few clients. They were kind and offered their condolences again but they all looked at him with the same expression, one that held hurt and disbelief that life could be so unfair. And along with that expression he often sensed a flicker of relief that if something so terrible had happened to Jack, it meant they might have escaped the wrath of fate.

Most people didn't know that Easton's body had never been recovered, but those who did understood. All a person need do was stand at the bank of the Snake and watch its unforgiving current to know how easily something could slip into the murky depths and never be seen again.

When Jack got home at nine o'clock that night, Hallie was asleep and Helen was dozing in the recliner, a book open on her chest. She had brought Hallie to his house so his little girl could sleep in her own bed. It was a kindness Hallie needed as she had always struggled with nightmares and losing half her family only heightened the problems. Jack approached Helen and tapped her shoulder.

Her eyelids fluttered and then she sat upright. "Goodness, I wonder how long I've been out. Is Hallie still sleeping?"

"She's fine," Jack said. "It looks like you've been working too hard." Jack motioned to the kitchen and living room. He could see that Helen had spent time dusting and tidying up. "Thank you."

"My pleasure." Helen closed her book and stood. "Hallie was so sweet today."

"Did she say anything?"

Helen's brows furrowed. "No, and I didn't push her. She seemed happy though."

Jack nodded. "Well, thank you again."

"How did it go?"

"It was difficult, but I'm glad I went. There were several things that needed my personal attention. Toby has been patient but I could tell he was glad I came in."

"Jack?" Helen scrutinized him. "Are you going to be okay tonight?"

She was just like her daughter. Gina could always tell when something was bothering him. He forced a smile for Helen. "Dealing with lots of memories today, but yes, I'll make it."

"See you for dinner on Sunday?"

"Sounds great."

He hugged Helen and helped her out to the car. After she drove away, Jack switched off the lights and sat in the darkened living room for a few minutes. When the image of Gina wouldn't leave his mind, he clicked on the TV to drown out the beat of his aching heart.

Jack awoke to a small hand patting his cheek. He opened his eyes and flinched when he met the gaze of Hallie standing at the edge of his bed. She grinned and patted his cheek again. Jack sat up and pulled Hallie onto the bed, cradling her.

"Good morning, Sweetheart. Did you sleep well?"

Hallie looked up at him, her dark eyes luminous. "Mommy sang to me last night."

Jack sucked in a breath, struggling for a response. Hallie had just spoken a full sentence—more words than he'd heard from her in over a month. His mind whirred with the counsel the doctors had given about not getting too excited when she spoke again—just act normal. Hallie was studying him, waiting for a response.

"That's nice, what did she sing?"

"The kookaburra song."

Jack smiled. Hallie loved it when Gina sang her the traditional Australian folk song about a bird sitting in a gum tree.

"Daddy?"

Again, Jack's chest tightened as he approached the conversation he'd been praying for—any words from his daughter.

"Mommy told me that Easton needs us. She said to tell Daddy to find him." Hallie sat up and looked him in the eyes. "Daddy, where is Easton?"

Jack opened his mouth, but no words would come. He closed his eyes before Hallie could see the pain in them. He felt her little hand on his cheek again.

"Mommy said to tell you she loves you and you need to find Easton."

"Oh, Hallie." Jack pulled his daughter to his chest. "I'm so sorry this happened. Easton isn't here, sweetheart. He is in heaven with Mom."

"But Mommy didn't have him."

Hallie slid off his lap and stood next to the bed, her eyes scrunched in frustration. Jack's throat tightened. He wanted to be angry; he wanted to swear, scream, anything to make

Hallie understand. Instead he brushed a curl behind her ear and leaned down to her level. "That was just a dream. I've dreamed of Mommy too. My heart is really sad and I miss Mommy and Easton so much. I know you feel the same way. Sometimes the dreams come to help us feel better."

Hallie stomped her foot. "No, Daddy! It wasn't a dream. I opened my eyes and Mommy was there singing to me. She told me it was important. She said, 'Make Daddy listen—find Easton.'" Her bottom lip trembled and tears spilled down her cheeks. "Why won't you look for Easton?"

Jack felt like he'd been slapped. He couldn't take this anymore. "Daddy has to shower. Go get dressed, Hallie." He grabbed his clothes and headed for the bathroom.

"Then can we go and look for Easton?"

The door clicked shut on her last sentence. Jack turned the water on, stripped down, and stepped inside the shower. He choked on the scream he'd held back and pounded his fists on the wall.

CHAPTER FOUR

"I'm ready to find Easton," Hallie said as soon as Jack exited his bedroom. She was dressed in a mismatched set of purple capris and a red shirt.

Jack swallowed and then knelt next to Hallie and hugged her. "Daddy's having a hard time today, Sweetie. I won't be able to help you. There isn't time before kindergarten." She had afternoon kindergarten and it was the best excuse Jack could come up with at the moment.

"I can miss school today. I already know my colors." Hallie looked at him eagerly.

"Daddy needs to go to the doctor today. Let's talk later about this." Jack turned and headed for the fridge. While he poured Hallie a bowl of cereal, he called Dr. Radkin's office and asked if he could move his Friday appointment up. He took the first opening they had at one-thirty that afternoon. Hopefully she wouldn't commit him after he told her what was going on.

All morning long Jack attempted to distract Hallie from searching for Easton. He kept checking the clock, 12:15

couldn't come soon enough. He dropped Hallie off for kinder-garten and drove slowly toward the red brick office building in Burley that housed the Snake River Counseling offices. He waited for ten minutes trying to fold himself quietly into a corner of the cramped waiting room, hating that he felt self-conscious about being there. It was a relief to sink into the ugly pink floral couch in Dr. Radkin's office and escape the consoling smiles of the receptionist.

"It's good to see you, Jack." Dr. Radkin shook his hand and then sat in a wingback chair near the sofa. "Tell me how things are going."

Jack liked his therapist. She didn't expect him to be cheer-ful, and her own demeanor was mild and straight-forward. She was probably in her fifties and kept her dark red hair cut short above her shoulders.

"I'm glad that I could get in to talk to you. I've been surviving, but I drove to Idaho Falls yesterday for the first time since Gina died. It was tougher than I expected."

"It's good to hear you're getting back to work." Dr. Radkin made a note on her legal pad. "Tell me about what made the day difficult."

With a deep breath, Jack launched into the events of the day before and then blurted out Hallie's upsetting dream. "I was so frustrated with her and I didn't know how to deal with everything that seemed to be happening at once." Jack paused and shook his head. "I mean, I felt like I was going crazy yesterday and then to have Hallie come at me with the same kind of stuff about finding Easton. What does it mean?"

Dr. Radkin studied Jack for a moment before answering, "You're not crazy. I'm not sure why you're processing things in this manner, but it's not necessarily unhealthy or abnormal. You'll suffer from a certain lack of closure over Easton's death because you didn't get to see his body."

Jack tried not to wince as he imagined the swirling waters of the river and Easton's once-happy grin.

"It might be helpful to write some of these things down," Dr. Radkin continued. "Allow yourself to experience the emotions, whatever they may be."

"What about Hallie though?"

"For now, don't argue with her. Just listen to her and see if you can use the dream as a talking point to delve deeper and find out what is most distressing to her. It's very likely that you're both suffering from the same problem with closure over Easton's death."

"But she kept asking me when we could go look for Easton." Jack leaned forward and put his head in his hands.

"If you don't know what to say, then give her a hug. Offer to sing her a lullaby. If you think it's best, be honest with her and tell her you just don't know what to do right now." She cleared her throat. "You're doing a great job with everything you have on your plate, Jack. Don't be too hard on yourself."

Jack looked up and met Dr. Radkin's gaze. "Thank you."

Dr. Radkin gave Jack a few articles to read to help with grief in young children and encouraged him to come back in two weeks for another appointment. He nodded, took the papers, but didn't schedule another visit. In the back of his mind, he hoped that things would somehow get back to normal soon.

Hallie didn't speak to Jack after he picked her up from school. The tightness in his chest increased. Dr. Radkin had told him to listen closely to Hallie but not to indulge her wishful dreams about Easton.

He tried engaging her in conversation during dinner, but Hallie kept quiet. It wasn't the same silence though. Jack could tell she was upset about her dream, but he wasn't ready to broach the delicate subject again.

They watched one of Hallie's favorite movies and she giggled a few times, but didn't speak anymore. After they got ready for bed, Jack read her a story and tucked her in with tickles on her bare feet. Hallie squealed once and then hid her feet under the covers.

"Hallie, I'm sorry that I couldn't be with you today. I hope you know Daddy loves you very much."

Hallie turned toward the wall clutching her teddy bear. Jack sighed and kissed her forehead. "Sweet dreams." He closed her door halfway and walked quietly down the hall. Instead of staying up late, avoiding his feelings with the TV, Jack took a sleeping pill and went to bed early.

Easton's cry brought Jack out of the realms of a deep sleep. He jumped out of bed, but stopped. Grief crashed down around him and he slid back on the bed. His body shook with ragged breaths. He felt as if each inhalation scorched his lungs as he fought against the pain of his loss. They were gone.

He checked on Hallie. Her breathing, slow and even, reminded him of the way Gina used to sleep. The clock's red numbers marked the time and they flashed to 1:09. The back of his throat burned, and he coughed back the ball of tears trying to inch up his throat as he burrowed into the covers. When he turned over, he caught a whiff of Gina's scent. Squeezing her pillow to his chest, he closed his eyes and tried to fall asleep.

His mind filled with Gina. She was holding Easton, and his head rested on her shoulder. She rocked back and forth humming deep in her throat. She had told Jack the baby could feel the vibrations of song as well as hear his mother's voice in the womb. Her love of Easton was so powerful. She hugged their sweet baby—no, clutched him—tightly as if the moment would slip away if she didn't hold tight enough. Then she moved from a hum to a gentle crooning; a lullaby about sweet dreams filled the room.

You have to find our baby. Find Easton.

Jack groaned and rolled over on his back. He gazed up at the ceiling, collecting his thoughts and reliving the memory. It was odd to dream a memory, everything was so vivid. It made his ache for Gina unbearable. He got up and swished cold water in his mouth, then stared at his shadowed reflection in the mirror.

Was the pain in his eyes visible to everyone else?

Jack drank more water, wiped his face and then padded softly to check on Hallie. She still clutched her teddy bear, sleeping peacefully. Jack returned to his room and pulled the comforter around him. He slept fitfully the rest of the night, almost afraid to dream or remember anything else. When the morning sun streamed through his window, the fresh smell of baby shampoo tickled Jack's nose. Before he could stop it, another memory from Gina crashed in on him. His sweet wife held Easton wrapped in a fuzzy yellow duck towel. She kissed the top of his head and inhaled. The clean scent filled the room and Jack saw Easton smile, his two bottom teeth poking up from pink gums.

Easton had been working on getting two more teeth when he—*No!* Jack heard Gina's voice in his head. *Easton is alive!*

"He's not," Jack cried out. "He's gone." For a moment Jack thought he heard her sobs and he looked up. The aroma of baby shampoo lingered in the air. The room was empty. Jack was alone. Would he always be tormented by this loss? It was different than grief—it was as if Gina were pressing her memories on him—as if she haunted him.

He got up, showered, and dressed before Hallie awoke. She was still subdued during breakfast. Once or twice she looked at Jack as if she wanted to say something, but then she looked down and continued slurping her cereal.

"Let's go to the park today and rake up a pile of leaves for you to jump in," Jack said as they cleared the breakfast dishes.

"Really?" Hallie jumped up and down, her chubby cheeks lifting into a grin.

"Yes. Go brush your teeth and I'll get the rakes." It was a good idea to leave the house and the oppressive memories weighing down on him and Hallie. He tossed a large fan rake into the bed of his truck and a purple child-sized rake for Hallie. He went back in the house, tidied up the kitchen and pocketed a few packs of gummies for a snack.

"Can I bring my bear?" Hallie asked.

"You're in charge."

She skipped to the garage and he buckled her in before driving six blocks to the nearest park. The air was crisp and Jack breathed in the chill, shaking off the grogginess of last night's interrupted sleep.

They raked leaves and Jack tossed Hallie into a big pile, laughing at her squeals. She played on the jungle gym while Jack checked a few emails on his phone. They'd been playing for nearly an hour and it was almost time to get Hallie home and ready for school. "You ready to go, sweetheart?"

Hallie approached the bench Jack was sitting on. He smiled, but her expression was nervous. "Daddy, I don't want to make you sad."

Jack held out his arms and pulled her into his lap. "You never make me sad, Hallie. I love you."

Hallie peered up at him, wispy strands of her hair floating on the breeze. "I want to tell you what Mommy said, but it will make you sad."

Jack had to be strong for his daughter, so he took a breath and forced out the right words. "Hallie, you can tell me anything and I'll do my best to be happy."

Her voice was barely above a whisper, "Mommy said, 'Don't give up. Help Daddy find Easton.'"

Jack cuddled Hallie. Only five years old. He tried to think of what to say, how to explain to her that Easton was gone. As soon as the thought entered his mind, Gina was there; he could sense her presence.

"Why are you haunting us?" He whispered, "You took Easton—isn't that enough?"

No! He felt more than heard her response and then she was crying again. A feeling impressed upon Jack of the care Gina took to always buckle the kids in tight. Jack shook his head—why hadn't she buckled Easton in the rest of the way that day? Or was there something faulty with the car seat?

No.

He felt the answer again and clutched Hallie tight to his chest.

CHAPTER FIVE

THE NEXT DAY Jack refused to feel or think anything about Gina. Hallie went to kindergarten and he buried himself in his work. Jack had almost finished checking through the last of the reports from his foreman when the phone rang.

"Hi, Jack?"

"Yes?"

"This is Emily Gray, Gina's old roommate."

Jack paused for a moment, trying to place the voice. He turned around and saw the framed picture of Gina and her three best friends, all roommates at Idaho State University. "Um, yeah. I remember." He squinted, picking out Emily right in the middle of the photo. She had short blonde hair that just brushed the tops of her shoulders. Her smile was wide and laughing, and it made her almond-shaped eyes almost disappear next to Gina's wide blue eyes.

"It's been a while. Gina was always good to come see me when I lived in Shelley."

"That's right. How are you doing? You're in Declo now,

aren't you?" Jack remembered how excited Gina had been that Emily was moving only fifteen minutes from them.

"Yes, I finally came back home." An uncomfortable silence passed. "Look, I'm sorry to call like this but I just keep thinking of Gina lately and well, I wanted to know if I could help you, uh, finish painting Hallie's room."

"Hallie's room? But how did you—"

"I'm a decorator and I paint murals. I promised Gina I would help her and then things got busy with the move. It took a lot longer than I hoped to sell the house after my divorce or I would've moved here long ago. I've been here almost six months and still feel like I'm settling in."

Jack cringed, the memories coming back to him. Gina had come to him in tears telling him all about her best friend Emily and how her lousy scumbag of a husband didn't want her to have kids because it would ruin her figure. Then she found out he was cheating on her. Emily was a couple years younger than Gina—only twenty-nine and she'd been divorced for almost two years.

"Uh, that might be nice." Jack thought about Hallie's room. Gina had been in the process of painting it. All the pictures had been removed, the old wallpaper stripped and a fresh coat of paint applied in robin's egg blue. Hallie had been so excited about the tree that Gina had told her about. He remembered now that she'd talked about having Emily paint a tree in the corner with birds and a rainbow. He could still recall how excited Hallie had been. "She's going to paint a rainbow too! And some clouds and flowers, and a bunny."

Emily cleared her throat. "I should have called sooner. How are you holding up?"

"It's been really hard. I went back to work, drove over the bridge." He leaned back in his chair, wondering why he'd just shared that bit of information with Emily.

He heard a gasp. "I'm sorry. That must have been so difficult."

Jack nodded. "I'm okay now. Everything has changed so much."

"I miss Gina. My memories of her seem so vivid the past few days."

Something in Emily's voice caught Jack's attention and before he could overthink things, he blurted out, "Hallie told me yesterday that she saw Gina in a dream or something."

"Oh?"

There was a note of something in Emily's voice, but Jack couldn't figure out what it was—curiosity or surprise?

"Jack, do you think I could come over today and take some measurements?"

"Today?"

"Yes. I know it's sudden, but I want to do this for Gina, for you, and Hallie."

Jack moved some papers and looked at his calendar even though he knew it was blank, just as the past four months had been. "Uh, okay. What time were you thinking?"

"I have an appointment at three, so how about if I come after that?" Emily asked.

"Sure, I should be back from picking Hallie up from kindergarten."

"See you then."

Jack hung up the phone and stood there for a moment trying to figure out what had just happened. Maybe this was Emily's way of coping with Gina's death. If so, he would try to understand. Besides, it might help distract Hallie from her mission to find Easton.

∿

When the doorbell rang at four-thirty, Jack felt a thread of anxiety running down his back. It had been a tough day and he didn't want to break down in front of Emily. He hesitated for three counts and then opened the door. Emily's blonde hair was pulled back into a ponytail; her hair had grown longer making her appear younger than he remembered. He hadn't seen her since the funeral and most of that time was a painful blur of black and gray colors tinged with sadness. Today Emily wore a pair of skinny jeans and a green t-shirt that highlighted the color of her eyes. Jack almost smiled when he thought of all the times Gina had talked about her best friend Emily and the fun times they'd had.

"Hi, come on in."

"Thank you." As Emily walked past him the hair on Jack's arms stood on end. The back of his neck tingled and she stopped mid-stride and turned to meet his gaze. He sensed that Gina was near. Jack felt a warmth as he looked at Emily. He watched her eyes widen and fill with moisture. She looked down at her feet and swiped her eyes. The feeling grew stronger, and then faded into the background. Emily lifted her head and Jack could see her throat tighten as she swallowed her tears. "I'm sorry. I didn't think this would be so hard."

Jack patted her arm awkwardly. "It is though."

"I miss her so much." Emily sniffed, shook her head, and then stepped back. "Okay, how about we look at Hallie's room?"

Hallie came running down the hallway. "Emily!" She hugged Emily's legs. "Are you going to paint my tree now?"

Emily glanced at Jack with a smile as she leaned over to hug Hallie. "Yes, I'm going to measure some things and if it's okay with your Dad, maybe I can sketch out a few lines today."

Jack nodded, smiling at Hallie's exuberant mood change and the words that flowed so easily. They pulled the shades in Hallie's room to let in the natural light. Emily took a few moments gazing at each wall, listening as Hallie chattered about her stuffed animals. She examined the bedspread and asked Hallie about her favorite things.

Fifteen minutes later Jack found himself grinning. Hallie was acting like her old self. She seemed right at home with Emily, and he noticed how attentive Emily was to everything Hallie said. After she took some measurements of the area that would be painted, Emily began sketching lines for the tree in the corner of the room.

"It's hard to believe how you can sketch a few lines and I can tell it's a tree," Jack said. "But if I did that same thing someone would think that Hallie had been scribbling on her walls."

Emily laughed. "As long as I'm the only one drawing on the walls, we should be safe. Right, Hallie?"

Hallie gave a serious nod and looked toward Jack. He chuckled and the action was so foreign, he started coughing. Had it really been so long since he'd laughed that he'd almost forgotten how?

Emily stopped sketching and looked at Jack. "I want to tell you why I called today, but I don't want to make things worse." Emily glanced at Hallie.

Jack cleared his throat. "Hallie, I need you to go and feed Skitter." The family cat loved to prowl around the wood pile out back. "And pet him for a minute because he looked lonely last time I saw him."

Hallie looked at the few pencil lines on her wall and frowned. "I want to see what Emily is drawing."

Emily knelt down by Hallie. "I have a little surprise. If you'll go outside, then I'll come get you when it's ready, okay?"

Hallie brightened. "Yes! I love surprises!"

With a laugh, Emily ruffled her hair and Hallie skipped out the door.

"You'd never know it, but last week she wasn't talking," Jack said. "Not one word, and less than a hundred in the last month."

Emily lowered her hand to her heart. "Really?"

"I've taken her to the doctor and a counselor. They all suggested more time for her to cope with everything, but it seemed like she was getting worse. Then a couple days ago she starts telling me all about this dream she had with Gina. She hasn't stopped talking since."

There was a beat of silence and Emily licked her lips. "I've been dreaming about Gina."

Jack leaned back against the wall, closing his eyes, bracing himself for whatever Emily had to say.

"I won't tell you about it if it's going to cause you pain," Emily whispered.

He opened his eyes. "It's okay." He had a feeling that Gina would make sure he got the message whether Emily told him or not. Better to get it over with.

"Gina came to me. She was holding Easton's blanket and she was crying." Emily sat on Hallie's bed and blinked rapidly. "It was awful. I felt so terrible because Gina looked heartbroken and she wanted me to help her, but I didn't know how."

Not again. He couldn't believe what was happening—it seemed as if Gina was everywhere all at once. Her closeness pressed on his lungs, made it hard to breathe. "Did she—was she holding Easton in your dream?"

"No, it was just his blanket," Emily answered. "I guess it stood out to me because it was the blanket I made for him. Do you remember the blue and white flannel one? I embroidered his name in dark blue with my sewing machine. Is it here?"

Jack put his face in his hands.

"Oh, no. I'm sorry." Emily stood and touched his arm. "I didn't want to make things worse, it's just—I've never had such a vivid dream before."

Jack rubbed his eyes and let his hands fall to his sides. "The blanket isn't here. It was his favorite. It was probably with him in the crash."

"I never thought it would be," Emily swallowed, and her voice dropped to a whisper, "this is hard." She stepped away and her shoulders shook with the cries she couldn't hold back any longer.

Jack stared at the mirror image of his own anguish, unsure of what to do or how to comfort Emily. She sank onto Hallie's bed, letting the tears fall. He watched her, the sorrow closing in on him again, the back of his head pounding with memories. Emily sniffed and wiped her eyes. "I'm sorry. I didn't want to tell you." She looked up at him. "But I can't explain. It was like this compelling feeling. I couldn't ignore it. Gina wants me to help you."

Jack sucked in a breath and leaned his head against the wall. The plaster on the ceiling swirled in different shapes and designs and he stared at the bright white until his eyes watered. If only he could understand what was happening with Hallie, with him, and now Emily. He closed his eyes and lowered his head.

"Maybe I should go. This probably wasn't one of my best ideas."

Jack shook his head. "No, I think you're right. Hallie needs this right now." He motioned to the blue walls. "I can pay you."

Emily stood and shook her head. "Absolutely not, and please don't offer again. I should have been over here months ago and done what I already agreed to. I was scared though. It didn't seem fair. I hurt so much in here." She put a hand over her heart and Jack noted the flush in her cheeks. "But I know it can't compare to what you're feeling."

"It's okay," he said. "It's hard to find the right words. No one knows what to say."

"So let's quit talking and I'll get to work." Emily forced a smile.

Jack nodded. "How can I help?"

She hesitated, turning slowly toward the wall. "Can you get me a stool? I have my measuring tape, but I can't reach high enough."

"Sure." Jack strode purposefully to the garage. He checked on Hallie. She sat on the back porch steps with Skitter in her arms, her head resting on the gray cat's puffy fur. The pain around his heart constricted as he watched her, sitting quietly, probably thinking of her mother and baby brother. Hallie had loved Easton so much. Gina often had to get after her for loving on him too tight. The poor baby was nearly smothered with little girl kisses.

He watched Hallie stroke the cat's fur. She had been alone until Easton came along and Gina always said the bond was immediate. Lots of people had warned them that Hallie would act out, even be mean to the baby out of jealousy—it happened with some kids. But not Hallie. From day one, she was vying for Easton's attention, packing him around the house every chance she got. Now she was alone again.

He stepped closer to the patio, his ears perking up at a familiar sound. Hallie was singing the Kookaburra song. Jack put his hand over his mouth and stepped back from the window. A searing pain shot through him. He leaned on the kitchen counter and stared at the flecks in the carpet. What if it wasn't a dream? Was Gina really there with them? If so, why?

For Easton.

He couldn't ignore her presence, but he also couldn't explain it. "I don't know what to do Gina," he whispered.

Find him.

Jack pounded his hands on the counter and groaned.

Emily stepped out of Hallie's bedroom. "Is everything okay?"

He shook his head. "I'll grab that stuff. I was just checking on Hallie." He hurried out to the garage, berating himself for the flush of emotions that kept stinging his eyes. With long breaths, he tried to clear his head and push the hurt away from his heart. He grabbed the step stool and walked back into the house.

Emily had pulled Hallie's bed away from the wall and was sketching lines with a heavy pencil. She looked up when he entered, her eyes questioning him. He pursed his lips and swallowed. "I'll be in my office if you need me."

"Jack, wait." Emily set her pencil on the floor and stepped around the bed. As she walked toward him, her eyes searched his. "Something is going on here. I can feel it. I know you can too. Can you tell me what it is?"

His hands trembled and he clenched them into fists. He shook his head. Emily reached forward and put her hand on his arm, looking intently at him. They stared at each other for a moment, a strange sensation arcing between them.

Emily squeezed his arm. "It's Gina, isn't it?" her voice was so soft, he barely heard it.

His chest swelled with a sense of rightness as he looked at Emily. He felt a strong urge to tell her about his dreams and about the memories he'd experienced from Gina's point of view. But he clenched his teeth and shook his head. He stepped out of Emily's grasp. "I'll be in my office." His voice broke on the last word and he practically ran from the room.

He closed the door to his office partway and forced himself to focus on the work he needed to finish up for the day. The house was eerily quiet as he logged into his accounts and began typing. A few minutes later, he heard Hallie open the sliding glass door and creep across the living room. Then he heard her squeal and giggle—apparently she liked the sketching Emily had done on her walls.

The weekend couldn't get there soon enough. He had to get himself together or Dr. Radkin would have him committed to Blackfoot. He smiled in spite of himself. The Idaho State mental hospital was located in Blackfoot—about an hour northeast of Heyburn. Gina had often joked with him that if he didn't stop balling up his socks she was going to end up in Blackfoot. She'd used that line when he put the Tupperware containers in the wrong spots and the cooking utensils in the wrong drawers. He could almost hear her rummaging through the drawers trying to find the right lids. "I'm going to end up in Blackfoot if I don't find this lid!" He had always laughed and teased her about her type A personality.

And there he was again, reliving those memories of Gina. He caught himself smiling before the sides of his mouth turned down again. Dr. Radkin had told him to indulge in his memories as they were a sort of balm to his soul. But it just seemed to add to his pain.

He heard a soft knock on the door and looked up.

"Hey, Jack," Emily spoke softly, averting her eyes from his. "I think I know what I need to get to finish the project."

He felt embarrassed about the way he had acted, but he

wasn't going to apologize because he didn't want to talk about it. "I'm happy to pick anything up for you."

"No, I can handle it." Emily leaned against the doorway and as Jack stood he saw that Hallie had her arm wrapped around Emily's leg.

"Daddy, come and see my room!" Hallie jumped up and down.

Emily laughed and Jack smiled as he followed them to the room. He pulled out his wallet and extracted two twenty dollar bills. "At least let me pay for the paint." He handed the money to her.

Emily shook her head. "No, I want to do this for Gina."

Jack grabbed her hand and pressed the bills into her palm, then wrapped her fingers around them. "I know how much work it's going to be to paint that mural."

Emily opened her mouth to speak, but Jack shook his head. "That isn't even enough to pay for all your supplies. Don't argue with me."

Her eyes registered surprise, and then she narrowed them. She pulled her hand from his. "Fine."

"Em, I want to help too." He flinched when he realized he'd called her by the nickname that Gina always used.

She stopped and turned to him, her features softening. "Okay." She pushed the bills into her pocket. "Is it okay if I come back on Saturday to start painting?"

"I think so. Hallie and I were going to do some yard work."

Hallie perked up. "Are we going to rake leaves?"

"We're going to make big piles if there's enough leaves."

Hallie clapped her hands. "Can Emily help us?"

"No, she'll be working on your room." Jack raised his eyebrows at Emily and was surprised to see red splotches appearing all over her neck. She covered them with her hand and cleared her throat.

"I'll see you two on Saturday."

Jack peeked out the window a moment later to watch her drive away, wondering why she'd been so nervous.

CHAPTER SIX

ON HER WAY HOME, Emily concentrated on keeping her hands from shaking. The heat of the red splotches on her chest and neck lingered. Jack had noticed too, she was sure of it. He didn't know. Gina hadn't given him the same message. Emily shrugged off a cold chill, her shoulders turning inward. She probably should have told Jack everything, but how could she? He was so shook up. She was certain that Gina was haunting him as well.

The dream had been so vivid that it came to her mind almost without thought. Gina had clutched the blanket and held it out to Emily. When Gina spoke her voice was ethereal, yet powerful. "Em, I need you to help Jack find Easton. He's alive."

Emily had opened her mouth to ask why, but Gina had looked at her with such pleading in her eyes that Emily had closed her mouth and nodded.

"When you find Easton," Gina continued. "I need you to help Jack. His heart is broken now, but he has such a capacity to love."

"No, I can't," Emily said. "I can't tell him that Easton is alive. He can barely go to work he's so distraught." Emily thought of the conversations she'd had with Helen about Jack's suffering.

"Which is why you have to help him." Gina stepped forward. "I have to go now. Please think about it."

"I'll try."

Thank you.

She had heard the words as she awoke in the dark stillness of her room. Emily sat up and flipped on her bedside lamp, but the room was empty. There was an afterglow of warmth and Emily lay back on her pillow, thinking over the dream. What did it mean? That was when she'd had the impression to call Jack and offer to paint Hallie's room.

When Jack had called her Em, it had nearly undone every stitch holding her together. It had felt right and she was scared, but she could be there to support him, to encourage Hallie to talk and remember the good things about Gina and Easton.

Easton. When she thought of Gina's sweet baby, it turned her inside out. Poor Jack. The horror of losing his wife and his son must be overwhelming. Yet, he'd held on, kept working. Even drove his route, right past the site of the accident. Jack seemed to be coping with his loss and trying to move on.

So what was bothering her? She thought of Easton again. Gina had delivered a message through that dream, but every logical bone in Emily's body argued with the idea that he could still be alive. And if he was, how would they ever find him?

Emily tidied up her apartment and allowed herself to think of Jack. The dark stubble on his face and the way he looked in his Wranglers and cowboy boots. She shook her head, embarrassed about the way her stomach flipped when she pictured how he'd looked at her, his dark eyes shining with emotion.

She still wasn't sure what she was supposed to do about Gina's urgent request from the dream, but at least Hallie would get her room painted. The little girl needed a dose of happiness.

~

Not long after Emily left, Alex Whitman called. "Jack, I know this is crazy but is there any way you can make it up here tomorrow at eleven?"

"What?" Jack pushed aside papers to see his desk calendar. "But I was just there."

"I know, but this is good. The main dude from the Idaho Potato Council is going to be here and I mentioned how well you've worked with us on our buildings and the new cellars. He wants to talk to you about a new project for the council and for him—Hansen farms, bro."

"Holy cow, are you kidding?" Hansen farms was one of the largest and most successful family farms in the state of Idaho. Jack was reeling from the possibilities.

"I thought it might be worth your while, if you're up for it," Alex said. "Of course, he'll understand if you can't. I told him your situation, but he's a busy man."

"I'll make it happen." Jack hung up and shook his head. It'd be hard to make another trip so soon, but this was the best decision for his job. Construction management was all about working with tight timelines. After Gina's death, he'd lost substantial income due to his inability to follow up on projects like he needed to. Even though Toby had tried to cover, some things had slipped through that Jack didn't have the emotional energy to deal with. The possibility of new projects with Hansen farms would more than make up the difference.

The standard life insurance policy he had on Gina had covered all of the funeral expenses for both her and Easton and left only enough for a small buffer that he held onto in case Hallie needed more specialized treatment.

He didn't have much of a choice. Crossing the bridge in Blackfoot wasn't a pleasant thought, but he would just have to man up. Jack tried to concentrate only on the positive while he prepared his go-to dinner for Hallie: macaroni and cheese and hot dogs. Life had changed drastically in the past few months, but at least he and Hallie weren't starving.

Less than an hour later, the dinner dishes clinked in rhythm with the dishwasher's agitator as Jack scrubbed the last of the dried mac and cheese from the table. He felt drained. It was only seven o'clock and Hallie was watching a cartoon, but he hadn't accomplished as much as he needed to that day. He tossed the rag in the sink and turned off the kitchen light. The fluorescent light faded to a dim glow in the darkness and the rag dripped in its own cadence to the background noises of Looney Tunes. Jack rolled his shoulders back and walked around Hallie sprawled out on the carpet with her blankets and pillows. He turned down the hallway toward his office, but stopped when the doorbell rang.

Hallie jumped up, but Jack put out his hand. "You know the rules. Only Daddy answers the door. Go watch your cartoon."

He flipped the deadbolt and opened the door. A police officer with short black hair stood on the porch, the backdrop of a beautiful sunset fading behind him, casting a pearlescent glow on the surroundings. "Vincent?" Jack recognized his friend from college—the same friend who had been one of the first on the scene of Gina and Easton's drowning.

He tapped his badge. "That's Sheriff Vincent Juarez, remember?" He winked and Jack chuckled. The trace of a Spanish accent was still evident in his friend's speech. Before the accident, it had been at least five years since Jack had talked to his college buddy. He wished Vincent was there to reminisce about old times, but the uniform indicated it was official business.

"Can I come in for a minute?" Vincent's hefty appearance belied the genuine care that he kept behind his deep brown eyes. With a hard swallow, Jack stepped back and motioned for him to enter. Time stopped and his mind raced back to the last time he'd seen Vincent. May fourteenth. Gina didn't show up for their lunch date and Jack couldn't reach her. He was frustrated and left several messages. Then he got scared. He remembered calling Helen, but she hadn't heard from Gina. Jack decided to leave Idaho Falls early and head back for Heyburn.

He wondered if Gina's car had troubles. It wasn't like her not to call. Thoughts crossed his mind, but he didn't entertain them—Gina would probably be home when he got there. At least he could surprise her and bring home dinner or something. He told Helen to call him if she heard from Gina.

He was almost to Blackfoot, where the freeway crossed over the Snake River when traffic slowed considerably. There was a huge bottleneck of traffic at the end of the bridge on the other lanes of northbound traffic. The cars crawled across the bridge like the snails he and Gina used to find around the smooth river rocks. Jack saw an ambulance and two fire engines, and as he approached the end of the bridge he saw another emergency vehicle clambering down the riverbank.

He pulled his car over to the side of the road, even though a police officer up ahead motioned for him to continue. Jack jumped out of the car and ran across the lanes of traffic to the other side of the bridge. It was a terrible feeling of dread that made him jump the barricade and head down to the river among the mass of emergency personnel.

The police officer shouted after him, but nothing could stop him. The back end of a silver Camry stuck out from one side of the river. Jack didn't even know he was screaming until a police officer had grabbed his arm and pulled him away from the water's edge.

"Sir, sir do you recognize that vehicle?"

Jack had been frantic, looking toward the ambulance, seeing the doors open with the empty gurneys still inside. He turned back toward the river and tried to jump into the water. But the police officer restrained him and called for help as Jack screamed, "My wife. Gina! My wife and baby are in that car!"

"Did you say there was a baby in the car?" the officer asked.

Jack looked at him and saw fear in his eyes. "His name is Easton. He's seven months old. Did you save him?"

The police officer stepped back and then hollered over his shoulder, "Gibson, there was a baby in the vehicle."

It was as if everyone froze then turned toward Jack. A second later they were jumping in the river, swimming around the submerged vehicle. That's when Jack crumpled to the ground. They already knew Gina was dead, but they hadn't seen his baby. Then Vincent showed up to start an investigation into the accident.

Someone was talking to him and his right eye was twitching. Jack snapped back to the present.

"Jack, are you okay?"

Vincent stood just inside the door, the worry lines in his forehead bunching together. "I probably should have called first. Are you having a flashback?"

Jack nodded. *That and a mental breakdown*, he thought to himself. Then he noticed that Vincent was clutching a black garbage bag and his first thought was of Easton followed by a painful impulse that felt like a slap to his face.

Easton is alive!

He put his head in his hands and leaned back against the door.

"Jack, why don't you sit down. You look all washed out."

Vincent led him to the couch, pushing the front door closed with his foot. "Take a breather and tell me when you're ready."

Jack leaned back onto the couch, angry at himself for not being able to keep it together. He took several shallow breaths, followed by longer, calming inhalations.

"Daddy?" Hallie put her small hand over his.

He looked up, meeting the worried gaze of Hallie. "I'll be okay." He lifted one corner of his mouth in a lopsided grin. "You can finish watching your cartoon. Daddy's just going to talk to Officer Juarez for a minute."

Hallie studied him and then stared at the police officer. She wasn't afraid. She appeared curious at the interruption.

Vincent smiled at her. "Your Daddy will be just fine. I promise."

Hallie's lips twitched and she backed up slowly toward her pile of blankets in front of the TV.

Once Hallie was concentrating on Bugs Bunny again, Jack turned to Vincent. "Please, have a seat." He motioned to the sofa.

Vincent sat on the edge of the sofa and cleared his throat. "I wanted to come by to talk to you in person. I'm sorry for all of this."

"It's okay," Jack murmured.

"We haven't found Easton's body, but a couple days ago a

fisherman's line snagged on this." Vincent opened the sack and pulled out a soft blue and white blanket.

The dark blue embroidery thread seemed to scream at Jack as he read his son's name: Easton.

"Where?"

"Downstream about five miles from the accident. He pulled it up, saw the name and remembered the story on the news. Guy brought it down to the station. We tested it for blood residue—there wasn't any. So the department had it cleaned. We thought you'd like to have it. I wasn't sure if it was the right thing to do. We don't want to cause you more pain."

Jack took the blanket, his fingers tracing the letters. He unfolded it. The edges were frayed and there was a large hole near one corner, probably where the hook had stuck and the fabric, weakened by the water, had begun to degrade. "Are they going to do another search?"

"We talked to Search and Rescue. They have a training coming up. They're going to focus on the area where the blanket was—they'll do their best." He leaned closer to Jack. "I don't want you to get your hopes up though. I don't think we're going to find Easton. I hate saying that to you, but it's better to accept these things than to torture ourselves with something we can't change."

Jack's heart pounded. He looked down at the blanket. The fabric wouldn't last long, but it was still warm. His fingers tingled as an icy chill descended on him and he knew it was Gina. "What if he isn't dead?"

Vincent's eyes widened. "What do you mean?"

"I don't know." Jack closed his eyes. He felt a pressure, an urging to say more but when he opened his eyes he saw Hallie sitting up and watching them. Vincent looked at him as if he were crazy. He couldn't risk losing Hallie and if the police thought he was unstable, they'd have social services there before he could blink. Vincent was his friend, but he was a good police officer too. "I'm sorry. I just wish he wasn't gone."

Vincent continued to scrutinize him for a moment, and then he nodded. "I've wished the same thing every morning these past months. We'll let you know if we find anything else."

Jack held the blanket and stared at the fibers until they blurred together.

"Is there anything I can do for you Jack?" Vincent asked. "You'd tell me, wouldn't you?"

Jack nodded. "It's rough, but thanks for bringing the blanket. It was nice of you to drive all the way down here."

"Well, I had some other things to follow up on in the area, so it gave me a good reason to come see you." Vincent pulled his bottom lip through his teeth. "I know it's probably painful, but if you ever need to talk, I hope you'll give me a call."

Jack couldn't speak. He wished he could be like Hallie and hold all those agonizing words inside so he wouldn't ever have to hear them— or say them—again. Words like dead, drowned, missing, sorry, tragic, filled up his quota every day. He swallowed hard and gave Vincent a weak smile. Vincent stood and put one of his large, dark brown hands on Jack's shoulder. "Hang in there, okay?"

Somehow Jack kept it together until Vincent left. He leaned against the front door, clutching Easton's blanket and willing himself to breathe normally.

"Daddy, that's Easton's blanket." Hallie stood in front of him, touching the edge of the soft blanket. "Mommy brought it back to us so we can find him." She yawned. "Are you going to look for him tomorrow?"

CHAPTER SEVEN

JACK CALLED Helen to see if she could watch Hallie and get her back and forth to kindergarten again.

"Of course I will," she said. "How are you?"

"Hallie's been talking."

"Really!" Helen sounded overjoyed. "What is she saying?"

Jack cringed, part of him didn't want to tell Helen but he couldn't lie to her. "Hallie said that Gina came to her in a dream and sang to her."

"Oh, Jack. That's wonderful."

"But it's not. Hallie has it in her head that Gina told her I need to find Easton."

He heard Helen's breath catch. "Oh the poor, sweet thing."

"I have something important to tell you." Jack felt terrible for being so blunt with Helen, but he didn't want to accept Gina's haunting experiences and there really was no way to soften the news he was about to share. "Vincent Juarez came by yesterday. A fisherman found Easton's blanket. It caught in his line five miles downstream."

There was silence and then he heard a muffled sob. "I'm sorry, Helen. I didn't want to tell you over the phone, but with everything going on I don't want to encourage Hallie. Easton is dead and we're not going to find his body. Search and Rescue is going to do some exercises in the area, but Vincent basically told me to put that hope away."

There was a long silence and he could tell that Helen was crying. "I'll see you Friday."

"Helen, I'm sorry," he said. She could barely get out a goodbye amidst her sobs. Jack's chest ached for the hurt they all felt.

Friday morning, Jack woke up earlier than usual, determined to escape the dreams and memories and put in a hard day's work. The razor nicked his jawline and Jack winced as red bloomed on his skin. He ripped off a square of toilet paper and placed it on the cut. The blade was dull; he needed new razors and several other things. It had been so hard to get used to doing all the things that Gina had done, things he'd taken for granted. Her lists were always so organized; she got in and out of the store quickly and kept the pantry stocked with everything they needed.

With a sigh, he looked in the mirror. Dark circles under his eyes had become a permanent fixture. He looked closer, noting the redness in the whites of his eyes contrasting with the deep brown of his iris. Gina loved his brown eyes. As he stared at the haggard remains of himself, the scene changed and suddenly he was in the middle of a memory.

Easton sat in the kitchen on the tile floor. His arms were so tanned that the creases in his fat rolls were white in comparison. He leaned over and blew a raspberry on the floor and then looked up and laughed. Jack heard Gina laughing along with him. Easton grinned, showing two bottom teeth, then bent over and blew another loud raspberry on the floor. His cheeks puffed out and Jack found himself smiling at the memory before he realized what was happening.

He clenched his jaw. "Easton is dead," he spoke barely above a whisper.

If he's dead then why am I here?

Jack jumped back and hit his head on the doorframe. He cursed and rubbed the crown of his head. He didn't know how, but he could tell she was crying. *If he's dead then why aren't you seeing him too?*

He jerked his head around and saw her standing there. Her yellow blouse looked wet where her hair curled over her shoulders.

I don't know how much longer I can help you, Jack. But if you don't do something now—if you don't find Easton—something bad is going to happen to him. I feel it.

"Gina, why are you doing this? I'm going crazy!" Jack yelled.

She looked at him with mournful eyes, then turned and walked down the hall. *I have to find him.*

He moved to follow her, but she was gone. Jack stood in the hallway for a moment, his breath coming in short gasps. His heart pumped hard—the only thing that kept him grounded in reality. He turned around and saw Hallie in her room curled up on her bed crying. His shoulders slumped and he shook his head.

"Sweetheart, I'm sorry I yelled." He knelt by her bed and rubbed her back. "Are you ready to go to Grandma's?"

She rolled over and the tears ran down her cheeks. "Why won't you listen to Mommy? Don't you want to find Easton?"

Jack felt like he'd been punched in the gut. The back of

his throat went dry and he struggled to swallow. "I'm going to look for him today, okay?"

Hallie sat up, her eyes brightening. "I know you can find him, Daddy. Please bring him home."

There weren't any words that would fix the problem. Maybe he could set up an appointment with his pastor. There had to be a way for Gina to find peace. As soon as that thought crossed his mind, he entertained the other that he kept pushing away. Maybe she was right. If he looked for Easton, what would he find?

He was living some twisted ghost story, and in every story he'd ever read, those who were haunted had to do something so the spirit could find rest. He should have felt lucky to see Gina, to talk to his wife. Instead, he was overcome by her anguish and grief. It was too much to bear. Jack rolled his shoulders back and looked into the hallway again. It was quiet, but a trace of her remained. Jack resolved to listen and really make an attempt to find out what it was Gina needed.

Helen didn't say much when Jack dropped Hallie off, so by the time he was headed toward Idaho Falls, he felt awful. Life was supposed to be hard—he got that—but not torture. His thoughts were jumbled and he tried to focus on his presentation, praying that it would go well. As he approached Blackfoot, he kept a mantra going in his head. *I'll look for Easton. I'll try to find him or whatever we need to do so you can have peace.* He hoped that Gina would get the message and give him some peace as well.

When he arrived at Whitman farms, he shook off the crazy thoughts swirling in his head and struggled to concentrate on the professional aspects of his life.

"Dude, you look bad," Alex said when he opened the door to his office.

"I can always count on your honesty, Alex."

Alex slapped him on the back. "Seriously though, go splash some water on that ugly face of yours and come back smiling."

Jack rolled his eyes, but he knew better than to argue with Alex. He hurried to the bathroom, the lights flickering on as he stepped inside. He glanced at himself under the harsh lights and had to agree that he didn't look any better than that morning. He stood up straight and wiggled his toes inside his dress shoes. He could do this. The gray and black tie Gina had given him for Christmas looked nice with his charcoal suit. Normally he wore Wranglers and work boots around the sites, but this meeting was different. Removing the jacket, he tucked the tie in his shirt and leaned over the faucet. The cool water felt good against the puffy skin around his eyes. He scooped up more and held it against his face, and a few droplets ran down the sleeve of his dress shirt.

The paper towels felt scratchy against his clean-shaven face, so he blotted the rest of the water from his skin. He picked up his shoulder bag and headed for the board room.

Frank Hansen chatted with Stan Whitman in the corner, flipping through the brochure Jack had designed showcasing previous projects with their completion dates and information. Alex gave him a thumbs up when he entered the room. He guided him over to Frank. "Jack just arrived and I told him you'd be glad he made it."

"That I am." Frank shook his hand and then covered the grip with his other hand. "I've heard you've had a rough time of it, son. I'm sorry for your loss."

"Thank you. It's been a particularly hard week, but I'm grateful for the chance to meet with you."

"Let's see what you have to offer."

Jack pulled out a folder from his bag and handed Frank a sheet with the statistics and forecasts used in the building projects for the Whitman's. "I work closely with my customers to ensure their satisfaction." Jack flipped over another paper and handed it to Frank. "We'd be happy to work with you to build up your business."

The rest of the presentation went well. Frank was prepared with several questions and concerns about going with a smaller construction firm versus continuing with the more complicated combination of working with the three large firms they currently had. The scale of the Whitman's project was specialized; the potato cellars equipped with the latest high-tech sensing materials for ultimate storage solutions for the potatoes. The technology included in the potato cellars measured air temperature with changes as small as a tenth of a degree recorded with accuracy. Jack made sure to show Frank how the new technology they were installing allowed farmers to read reports and make changes to humidity and temperature levels from their cell phones.

"Now that's something I never would've believed twenty years ago," Frank said. "Well, son, this all looks great." He scooped up the papers Jack had given him and stacked it neatly against the table. "I'll take this back to the board. Expect to hear from me within a week."

Jack smiled and it felt genuine. "Thank you."

"But as far as my own personal business," Frank paused and looked down at the folder of samples. "How about we get a visit set up about two weeks from now?"

With a grin, Jack pumped Frank's hand. "That sounds excellent."

Jack left the building, sort of floating on a high. The sense of relief was so foreign to him after four months of constant worrying. The Hansen account alone would most likely prove to be a five percent increase in his salary. It would make it possible for him to relax a bit more at home and really be present for Hallie's needs.

He inhaled the musky scent of potatoes and could almost taste the dirt in the air. A ten-wheeler bumped along the washboard road into the packing plant with a load of spuds teetering right near the edge. The driver honked and whistled at a woman as she climbed into another truck. She looked like she was barely twenty. She flipped her dark ponytail and waved. Jack couldn't help but smile at the interchange. Gina used to drive during spud harvest and she loved regaling him with tales of the hunks of junk she drove, holes in the floorboards, grinding gears, spuds falling off and hitting cars on the highway—harvest season was always an adventure.

The Snake River meandered right through the heart of Idaho Falls. Jack followed the major highway into the city and stopped at his favorite sandwich shop for lunch. Betty's Baked Clubs was busy as usual so he ordered it to go and prepared himself to face his fears.

Before Gina's death, Jack followed the same routine. Each week after his commute into the city, he'd stop for a sandwich at Betty's and jump onto Memorial Drive. The road ran parallel to the green belt on the river. It was a beautiful area with large shade trees, vibrant green grass, and a scenic overlook that couldn't be beat. Sitting on the grass and eating his lunch was the most peaceful part of his day. He had honestly thought he'd never be able to venture near the river again, but he felt different after his meeting with Frank. His promise to Gina echoed in his ears and he felt as if she pulled him toward the river, as if there was some connection to Easton there.

The sunlight caught the spires of the Mormon temple a half mile down the river. The building's pure white stone made it appear as some kind of beacon floating on the Snake. Jack removed his suit jacket and sat on the grass watching puffy clouds pass by the temple spires.

Chewing slowly, he tried to concentrate on the thoughts filtering through his mind. There were too many coincidences to ignore. Gina was haunting him, but he didn't know why. She said it was because of Easton, but that didn't make any sense. How could his son still be alive? They had found the car seat and then his blanket. Jack refocused his thoughts on the car seat. He still couldn't fathom how the car seat made it out of the Camry. The thought had barely entered his mind when he heard a baby cry. His heart jolted and a chill crept up Jack's spine. He set down his sandwich and turned his head toward the sound of the cry.

A woman sat near the river on a patchwork denim quilt. A baby boy cried as she tried to distract him from the leaf he was chewing on. The shrill cry pierced Jack's soul. He leaned forward. The woman was only thirty yards from him. The cry sounded just like Easton, and the baby's dark hair reminded him of Easton. Jack rubbed a hand over his face and took a deep breath. He turned and took a sip of orange Mountain Dew, struggling to compose himself. This had been a bad idea. Coming to the park to relax just opened up his mind to all the problems he'd been having lately.

The baby cried again and Jack couldn't help but turn and study the woman and her child. The baby boy was chunky, his little hands were pudgy with fat rolls going up his arms, just like Easton's had been. The woman picked him up and nuzzled his neck. The baby giggled, but then started crying again.

That little laugh made Jack's breath catch in his throat. His ears were tuned to every sound as he analyzed his memories of Easton with the baby almost within reach. Everything reminded him of his own baby boy. Jack was just about to write himself off as crazy when his promise to Gina pressed up against his skull. It wouldn't hurt anything to get a little closer—take a look. Maybe doing so would trigger something important that he'd forgotten. He pushed himself off the grass and walked toward a tree that was about ten yards from the woman.

The baby looked so much like Easton—the same olive skin that Gina had given both of their children. His dark hair looked glossy and straight, a bit longer than Gina would have liked to keep it. Jack shoved back the doubts and watched the woman. He couldn't see a ring. She was young—maybe mid-twenties. She cooed at the baby who continued to cry. Jack couldn't ignore the similarities.

With half of his conscience telling him he was nuts and the other half staring at the baby with longing and Gina's haunting memories urging him on, he pulled out his cell phone. He held it to his ear, carefully pushing the camera button. Then he pretended to text while tipping the phone slightly. When he got the right angle, he zoomed in on the baby and held his breath. It took a few seconds for the camera to focus, but when it did, he captured the picture. What he saw brought goose bumps to his skin.

When Easton was born, he had a red mark on his forehead in between his eyes. The doctor called it a stork bite, but the nurse corrected him and said it was an angel kiss. She said it probably wouldn't fade until after Easton was two years old.

It wasn't noticeable unless Easton was crying, pumping blood to the area made it flush and the mark was easy to see. Otherwise, it appeared as a faint red splotch. Gina always kissed him there—told him that he was her angel.

The baby in the picture was crying and he had an angel

kiss in the exact same spot as Easton. Jack moved to the other side of the tree and took a few more pictures with his phone. He zoomed in on the woman. She had black hair, probably dyed, and light colored eyes. Perhaps they were close to the same crystalline blue of Easton's. Jack scrolled back to the picture of the baby's face and the angel kiss. The baby could have easily passed as the woman's son, but he wasn't hers. It was Easton. The logical side of Jack immediately tried to argue, but pressure built in his chest as his heart beat faster with the possibilities.

The blood pumping in Jack's ears muffled Easton's cries as Jack thought about what he should do. He could walk over and talk to the woman—mention how cute her baby was, but he felt a strong impression not to get any closer. He considered the impression just as the sun came from behind a group of clouds, the bright sunbeams filtering through the leaves of the tree. The glare made Jack turn and close his eyes. When he opened them, the woman had gathered up all the toys and had the baby under her arm as she picked up the blanket.

Jack looked in the direction of the sun and smiled. Then he turned toward his baby boy. When he saw Easton, he realized why Gina had followed him for the last several days. She'd been preparing him. He would have gone up to the woman and talked to her, probably said how her baby looked just like his son—and she would have run. Jack might've called the police, but the scenarios flashed through his mind, all with predictable endings in favor of the woman who had stolen his son. Jack wouldn't have had a chance to save Easton if he tried going that route. Gina was helping him. Maybe he wasn't crazy after all.

A bird chirped and Jack scanned the trees for the remains of a nest. He found it sitting snug in the notch of two branches. A few months ago, that nest held baby birds and now they were stretching their wings, testing the currents of air. A few months ago, he'd taken Easton outside to see the new life all around them and shortly after everything had changed. He turned his head to watch the slow retreat of the woman and the baby who he thought might be his son.

Jack walked purposefully toward the parking lot. He pulled out his cell phone and began carrying on a fake conversation with himself. "Sure, I can get those documents to you. It'll probably be later today."

As he talked, the woman unlocked a white Elantra and Jack squinted, noting the license plate number. He pulled a pen from his inner pocket and scribbled the plate number on the back of his hand as he hurried to his car. The engine started on the woman's car and Jack panicked. He bolted for his truck, fumbled with the keys and gunned the engine. It took everything he had to back slowly out of the parking space and pull out onto the road two cars behind the Elantra.

CHAPTER EIGHT

JACK'S HEART pounded in his chest and his breath came in short gasps. It was Easton. Everything was turned on its end. Jack had a picture, a license plate number, and a general location. And he had Easton's angel kiss burned into his retinas. It was all he could do not to jump out of the car, screaming for everyone to help him get his son back. Easton was alive!

The car turned and Jack cursed when yet another vehicle blocked his view. He sped up and made a sharp right turn off the highway. He glimpsed the white car go around the corner and felt a tightness in his chest. The cell phone lay in his console. It would be so easy to dial 911 and give the police the plate number, but there was one problem—according to them, his son was dead. Jack had to have more than an angel kiss to prove that it was his son.

In only four months, Easton had changed. He was still chunky, but not like the pictures of when he was six months old. His hair was longer now, a bit darker than Jack remembered from last spring.

He fell back another car length. It wouldn't do any good

to tip the woman off that she'd been discovered. He was certain she would run. He'd seen the way she'd scanned the park, noting the occupants as she held onto Easton. "Gina, what should I do now?" Jack was frantic as he watched the car go around another bend in the road. "I can't mess this up. I'm sorry I didn't listen to you. Help me!"

Just as he was about to make the left hand turn, he felt her presence; they were in sync somehow. Jack wanted to keep following the white car, but he knew what Gina would do, what she wanted him to do. He made note of the street and turned his truck around.

With his heart thumping so hard he felt it might explode, Jack drove back the way he had come. He pulled into a convenience store parking lot and found a receipt in the side compartment of his door. He flipped it over and began writing. He jotted down the number of the street, the make and model of the car including the license plate number he'd written on the back of his hand. Closing his eyes, he focused on the encounter with the woman. He had her picture, but he wanted to be sure he took down every detail he had noticed.

He smoothed out the receipt. Maybe Vincent could help him. Jack found his number and called the Sheriff's office. "Vincent, I need your help. I'm in Idaho Falls and I know this will sound absolutely nuts, but I need you to hear me out. I just saw a woman with my son, Easton."

"Whoa, Jack—"

"No. I know what you're going to say and I don't care. This baby has a red mark on his forehead just like Easton's. He's the same age as Easton. He has Gina's blue eyes."

"Jack," Vincent cut in, "your son died in the river last May."

"But what if he didn't?" Jack cried. "What if this is him?

How did the car seat get out of a vehicle submerged in water?"

"Okay, take a breath and think about what you're saying here," Vincent said. "If this baby is your son, why does some woman have him?"

"I don't know," Jack spluttered. "But it's him."

"But why do you think it's him?"

"Listen, the only way that car seat made it out of the car is if someone took it out. So if that's the case, my next question is, did that have something to do with Gina's accident?" Jack heard the hysteria in his voice and willed himself to calm down.

"I don't have all the answers," Vincent replied. "But I do know one thing. Evidence. That's the number one rule, Jack. Even if the baby looks just like your son, the only way to prove it is by a DNA test. We don't have Easton's DNA on file because he was declared dead, so that means you'd have to get this woman to allow you to test her baby's DNA."

Jack rubbed his hand over his face, the possibilities and implications of what Vincent had explained crashing over him. "What if I had a picture of him? Would that be enough to get a court order for it?"

Vincent sighed. "You took a picture of this baby?"

Jack wasn't sure whether to lie, so he decided to skirt the direct question. "I'm saying if I had a picture of him and another picture of Easton, could you do anything?"

"Jack, you know how quickly babies change as they grow. And babies look so much alike. One picture is not enough evidence."

"What kind of evidence do you need to get a warrant for a DNA test?"

"I'd need something to tie the woman and the baby to your case, probable cause, witnesses...I'm sorry, bro."

Jack looked at the plate number written on his receipt with the description of the woman. He leaned back against his seat. "It's okay. I—I'm sorry to bother you."

"It's not a bother. You're going through a rough time. What you've just encountered is actually pretty common. People who have lost their children see them everywhere, or at least they think they do. I advise you to get some counseling to help you through this."

"I will. I mean, I have. I'm going to text you the number of my therapist because I know you think I'm crazy. I have to go now. Thanks again." Jack ended the call quickly. What a mess. Now Vincent thought he was unstable. Of course, if the tables were turned, Jack would probably think the same thing, but his gut wouldn't let him shrug it off.

There had to be some way to check into this woman. He thought briefly of Jason Edwards. As an FBI agent, he had ample resources to check out anything and anyone. Jack smiled when he recalled that he had been a suspect in a marijuana-growing operation in a potato cellar. When Jason discovered Jack's name tied to the construction of the high-tech indoor growing operation, it only took a few phone calls to clear him and then bring him on as an expert witness. The two had been friends ever since. But even that friendship wasn't enough to keep Jason from thinking that Jack had gone crazy. As much as Jack wished that Jason could help him, there must be another way. He took a deep breath as a thought entered his mind.

Jack leaned forward so fast he bumped his head on the visor. Toby. His boss had been nagging him for weeks to go out with a woman who worked as a private investigator. If an investigator could help him, he could at least find the details about the woman and her baby to prove to himself that he wasn't crazy—he was a grieving father trying to make it through each day. Jack dialed Toby's number and he answered on the second ring. Jack infused a light note into his voice. "Hey, man, remember when you mentioned you had that friend—the private investigator you wanted to set me up with?"

"Well, yeah, but you bit my head off." Toby chuckled. "A guy knows when to leave well enough alone."

"Could you give me her number?" Jack gripped the steering wheel, his heartbeat pounding in the palms of his hands.

"Sure, but I can talk to her if you want first."

"C'mon, I know you already told her all about me. Just give me her number and I'll cut to the chase."

Toby laughed. "Man, how can you read me so well? Hold on. I'll text you in ten minutes. I'm driving right now and I can't look it up."

"Thanks." Jack hung up. "Don't worry Gina," he whispered. "I'm not interested in dating, but I *am* going to find our son."

Toby's text came through seven minutes later—Jack watched every minute tick by on the car's console.

Danika Corbin: age 35, smart, sexy, divorced five years ago, no kids. Did I mention she is fine?

Jack shook his head. Hopefully Toby wouldn't try to interfere. Jack would take Danika on a date if she'd agree, but he wanted to keep this strictly business and on the down-low.

CHAPTER NINE

FOR A FEW BLOCKS she felt as if she were being followed. Janette Baker pulled into the circular drive of another home under a large elm tree and waited. "It's okay, honey," she cooed to the baby in the back seat of her white Elantra. "Andrew, you're being so fussy today. Don't worry, Mommy will help you feel better."

Janette watched the street for five minutes, but she didn't see anyone suspicious drive past. She would do anything to protect her baby. "I love you, Andrew," she whispered. She shrugged off the premonition of danger and pulled back into traffic. Her home was only a mile away. She looked at the clock and grimaced. "I forgot to take my meds today." The anxiety lessened somewhat—it was nice to have an explanation for her nerves.

Janette pulled into the driveway and carried Andrew inside. The tiny house was seventy-five years old with antique lace curtains and the faint smell of an old person. Janette's great-aunt Martha had left her the house when she died six months ago. Janette's messy divorce was just wrapping up, irreconcilable differences noted, but Janette and Trent knew the real reason for the dissolution of the marriage. They had tried for a baby for the past six years. A miscarriage, infertility, artificial insemination and finally a round of IVF had all failed. All her life, she'd planned to be a stay-at-home mom; instead Janette taught school for meager wages and fought with Trent over the debt they'd gone into to try to have a baby. The strain had been too much.

When Janette received the notice that she had a house in Idaho, she quit her job and took two weeks of sick leave she had saved up. She could have finished the last couple months of teaching in New Hampshire, but something compelled her to run. She applied for positions at each of the top recommended preschools in Idaho Falls, Idaho. When she received notice of interviews at two of them, she bolted.

Janette handed Andrew his sippy cup and kissed his cheek. She remembered how everything she owned had fit in the Elantra and she'd driven as fast as she could to put nearly three-thousand miles between her and the aching hole of failure that was her past. She focused on the sweet baby on her hip and smiled. The past couldn't haunt her anymore.

Poor Jack Bentley. Officer Vincent Juarez hated delivering bad news, but that was exactly what he'd done. Some people at the precinct said not to take the blanket—that it would just cause more pain. But Vincent had thought about his three children and how he would feel if one of them died. He would want the blanket.

It might've been a mistake though because Jack seemed

distraught and now this crazy accusation about some woman stealing his child? Jack insisted that he wasn't crazy—had even given Vincent the number to his therapist. He kept asking him over and over, "How did the car seat get out of a vehicle submerged in water?"

Vincent didn't have the answer to that question and it bothered him that Jack had pushed on the hot button of the case that had always felt wrong. He'd seen dozens of car accidents and those car seats stayed in the car—even in that rollover where they figured the pickup had rolled fourteen times. Jack had said that someone must have taken the car seat out of the car.

The accident was a hit and run. There were witnesses, but they never found the pickup that caused the accident, broadsiding Gina and pushing her into the river. Some of the other officers had speculated on foul play, but there was no motive. Now Jack was bringing up the only motive Vincent could come up with and it was ridiculous, which was why Vincent hadn't voiced his thoughts.

He picked up the phone and dialed the head of Search and Rescue. "Is there any way you can move that exercise up a few days?"

It was a futile effort to avoid the nagging evidence at the back of Vincent's mind. A few days after the accident, when it was broadcast that Search and Rescue was looking for the body of eight month old Easton Bentley, they'd received some tips. There were a few strange reports of a woman on the side of the road about a quarter mile south of the accident. She was carrying a baby—they reported that the woman was wet. They said she got in her car with the baby.

People said it was the ghost of Gina and Easton. Other officers agreed because by then, they had found the empty car seat. Vincent had spared Jack from hearing the news, doing his best to quiet the rumors. They'd searched the area and found no sign of anyone, but he had always wondered. Vincent rubbed a hand over the stubble on his jaw. Now wasn't the time to investigate ghosts.

CHAPTER TEN

EVERY NOISE MADE Jack flinch and he struggled to keep his patience with Hallie. Saturday meant sleeping in and cartoons, but no kindergarten to keep his little girl busy. His real stress didn't have anything to do with Hallie, if he was being honest with himself. He had a date lined up that evening with Danika Corbin and hopefully would be hiring her to find the woman who had Easton. Last night he'd uploaded the pictures from his phone to his computer and printed off a copy. When Hallie was asleep, he'd taken one of Easton's baby pictures and compared it. There was no doubt it was the same child, but the police wouldn't even consider it.

The phone rang and Jack answered on the second ring.

"Hi Jack, this is Emily. I hope it's still okay if I come over. I picked up the supplies and I should be to your place in fifteen minutes."

Jack barely kept from cursing out loud. With everything that had happened he'd completely forgotten about Hallie's room. "Uh, yeah. How long do you think you'll need today?"

"I have another appointment at four, so I thought I'd work until then."

"But that's over five hours—how long is this going to take?" Jack realized how that sounded right after he said it. "No, wait, that's not what I meant. I mean I'm worried about you doing all this work for free."

"Jack," her voice held a warning note. "We discussed this already. You're going to let me do this and you're not going to complain because Hallie needs this and I'm keeping my word to Gina."

Jack opened his mouth and then coughed as he tried to think how to respond. "You're right. I'll keep my mouth shut."

"See you in fifteen."

Jack looked at the phone and shook his head. He thought he remembered Gina always saying how timid Emily was, but this woman had some footing. He glanced around the room, assessing the mess level and shrugged. Emily would understand and besides, Hallie was happy setting up her stuffed animals all over the couch for a tea party.

"Hey Hallie, you might want to go pick up your room because Emily is coming to work on it right now."

Hallie dropped the stuffed animal she was holding, squealed, and ran down the hall to her room. At least Emily's visit would distract Hallie from her constant reminders to Jack to search for Easton.

Emily arrived promptly and Jack forced a smile when he opened the door. His mind was racing with the details of the investigation he planned to pursue. "I'm glad you could come. Let me help you unload." Jack took some of her supplies and set them in the hall outside Hallie's room.

"Sorry about sounding so bossy on the phone," Emily said. She followed him and set down a can of paint. "Gina always encouraged me to break free of my turtle shell and be my bold self. I guess after I had that dream about her, I realized that I couldn't let you talk me out of what I'm supposed to do."

Jack took the sack of supplies from her. "And I'm sorry about what I said. I don't want you to get the wrong idea. I'm grateful that you're doing this. It's just hard to accept such a gift."

Emily smiled at him and held out her hand. "Truce?"

Jack shook her hand. "For now." A slow smile crept across his face and he raised his hand and tugged on her ponytail. Emily's eyes widened, but she forced a laugh.

"Uh, I'll get the rest of the paint." Jack hurried to the front room, wondering where his senses had gone. He was just teasing Emily, but he didn't know her well enough to do something like that.

When he entered Hallie's bedroom, the little girl giggled and jumped around on the plastic drop sheet Emily was shaking out. Emily glanced over her shoulder and smiled at Jack. He noticed a bit of redness on her cheeks before she turned back around.

"Now, Hallie, you can't be in here if you're going to be bugging Emily the whole time." Jack leaned against the door frame.

"I won't, Daddy." Hallie stuck out her lower lip. "I'm helping her."

"She's going to be my big helper," Emily said. "She promised to listen to my instructions."

Hallie smiled at Emily and then turned to look at Jack with a serious expression. "Emily said I can help paint the tree."

Jack lifted his brows. "Are you sure that's a good idea?"

Emily pointed at him with a paintbrush. "Aren't you?"

He couldn't help but smile at the way her freckles stood out when she grinned. A light smattering across her nose made her look like a pixie with her vivid green eyes. Jack shook his head and left the room to retrieve the last of the supplies.

The house felt different with Emily in it. Jack did his best to pay attention, but he didn't sense anything from Gina. He wondered how their connection worked—why he couldn't see her or talk to her all the time. Now that he was on track to search for Easton, would he still have contact with his wife?

He heard Emily's laugh accompanied by Hallie's giggles as he walked down the hallway. It was nice to hear his daughter laugh again. Emily's personality brightened the atmosphere and he could tell she was trying hard to stay positive in the home where one of her best friends used to live.

When he walked into the room, Hallie stood next to Emily, her brown curls bobbing in tandem with her happy feet. She bounced up and down as Emily dipped her paintbrush and created a dark brown line on the blue wall. Hallie squealed and bumped Emily's leg, making the paintbrush zigzag out of the lines she had sketched.

Jack held his breath, reluctant to scold Hallie and at the same time wondering how Emily would react.

"Oops! Hallie, you'll have to make sure not to touch me when I'm painting, see?" She pointed to the line and Hallie's shoulders slumped.

"I'm sorry."

Jack could hear the wobble in her voice and was just about to suggest that Hallie go outside with him. But Emily crouched down beside her and caught Jack's eye. "No worries. We'll just make that line into a branch, but we can't have all branches, so no more bumping, okay?"

Hallie lifted her head. "Okay, but can I still help?"

"Of course. I always keep my promises." She tilted her head toward Jack. "Are you going to help us paint too?"

"Um, I'm not very good at drawing, but if you need any newspaper. . ."

"Actually, I'd love some. I like to practice with the paint colors when I'm mixing to get them just right."

Jack pointed at himself with a thumb. "I'm your man. Be right back."

He brought back a stack of newspapers from the garage and Emily laughed. "I don't need the whole forest, just a few sheets."

"But I thought that's what you were doing is painting a forest," Jack quipped. Something about Emily brought out the teasing side of him that had always made Gina smile.

Emily painted another branch that reached out toward Hallie's light switch. "Sure, it's a forest. With *one* tree." She scrunched her eyes in concentration as she outlined the higher part of the tree trunk. "Since you're still here, why don't you start on the clouds?"

Jack shook his head. "I told you, I don't draw."

Emily placed a yellowish sponge in his hand. "Clouds don't take any artistic ability, trust me."

Jack looked at the sponge and tried to ignore his desire to stay in the room with Emily and Hallie. "I'd like to, but there's just this little problem of me not wanting to mess up your mural."

"Don't be a whiner. I'll show you how." Emily didn't look at him, just motioned with her paintbrush to the wall next to her.

"Yeah Dad, no whining, remember?" Hallie bounced on her bed and then stilled as she watched Emily paint.

Emily laughed and tucked a strand of hair behind her ear. She left a trail of green paint along her cheekbone and her ear in the process. Jack lifted his eyebrows and tried not to laugh.

Emily noticed. "What?"

"You just painted yourself."

She looked at her hand and groaned when she saw the green smudge on her fingers. "Oh, well. I do that at least once every job. It comes off."

"It's a nice touch."

Emily quirked an eyebrow. "Really?"

"Well, in a good way. I mean, it's cute, or—uh, I'll just stop talking now. Maybe I should go work on the yard."

"You're not getting out of clouds that easy." She took a white towel and rubbed her face, missing most of the green paint, and then pointed to the sponge he still held in his hand. She placed her hand over his and helped him dab the sponge in some white paint. "Now all you do is let the sponge feather-kiss the wall, like this." She took the sponge and tapped it lightly on the wall, moving in a circular pattern. "Now you try."

He looked at the sponge and back at the wall and moved forward. But instead of a gentle kiss, he put too much force behind the sponge and left a gloppy splatter of white paint.

Emily stepped back and eyed the gloppy cloud with one hand on her hip. "Hmm, I could have sworn this didn't take any artistic ability, but it looks like I was wrong."

"I tried to tell you." Jack handed her the sponge, but Emily just shook her head.

"Let me help you." She clutched his hand and showed him how. "You don't want to feel the sponge touch the wall—just a feather kiss remember?"

"I don't really know what a feather kiss is," Jack said.

"Maybe this would help." She took the sponge and looked at it for a second and then reached out and dabbed Jack's face. Emily burst out laughing and Hallie squealed.

Jack touched his cheek and felt the wetness on his fingertips, the sharp smell of fresh paint reloading his senses.

"Daddy, you look like a clown!"

"Sorry," Emily blurted out before she laughed again.

"Is this the work of a true artist?" He motioned to his cheek, then grabbed the sponge from Emily and brushed it over her nose. The surprise on her face was so funny that Jack laughed, and before he could stop and retrieve the somber mood that shadowed him daily, he laughed again. He daubed the tip of Hallie's nose with the white paint and she shrieked running around the room. And he couldn't stop laughing. Emily collapsed onto Hallie's bed with a sigh and Jack wiped at the moisture in the corner of his eyes.

He sank to the floor, the tension over the past few weeks draining out of him. Hallie hugged him. "I like playing with you and Emily."

Jack tousled her hair. "It's been too long since we've laughed like this."

He saw Emily's mouth turn down, but then she sat up, smiling at them both. "Me too. And we're barely getting started." She pointed to the thick brown lines outlining the trunk of the tree. "Now that we have our giggles out, you can color in the trunk, Hallie."

Hallie clapped her hands. "I won't go out of the lines."

"I know, but do you think we should let your dad have another chance at those clouds?"

Hallie turned and examined the white smudge on the wall with a serious expression, and then her features softened. "Maybe one more try, but don't make it ugly, Daddy."

"Aye, aye, Captain." Jack saluted and carefully lifted the sponge.

"Here let me do one full cloud and you can look at it as kind of a pattern." Emily took the sponge from him and dipped it in the paint. "Then when yours goes off on a tangent, it'll look natural."

With a chuckle, Jack stood back and watched her work. He could see a tiny bit of green paint in the hair by her ear. He felt reenergized after laughing and a bit out of sorts. For four months, Jack had constantly swallowed the ball of grief stuck in his throat. But he had laughed again. With Emily. Watching her work, Jack couldn't ignore the good feelings he had for her, but he wouldn't dwell on that. He mentally shrugged. Maybe his mood wasn't all because of Emily. It probably had something to do with meeting Danika that night and a possibility that his son was actually alive. Suddenly, the world held promise again. Even though one part of him wanted to agonize over the separation between him and Easton, he only felt a calmness settle around his heart that all would be right.

And Emily was here, adding to that rightness. He hadn't ever spent much time around her, but he felt like he knew her because of how much Gina talked about her. Emily had a freshness about her that was attractive and he recognized why Gina had gotten along with her so well.

Emily turned and held out the sponge, interrupting his thoughts. "See, that's how it's done."

"I'll give it a shot."

Twenty minutes later, Jack could see that Hallie's help was turning into more of a hindrance. Emily was incredibly patient with her, but his daughter was going to make the job take twice as long. "Hallie, let's go set up a cartoon and then maybe Emily can surprise you."

"Hmm, that might be a good idea. Maybe I can get the

first bird painted." Emily crouched down and looked into Hallie's dark brown eyes. "Does that sound okay?"

Hallie stuck out her bottom lip. "I just wanted to help."

"And you can, after your cartoon." Jack steered her into the living room. It was eleven-forty-five, so he decided to make Hallie some lunch first. She helped him get out the ingredients for cheese sandwiches, tearing the bread as she tried to butter it. He turned the griddle on and then walked back to Hallie's room.

"Would you care for a gourmet cheese sandwich?"

Emily turned and he smiled at the green smudge on her cheek. "I love cheese sandwiches, how did you know?"

"Lucky, I guess. That and my chef repertoire is so extensive, you know."

Emily laughed. "Let me know when it's ready."

Jack added a slice of ham to the sandwiches and cut up a pear, carefully arranging the slices in a spiral pattern for Hallie. He repeated the process for Emily. He warmed up a can of bean with bacon soup and set the table. Then he used a rag to scrub the paint off his face and Hallie's.

"Soup's on," he hollered.

"Be there in two minutes."

Jack heard the bathroom door close and when Emily returned, her cheeks and nose were freshly scrubbed and only a few flecks of paint remained.

"Aw, you took off your makeup."

Emily shook her finger at him. "So did you."

"Daddy, can I say the prayer?" Hallie asked.

"Sure, sweetheart." Jack noticed how Emily's features softened as she looked at Hallie and bowed her head.

"Dear God, please bless the food. Bless Daddy to be happy and bless Emily to paint my tree and my bird and my bunny. And bless Easton to come home."

Jack didn't flinch when he listened to Hallie's prayer. He didn't correct her or argue with her because he had been saying the same prayer all morning.

When he opened his eyes, he saw that Emily had been watching him but she quickly averted her eyes. "This looks delicious." She picked up her sandwich and took a bite.

They all chewed in silence for a few moments until Hallie started chattering about her tree and how Emily needed to make sure one of the leaves had a butterfly on it. They finished the meal and Jack started a cartoon for Hallie. Emily helped clear the dishes and Jack followed her back to Hallie's room. He wanted to tell Emily that he had seen Easton, but he worried that she might think him crazy. He was trying to think of a way to bring up the subject when Emily handed him the sponge. "That wall needs a few more clouds."

"So you approve of my cloud painting abilities?" Jack asked.

"I do." She hesitated, her paintbrush poised over the beginnings of a leaf. "Jack, I want to ask you something, but I don't want to make you uncomfortable."

A couple days ago, Jack would have shied away from the start of that sentence. "Em, if you have something to say, I trust you. You can say anything."

Her eyes darted to him and down to the floor. She turned, but not before the red splotches on her neck appeared. Maybe he didn't want to hear it; she seemed uncomfortable just contemplating the conversation.

She cleared her throat. "Do you believe that people who have died can communicate with us?"

Jack could see where this was headed, but he noticed how Emily was struggling so he decided to shut up and let her speak. "I do."

Emily looked relieved. "That's good, because well, I've

been wondering about something. I mean, do you think that spirits get trapped here on earth sometimes?"

"Trapped? Like they can't get into heaven?"

"I don't know if it's that they can't get in, more like they can't leave earth until things are resolved."

"Emily, I'm guessing you're talking about Gina. Are you thinking about your dream?" She set the paintbrush down on the tray and turned to Jack. There were tears in her eyes and he could see a slight tremor in her chin.

"I'm not sure what's happening, but I feel her."

"Gina?" Jack saw the emotion in Emily's eyes. Was it possible that Gina had been seeking out help from anyone who would listen to her? He thought about the dream Emily had shared with him about Gina holding Easton's blanket. He needed to tell her about the blanket, to show her.

"Just a minute. I need to show you something." He went into his bedroom and retrieved Easton's blanket from a shelf in the closet. He had placed it inside an old, dark blue pillowcase. He rubbed his thumb against the flannel as he walked back into Hallie's room. When he pulled out the blanket, Emily gasped.

She took a step forward, reaching out her hand to touch the fabric. "I thought you said you didn't have it."

"I didn't then. A fisherman found it." Jack clenched the blanket tighter and then released his grip. "The sheriff on the case brought it to me the same day you told me about your dream."

Emily covered her face with her hands. Her shoulders shook and Jack set the blanket down. He wasn't sure what to do. He hated seeing her cry. He remembered the first time he'd seen Gina cry—he'd felt so helpless until she'd told him to just hold her. But this was Emily, Gina's best friend.

Hold her.

The impression felt so strong that Jack looked for Gina in the room. She wasn't there, but a compelling feeling moved him toward Emily. He stepped closer to Emily and took her into his arms. Her body trembled and she cried into her hands. "Shh, it's okay."

"No, it's not," she sobbed.

Jack patted her back as she cried. He tucked her hair behind her ear and felt a shuddering breath as she moved her hands from her face. Emotions welled in his own chest as he comforted her. He had missed the closeness of a woman, Gina's soft curves and gentle touch. Thinking of his wife didn't make him feel guilty as he held Emily. He wondered at that, what it meant for the state of his heart. Emily's hands were small, yet strong against his chest. She put her hand on a wet spot on his shirt and moved her head. "I'm sorry. I don't know what's happening to me."

"Just tell me, Em," Jack whispered.

She tipped her head back, her green eyes luminous with tears. "Gina keeps showing up in my dreams and I don't know why."

He wanted to keep holding her, but she stepped out of his embrace. Jack bit his lip. "I think I do." He closed his eyes and inhaled. "It's about Easton."

"That's what I thought at first when I dreamed of Gina holding the blanket, but what does it mean now that you have the blanket ? Are they still looking for his body?"

Jack shook his head. "I think Easton might be alive."

Emily's eyes widened. "How?"

"I don't know, but come with me and I'll show you something." He took Emily's hand and led her to his office. She gripped his fingers and followed closely behind. Jack wondered if Emily was as starved for comfort as he was. He closed the door and picked up the folder tucked behind his monitor. "I haven't said anything to Hallie because it's obvious that Gina has a message for her too. I think she was trying to find someone who would listen to her."

Jack handed the folder to Emily. She opened it and flipped through the pictures of Easton. She looked at Jack, covering her mouth with her hand, her eyes widening. She clutched the folder. "What is this? Who is this woman?"

"I don't know." Jack took the folder from her. "But I'm going to find out. I saw them in Idaho Falls by the river. I thought I was going crazy and then I decided to start listening to my wife."

"Did you call the police?"

"Yes, I called my friend who is a sheriff and felt him out first. Told him I thought I saw my son and asked what he could do to help me. They think I've cracked. But what's more important is Vincent told me that they didn't have any grounds to investigate." Jack set the folder on his desk. "I'm going to hire a private investigator—I'm meeting with her tonight. I just need more evidence."

"But this woman who has Easton, what if you can't find her?"

"I thought the same thing, but every time I started panicking I got this feeling right here." He put a hand over his heart. "And I just felt like everything was going to be alright. I was so close to him, to this woman. I could have walked up to them, but then I realized that if I did that, she would run and I'd never get my son back. She's hiding somewhere, but I have her license plate number, her picture, and I saw her in Idaho Falls. How long do you think it would take a P.I. to find her?"

"Hopefully not long, but Jack, how did this woman end up with Easton?" Emily folded her arms. "I thought they found the car seat in the river."

"It's crazy, but somehow she kidnapped him. I'm not sure if the accident was intentional since they never found the other driver. I always assumed it was somebody with no insurance or a record."

"I want to help you," Emily said.

Jack took her hand and squeezed it. "You already have. When you told me about your dream and then Vincent showed up with the blanket—I decided to start looking."

"Daddy, did Emily finish the surprise yet?" Hallie poked her head into the office.

"Not yet, Sweetie, but I'll hurry and get back to work," Emily answered.

She studied Jack for a moment. "It's going to be okay, isn't it?"

Jack nodded. He steered Hallie back to her cartoon as Emily retreated down the hallway. Emily spent another hour painting in Hallie's room. Jack finished the clouds and helped Emily clean up the supplies. Hallie bounced around the room chirping like a bird when she saw the robin Emily had painted on the branch of her tree.

Before Emily left, Jack hugged her. "Thank you. This is just what Hallie needed. You wouldn't believe the difference in her from last week to now."

Emily put her hand on Jack's arm. "Please call me if you find anything."

He covered her hand with his. "I will."

CHAPTER ELEVEN

JACK HIRED A BABYSITTER FOR HALLIE. Helen would be hurt if she found out he hadn't asked her, but he didn't want to explain what he was doing. Danika had agreed to drive from Twin Falls to meet him in Burley at a Mexican restaurant. Jack pulled up at five after seven and parked in front of El Caporal and hurried into the building. He caught sight of long legs, a mini-skirt, and flaming red hair as the doors whooshed shut. The woman in the entryway assessed him quickly and tilted her head.

"Jack Bentley?"

"Sorry, I'm late." He held out his hand and she shook his, her silver bracelets jangling.

"No problem. They have a table ready for us."

As she turned he saw a purple streak in her hair and he smiled. Toby definitely didn't know his type, but if Danika could help him he was willing to do a little flirting.

After they placed their orders, Jack noticed Danika's low-cut blouse, which was probably exactly what she wanted, so he averted his eyes. She wore a silver heart pendant that kept dipping down into her cleavage. When she took a drink of her diet Coke she left a smudge of dark red lipstick on the glass. The waitress brought out their meals and after a bit of chitchat, Jack wiped his face with the cloth napkin and smiled at Danika. "Toby said that you're a private investigator." Jack decided to broach the subject that was currently giving him heartburn. "Does that keep you pretty busy?"

"It all depends on how many cases I'm working at once. Sometimes I have lean months and other times I have to turn people down."

"Have you ever helped with any kidnapping cases?" Jack tried to act nonchalant, but he could hear the tension in his voice.

Danika frowned. "I have. Usually by the time someone hires me, the case is cold. It's difficult. Lots easier to take pictures of some guy cheating on his wife."

Jack cringed. Her answer should have made him change his mind, but he was desperate. "I'm sure Toby told you about my history."

Danika nodded. "I didn't want to bring it up. I'm sorry."

"No, no, it's fine. I just—well, I'd like to reopen the case of my son, my baby. I think there's a chance that he could be alive."

"I'm listening." Danika arched an eyebrow.

Jack leaned forward and in quiet tones told her about the woman he'd seen in Idaho Falls with Easton. When he finished, he gripped his glass of iced tea tightly, the condensation running over his fingers.

"I don't know," Danika said. "That's a pretty big stretch. But you do have some good basic information."

"So, you could help me?"

Danika took a sip of her drink. "I don't want to get your hopes up."

"They're not," Jack's voice was flat. "I just need answers."

"Let me guess. You called the cops and they said you were crazy." She folded her arms.

"More or less," Jack said.

"They could be right, but you don't strike me as the crazy kind."

"I'll take that as a compliment," Jack said. "How about we finish eating dinner, you think about it, and let me know. I won't try to twist your arm."

"Okay, I'll consider it, but only because you're hot."

Jack choked on his drink, but luckily the waitress came to check on them before he could respond. He tried his best to focus on other things during the meal, asking Danika about her interests and answering some of her questions, but he was only interested in finding Easton. After Jack paid the bill, he walked with Danika to her car. The parking lot was full and she had parked near the back where the lighting was dim. Jack was trying to think of a way to segue into his earlier request to investigate Easton when Danika slipped her arm through his.

"You've had a lot of adjusting to do, being a widower." She sidled up to him. "I know it can get lonely. Why don't you come back to my place?"

"I don't know." Jack felt like his head was on fire. He wanted to run the other way, but he stood his ground. "My little girl is at home with a sitter. I told her I wouldn't be too late."

"It doesn't have to be late." Danika smiled and squeezed his bicep.

"I'm sorry, Danika. I just don't think it's a good idea. I really need your help to find Easton."

Danika pouted. "I only take cases that I think can keep my attention."

Jack hesitated. He dreaded having to look up another investigator. He could tell from their conversation at dinner that Danika had good resources and her no-nonsense personality meant she probably had a fair amount of success.

"Now you," her voice was husky as she tapped his chest. "You have my attention." She wrapped her arms around his neck and stood on her tiptoes. She covered his mouth in a hot kiss. Jack froze and he felt his blood flash with heat. It had been a long time since he'd felt anything like this. His emotions had been total grief, his hormones covered with sorrow. She pressed against him, kissing him softly, and for a half-second he kissed her back, but it wasn't a good feeling. He disentangled himself. "I'm sorry, Danika. It's just too soon for me. If you can help me, I'd like to hire you for the case, but I'm not really ready to date."

Danika's lips twitched, her face was flushed. Then she smiled. "I like a challenge. I'll take the case. I bet I can get you the info in forty-eight hours."

Jack's jaw dropped and Danika put a finger on his chin. She leaned in close. "You could still come by my house. We don't have to date. You could help me get a head start on the case."

"I—uh, I don't want to complicate things." Jack's mind was racing. He was completely out of his league with this woman and not sure how to turn her off, while still needing her help. "I hope you understand."

"Sure," Danika chuckled. "My retainer is usually five-hundred, but if you'll write me out a check for two-fifty, I'll get started tonight, since I won't be otherwise occupied." She winked.

Jack pulled out his checkbook. It was hard to keep his hand from shaking as he wrote out the check. He promised to send Danika the pictures as soon as he got home.

He returned home before ten o'clock and paid the babysitter, checked in on Hallie, and then emailed Danika the pictures and information. He switched off his computer and headed for a hot shower. He wanted to wash away Danika's kiss. He felt guilty. He'd never entertained thoughts of another woman before—he'd never had to because Gina was his world. She still was, but someday the lack of a mother would affect Hallie. Immediately, Emily came to his mind with those freckles scattered across her nose. She was everything Danika wasn't and yet, Emily was different from Gina too.

With a shake of his head, Jack dried off and got ready for bed. It was too soon to be worrying over women. When Jack crawled into bed, he searched for Gina's presence in his mind. "I love you, Gina. I always will. I don't understand these feelings I'm having for Emily." He felt like he was betraying Gina's memory, but he couldn't ignore the impressions he'd felt earlier when Emily had needed his comfort.

Talking with Danika had given him courage. He had a plan and he needed Emily to help him carry it out. Perhaps that was why Gina had placed her in his path. An image of Emily came to his mind, the green smudge of paint on her cheek, her eyes dancing with laughter. He didn't feel any guilt over holding her earlier today—nothing like how he felt when Danika kissed him. Emily was different. The way she interacted with Hallie, how her nose scrunched when she concentrated on painting the bird on the tree. She was Emily, and he felt safe thinking of her.

Jack smiled as he fell asleep.

CHAPTER TWELVE

A SCREAM PULLED EMILY from the nightmare and she bolted upright in bed before she realized that the scream was her own. She turned on the light, and then covered her face with her hands, taking in shaky breaths. She had dreamed of Brett, his face contorted with anger standing next to the brunette he'd been sleeping with. "You were never enough for me!" he'd yelled at her. It had been almost two years and her heart still hadn't healed. The fissures were deep, filled with Brett's rage and unfaithfulness. She shivered.

The clock's red digits changed to 1:45. Emily got up and wiped her face with a cool cloth, then downed a glass of water and crawled back in bed. As soon as she closed her eyes, her mind shifted to Jack, his face creased in laughter. The smudge of white paint on his cheek and how he'd painted her nose made her giggle.

Emily's stomach flipped and she smiled, reliving how it had felt to have Jack pull her into his chest; his arms wrapping around her, determined to keep her safe. She had rested her head against his chest and cried and felt his heart beating in her ear. Something was happening to her and she couldn't help but think of her dream and Gina's urging to heal Jack's broken heart. Earlier, it had seemed as if they were both helping each other. Gina was a bond between them. Was that the only reason Emily felt compelled to spend time with Jack and Hallie?

Easton. After what Jack had showed her, Emily knew that was the real reason—the true connection. Jack had asked her to help and she had agreed. She didn't dare hope, but the pictures had looked remarkably like Easton. It was bizarre and Emily wasn't sure if they were both crazy. She put a hand over her heart, and the corners of her mouth lifted in a slight smile. Thinking of Jack had driven the nightmare of Brett from her mind. Jack was ten times the man Brett was, and after seeing Hallie, Emily could see what a good father Jack was and how much he loved his family. Gina was right. Jack would never betray the ones he loved.

Emily couldn't shake the feeling that the things Gina had told her in the dream were important. She struggled to remember everything Gina had shared. At the same time she yearned to see Jack and Hallie again.

CHAPTER THIRTEEN

THE ACCOUNT AGREEMENT came through from the Idaho Potato Council on Wednesday and Jack spent the day prepping for his commute to Idaho Falls the following week. Hopefully, the presentation he would give in front of some of the top potato farmers in the state would gain him more clients. His construction business had really been taking off right before Gina died, but then he'd lost the will to pursue new clients and things had been sluggish. But now with the hope that Easton might be alive, Jack had a new desire to build his business and provide for his little family.

At three o'clock, just before Jack was leaving to pick Hallie up from kindergarten, Danika called.

"Found her."

Jack nearly dropped the phone. He sat on the edge of the table. "You're sure?"

"I'm never wrong. Her name is Janette Baker. She lives in Idaho Falls and works at a daycare so Easton is always with her. I'm sending you an email with her address and the other information I found on her, including pictures of her with your son.

Jack struggled to get his voice to work. He let Danika's words repeat in his mind. "Do you think the police would help me now?"

"Unfortunately, no. We need proof and short of a DNA test, I don't know what you can get to prove he's your son."

"I can get a DNA test."

"How?"

"I don't know. I'll figure something out." Jack didn't tell her that he already had a plan.

"Jack, I don't want you to do anything rash," Danika said. "She is jumpy, paranoid, and definitely a flight risk."

"She has my son." Jack stood up and paced back and forth through his kitchen. "I have to do something."

Danika hesitated and he heard her typing on her computer. "Let me talk to my contacts at the police department and see what they say."

"They'll say I'm crazy. I've already tried that route. I'll get my evidence and then I'll call the police."

"So, do you want me to keep tailing her?"

Jack liked how Danika didn't argue with him. "Yes, I need to know her schedule, her patterns. Keep a log of the time and see if you can predict where she's going to show up."

"Easy enough. How about I gather this info and we meet for dinner?"

She definitely didn't give up, Jack had to give her that, but he refused to go down that path. "I don't think that's a good idea right now. My little girl is having a hard week."

"I'll take a rain check, but I'm not letting you off that easy, Jack."

"Okay, I'll think about it," Jack replied, knowing that he was giving her a half-truth. "Thanks for the great work."

Jack ended the call, adrenaline coursing through his body. Crazy with the knowledge that Easton was still alive, he wanted to drive to Idaho Falls right then. He forced himself to take a few breaths, thinking of Gina and her rational ways. What would she tell him to do?

He thought of his FBI friend, Jason Edwards. Jack didn't want to talk to the local police again, but maybe his friend could help him. Jack hesitated a few seconds before pulling up Jason's number and calling him.

"Jack? Man, it's been too long," Jason answered and launched into conversation as usual. "How are you doing? How's Hallie?"

"It has been too long. I'm surviving, and Hallie has been struggling, but is doing better the past week." Jack bit his bottom lip, trying to decide how to broach the subject. "Are you still dating that girl you rescued?"

"Courtney? Yes, I am," Jason replied and Jack could hear the smile in his voice.

"Sounds like you're happy about that," Jack said.

"I am very happy, but that's not why you called. What's up?"

Jack sighed. "Please don't think I'm crazy, but I need your advice."

"Okay, shoot." Jason cleared his throat. "And I know you're not crazy, but that's not a great leading statement."

Jack chuckled. "It's about Easton. I think he's alive." Before Jason could interrupt, he launched into a full explanation of what he'd seen in Idaho Falls, hiring an investigator, and discovering the identity of the woman.

"Jack," Jason's voice was quiet, yet strong. "I wish I could help you with this, but you're right. We don't have a way to prove that he's your son and I doubt any mother would submit her child to a DNA test under the circumstances."

Jack swallowed. Jason didn't think he was crazy and it gave him a sliver of hope. "There has to be some way to prove that he's my son."

"DNA is the only way because it has to be fool-proof."

"But you just said we can't get a DNA sample." Jack rubbed the sweat from his forehead. The intensity of having Easton so close and yet out of his reach made his lungs tight. He forced himself to take a slow breath.

"There is a way if we can connect the woman to any sort of investigation," Jason replied.

"But I can hear in your voice that it would be a long shot," Jack said. "I can't just give up. She has my son. I know it's Easton."

"Let me do some checking, okay?" Jason rustled some papers and Jack heard the clicking of his keyboard. "I'll ask around and see if I can come up with an idea."

"Okay," Jack tried to hide the defeat in his voice.

"Jack, don't do anything stupid. You don't want to mess this up. If she really has your son, then we need time to gather evidence."

"But time doesn't matter if no one is doing anything," Jack responded. "I already told you that my friend on the force thought I was completely nuts."

"I get that, but here's the thing. If we can find a reason to move forward, I can help you because it will be a missing persons case and that is under the FBI's jurisdiction. But you have to exercise some patience in the meantime. It could take weeks to get enough information to request something like a DNA test—that's serious stuff."

"But my P.I. said that the woman is paranoid and jumpy. What if she runs with Easton?"

"It's been four months, Jack. I don't see a reason for her to run. Send me the info you have and I'll get to work on it in between the case I'm working right now."

"Thanks, man. It means a lot that you'd at least hear me out."

"I'm doing more than hearing you out. Now get back to work and get your mind off this for a few days," Jason's voice held a note of authority.

"Okay. Take care."

After Jack ended the call, he took another deep breath. Jason had listened and he was definitely qualified as an FBI agent, but Jack felt an urgency that he couldn't explain. He wasn't willing to wait weeks to find out if there could be a start to an investigation. A start that might not go anywhere and might not even garner DNA evidence.

His heart was still pounding and if anything, he was more wound up than before he spoke with Jason. He needed to talk to someone who didn't think he was crazy from grief. Emily immediately came to his mind. Jack called her on his way over to the school to pick up Hallie. "Hey, Em. Can you come with me to Idaho Falls tomorrow? I know where Easton is."

"What? But it's only been a few days." Her voice went up several notches. "Are you sure?"

Jack grinned. "My private investigator claims 100% certainty."

"Are you meeting the police there?"

"No," Jack pressed his lips together, trying to decide how much he should trust Emily. "They can't help me unless I get a sample of Easton's DNA to prove that he is my son."

"I don't understand. How are you going to do that if the police won't help you?" Emily asked. "Did you call them?"

"Yes, and I'm not calling them again. Em, they thought I was crazy." He left out the part where he had contacted Jason.

"Okay, whatever you need me to do, I'll be there."

Jack put a hand on the back of his neck and took a deep breath. "Thanks. That means a lot."

"You're welcome." Emily's voice was soft.

"Can I pick you up at nine tomorrow?"

"Sure," Emily said. "But Jack, I want you to know that I'll be praying and I hope you will too."

"It's all I've done since I saw him."

After Jack hung up the phone, he could hardly focus the rest of the day. Hallie knew something was up. "Daddy, did you find Easton?"

Jack decided to answer her question. "I'm looking very hard. I'll do my best."

Hallie nodded and hugged her teddy bear tight.

After putting Hallie to bed, Jack holed up in his office. He printed out a map and circled several locations around Janette's home. Danika had even found the location of the gas station Janette used. His plan was simple; he only hoped that Emily would go for it.

The next morning Jack dropped Hallie off at Helen's and then drove over to Emily's house. He waited until they were on the freeway to share the details of his plan with Emily. She listened, her eyes widening and then shook her head. "It's too risky."

"All you have to do is swab his mouth. We'll wrap a bandage around your finger—the cotton stretch kind. Stick your finger in his mouth like you're noticing his teeth, get enough saliva. I've read up on the internet and that's all we need."

"But what mother is going to let some stranger put a finger inside her baby's mouth?"

"Do you have another idea?"

Emily looked out the window and then turned to Jack. She reached over and squeezed his hand. "No, it's a good plan. But what are you going to do if it doesn't work? If we don't find an opportunity to get near Easton?"

Danika has tailed her for three days. She's stopped somewhere every day after she gets off work. The gas station. The library. The city offices. All we have to do is follow her to her next errand."

Emily drummed her fingers on the table. "You're hoping for a grocery store, aren't you?"

"Why not? She hasn't gone this week. Everyone needs milk and eggs."

"Okay, I'll try." Emily rubbed the wrapper of the bandage. "I still don't understand why the police won't help you."

Jack tightened his grip on the steering wheel. "I didn't ask for their help."

"I thought you said you did." Emily folded her arms. "You have to be honest with me if you expect me to put myself at risk for you."

"I am being honest," Jack said. "I gave a scenario to a police friend of mine. He told me that they'd have to get a court order to collect DNA. Easton has a death certificate. He has a headstone. To everyone else he's dead and I'm a crazy person. Think about it Emily, if you hadn't seen Gina in a dream, would you be here now?"

Emily rubbed her arms and then released her hands to her lap. "You make a good point."

"If there was another way, I'd do it, but the justice system isn't set up for a situation like this, so I have to take matters into my own hands. It takes six business days to get the results back for a paternity test based on DNA. Danika will keep an eye on Janette and Easton. As soon as we get the results, we'll go to the police."

"I'm scared," Emily whispered.

"I am too, but that woman is no match for Easton's mother." Jack smiled and Emily seemed to relax a bit.

Once they arrived in Idaho Falls, they drove the routes Danika had outlined to familiarize themselves with the area. They stopped at each of the places Janette had been seen and found ideal parking spots, doing their best to remain inconspicuous.

Jack's stomach was tied up in knots and they still had some time to kill so he took Emily to Betty's Baked Clubs for lunch. They took their sandwiches to the park and ate overlooking the Snake River. The water was a constant, as it always had been in Jack's life. He vowed not to be afraid of its force. He was going to get Easton back, and maybe then Gina would be able to rest in peace.

CHAPTER FOURTEEN

A SHORT BLONDE woman put a carton of yogurt in her basket and smiled in Janette's direction. She pushed her cart toward Janette. "What a darling baby. How old is he?"

Janette smiled back, nodding toward Andrew. "He's eleven months."

"That is so sweet, look at those chubby cheeks."

Andrew grinned at the woman and he reached out for her. "Hey there, buddy."

Janette bumped the cart forward just as the woman reached out for Andrew's fingers. His smile widened and he leaned farther over the cart toward the blonde.

"He looks so happy. Do you mind if I hold him for a minute?"

"Oh no. He smiles at people, but if they try to pick him up, he screams."

The woman frowned. "Oh that's too bad. I love babies."

Janette forced a smile. "Well, thank you. Have a good night."

"Uh, okay. You too." The woman stared at Andrew and

then flashed a tight smile to Janette. She turned and picked up a carton of eggs. Janette pushed the cart faster toward the bread aisle. Only three more things on her list. People noticed Andrew all the time. His dark hair and sky blue eyes drew their attention. She hated how people thought it was okay to touch him, to squeeze his fat rolls. Andrew was so good-natured. He always gave his toothy smile and reached out with chubby fingers, but Janette worried. She looked behind her, but she didn't see the blonde woman.

Janette grabbed a loaf of bread, and then headed to the diaper aisle. She turned the corner and her cart bumped into the blonde woman's. "Oh, sorry about that." The woman looked up, a sippy cup in her hand. "Oh, it's you. That's perfect timing. I was just trying to figure out which of these cups works best. My friend is having her first baby and the shower is tomorrow. I sewed her a blanket, but I wanted to put a few things with it. Which one does your baby like?"

Janette narrowed her eyes and turned toward the shelf. She pointed to the sippy cups Andrew used. "These are the best. They don't leak all over and the stoppers are easy to remove so you can clean them."

The woman brightened and stepped toward her. "That's so kind of you. I wouldn't have even thought of that." She looked down. "I don't have any children."

Janette's heart beat increased. She saw the woman glance at Andrew and wiggle her fingers at him. He smiled and reached out toward her. The woman reached her hand out to touch his cheek. Janette jerked the cart back. "I've got to go."

The wheels of the cart rattled as she pushed it so fast that a breeze tickled the hair back from Andrew's forehead. She glanced behind her and saw the blonde woman, picking up a box of baby cereal. Her throat constricted and she felt a panic attack coming on. That woman didn't have any children. What if she tried to take Andrew?

Andrew babbled and Janette mentally shook herself. Everything was fine. It was time to take her meds again. No one would hurt Andrew. "You're safe with me," she whispered to him and stroked his cheek. She went through the express lane and ignored the veiled glare from the checker as she piled on nearly forty items instead of fifteen.

She couldn't get home fast enough and she practically ran inside when they arrived. She walked through each room with Andrew on her hip. When Janette had first moved to Idaho, she'd discovered that the house needed work and she didn't have much money. Broken pipes needing repair, a new water heater, and a leak in the roof had drained her savings. Only three weeks after moving in, the basement flooded during a heavy spring rainstorm. The contractor suspected a crack in the foundation and that's when Janette had a nervous breakdown.

After a visit to the emergency room, the doctors recommended she spend a few nights at the mental hospital in Blackfoot where they kept her on suicide watch. They gave her three different medications, but nothing really helped. After five days, Janette made a decision. She pretended to be feeling much better and acted like a different person. With no family to contact and Janette's own voluntary admittance, the hospital had to release her when she requested it. She checked out and headed back to Idaho Falls with a plan. As she approached the two bridges spanning the Snake River, she pulled her car over to the side of the road. If word got out about her breakdown, she'd never get another job. Things looked worse by the minute, but she was ready for peace, for a rest. Janette had walked calmly down the bank of the river, several hundred yards from the freeway.

The water swirled and frothed, looking almost angry as it tumbled over large rocks near the west side of the river. Janette felt like a complete failure. Her life was empty because she couldn't have children, and it always would be. She took two steps into the water; it was icy cold and she noted how fast the current was moving. For a moment, she wondered if her body would even be found.

She bent her knees, ready to jump in when she heard a series of loud noises—screeching, honking, a crash. Janette still didn't know what had compelled her to do so, but she turned and began running toward the sounds of the accident. She'd arrived less than two minutes after she'd heard the commotion. She heard screams and looked out at the river in time to see a silver Camry sinking into the water. Someone was calling for help as the current pulled the car away from the bridge toward the riverbank. Janette didn't know what to do. She wasn't a strong swimmer. She looked toward the bridge but she didn't see anyone else coming.

That's when God had given her a sign. She looked back toward the car; it was on its side, the front end sinking rapidly. Then she saw a child's car seat balanced precariously on the side of the door. She saw an arm and heard more screams for help. "Please, don't let him drown!" a woman cried out frantically.

The car was probably only ten yards from the bank. Janette knew what she had to do. She splashed through the river, going under for a moment as the bottom dropped off. She came up spluttering. The silver car was mostly submerged and Janette paddled frantically toward the car seat as it slid off the car and into the water. She reached the baby just as the water washed over his face. With a force that she still didn't comprehend, Janette pushed the car seat toward the riverbank, lifting it out of the water as she kicked her legs and then stumbled to find solid footing.

The baby coughed and gagged on the river water as Janette struggled to release the restraints. Almost in hysterics, she pulled the baby from the car seat and put him on her shoulder, pounding out any water. The baby cried and Janette felt a surge of relief. Crying meant breathing.

Janette looked back to the river and her stomach tightened. The driver of the car hadn't made it out. The river ran over the front of the car, the back end bobbing out of the water. That was the moment Janette's life had changed—her sign from God. She looked up and saw that the tree blocked her view of the highway. The thick bushes along the riverbank would make it nearly impossible for someone to have seen her pull the baby from the water.

She had saved him.

The decision was immediate. Janette buckled the top harness in the car seat, but left the leg harness undone. Then she pushed the car seat back into the river. She backtracked to the road where she'd parked her car—putting distance between herself and the river she'd almost given her life to. Instead, the river had given her new life. The baby whimpered against her chest and she rubbed his back.

"It's okay, Andrew. I'm your mommy now. I won't let anything happen to you."

When she reached her car, the first police troopers were arriving on the scene. She grabbed the extra blanket from her trunk, wrapped the baby up tightly and placed him carefully on the floor of the back seat. He wailed for five minutes and then was quiet. Janette took him home to Aunt Martha's little cottage.

She pawned some things and used what little money she had left to buy baby supplies: a crib, diapers, a new car seat and stroller. When the neighbors commented that they didn't know she had a baby, she replied that she was a very private person.

Janette shook off the memories as she checked the locks on the front door again. Andrew was dozing in her arms and she carried him to his room quietly, placing him in the crib.

Her lungs felt heavy, and an anxious sensation kept her wondering if someone had been following her again. She took two pills and looked out at the front yard. The white birch tree held tight to its few leaves. The tree was the first thing Janette had planted after she brought Andrew home—a symbol of the potential for her little family.

Trent paid her five-hundred dollars a month for alimony and just last month she had received about ten grand in the divorce settlement. It didn't amount to much back in New Hampshire, but in Idaho the property taxes were significantly lower along with the cost of living. After she rescued Andrew, she applied to several daycares nearby. He was her little good luck charm. Sunrise Daycare offered her a part-time position which worked perfectly. She could earn enough money to pay for groceries and stay close to Andrew.

The scariest part of her day was when she had to leave for work. The outside world pressed down on her with worries of being discovered, but Janette wanted to provide Andrew with a good life, so she pushed back her fears and inadequacies. She wouldn't be able to work at the daycare forever, but for now it was a solution.

She had heard something at work last week. The daycare owner had referred to the terrible accident last May when a woman and her baby drowned in the Snake River. Janette's throat had tightened with fear and her conscience prodded her, but she wouldn't let doubt overcome God's will. The news story she had found reported that the baby had drowned but his body hadn't been recovered. Janette knew it was her miracle that she had found sweet Andrew. She had saved him, and it was because God loved her and wanted her to have a second chance at life. Both of them had been given an extension on life and she was determined not to waste it.

Janette took a deep breath and checked on Andrew. His breathing was almost silent it was so soft. She checked the windows and the locks, but she couldn't shake the feeling that someone was watching her, following her, waiting for their chance to take her baby. The house was the only thing keeping her in Idaho Falls, but Andrew was more important than a house. It was time to move.

CHAPTER FIFTEEN

EMILY CRIED FOR FORTY-FIVE MINUTES, with Jack trying to console her. She couldn't be comforted, so finally he pulled the car over.

"Emily, you have to stop this." He took her by the shoulders. "This isn't your fault."

"He was right there. I should have just grabbed him and ran." She broke down again, letting her head drop to her chest.

Jack felt like crying too. Their plan had failed, but falling apart wouldn't solve anything. He would just have to try again. Maybe Danika could help him. Jack pulled Emily to his chest, wrapping his arms around her. She burrowed her head in his chest.

"I'm so sorry," she murmured. "She was just so skittish. She's definitely paranoid. You should have seen the way she looked at me, as if she expected me to try and take her baby."

"We'll get Easton back. I'll call Vincent again and see if there's any way he can help me. I have a friend who works for the FBI and he said he'd see what he could do. We might just have to wait."

"I should've tried harder." Emily sniffed.

"No, you did right. You would have just scared her off. We need her guard to be down."

The drive back to Heyburn was torture because Jack was sure he'd left his heart back in that grocery store parking lot. For Emily's sake, he remained stoic, reassuring her that it would all work out. He couldn't silence the doubts in his own head though.

It wasn't until he'd dropped Emily off and tucked Hallie into her bed that his wall began to break apart.

"Daddy, did you find Easton today?" Hallie murmured in sleepy tones.

"Oh, Hallie. I tried." Jack's voice cracked and he hurried from her room, biting his fist and wishing that Gina was there to help him.

Friday afternoon about ten minutes after Jack had dropped Hallie off to kindergarten, the doorbell rang. Jack opened it to see Emily standing there with her box of painting supplies.

"I'm sorry I didn't call, but I had to come today. Please?" Emily said in a rush before Jack could even think about saying hello.

He could tell by her bleary eyes that she was still upset, so he stepped aside and motioned for her to come in.

"Thank you," Emily said before heading down the hall to get to work. Jack gave her space and waited an entire hour before checking on her. The truth was that he didn't really know what to say or what the next step should be in trying to get his son back. His heart thumped hard when he looked in the room and saw what Emily had accomplished.

The tree was taking shape. Emily had finished painting the trunk and had several branches extending along the wall. In addition to the robin, a fat black and orange caterpillar perched on a leaf, farther up a tiny cocoon hung from another leaf, and finally a multi-colored butterfly emerged from an upper branch.

"This is amazing," Jack said. "I had no idea you were so talented, Em."

She turned and he recognized the red splotches on her neck that appeared whenever she was nervous. "Thanks."

"I mean it, you shouldn't be embarrassed. It's remarkable."

Her hand fluttered near her neck and he saw the flush creep up to her cheeks. "It's not that. It's just, I'm so glad that you can see it."

He caught himself before he asked, See what? He took another look at the tree, and then he did see it. The beginnings of a rainbow swept across the sky, touching on the clouds that Jack had helped create. One of the clouds had a gold halo on the right edge and he could see how the outline of the cloud looked like a G. He stepped closer and saw Gina's name painted on the cloud underneath the halo.

He immediately scanned the rest of the room, looking for any sign of a halo for Easton. When he didn't find one, he turned to Emily.

"I know it was him, Jack, and I know you don't want me to feel bad, but stop." She held up her hand as he approached. "I get it. This is all happening because Gina knew that Easton was alive." Her lip trembled. "And I failed her."

"No, you were wise. We're going to get another chance. Danika is watching her, figuring out her patterns, trying to discover if there is some evidence to give us a way to open an investigation."

Emily turned around and started working on another branch. Jack could sense the turmoil by the tension in her shoulders. He felt her pain, and he wanted to take it from her. He lifted his hand, hovering for a second above her shoulder. "Em?" he placed his hand on her shoulder and she flinched. He squeezed gently and she turned around.

Tears shimmered on her lower lashes.

"I want to ask you to help me, but I can't unless you grab onto that hope that Gina gave us all. I was crushed too, but instead of being depressed today, I've just felt this determination to get this right, to get Easton back. And I don't know why, but in here," he put a hand over his heart, "it feels like it's going to work."

Emily set her brush down and turned to Jack, blinking rapidly. "I'm trying to have faith, but my fear is overshadowing everything."

She stood close enough that Jack could smell the fresh citrus scent of her perfume. He breathed it in, trying to think of the right words to say. "I'm plenty afraid, but the need to get Easton back is more powerful than anything. It'll be okay." Jack put his arms around Emily and pulled her in close for a hug. She put her arms around his waist and leaned her head on his chest. They stood there for a moment until Emily looked up at him.

"I'd better hurry and get Hallie's room done then, so we can start on Easton's mural next."

CHAPTER SIXTEEN

JANETTE'S NERVES hadn't improved and she couldn't risk another breakdown. A change of scenery would probably be the best cure for both her and Andrew. Since her scare at the grocery store last week, she had kept a close eye on job openings in other states, but nothing satisfactory had come up yet. The problem was that she didn't know how long it would take her to sell her home. The realtor she called had listed it for sale the next day. It had already been shown three times. If it sold too fast, she'd have to move somewhere else before she'd had time to study the area thoroughly. Janette had intended to finish out the year in Idaho and then move far away from anyone who might remember the details about the woman who drowned.

She checked for job openings and found an urgent call for a long-term substitute in a specialized preschool daycare center in Boulder, Colorado. It was only fourteen hours away —a drive that she could do with Andrew, although it would be difficult. Janette clicked the request for an application. She had been foolish to stay in Idaho; she should have left the state as soon as she found Andrew, but she had been too frightened, too broke, and didn't want to draw attention to herself. She had thought of every option and then proceeded according to those that would bring the least scrutiny.

But maybe Andrew would suddenly develop a serious allergy—triggered by the harvest season. Leaving her job would be difficult, and it wouldn't look good on her resume but Janette couldn't risk losing Andrew.

Janette's cell phone pinged with a text. She opened the message from her realtor.

Good news. We may have a potential buyer.

She smiled, so grateful that God's hand continued to be in her life. Everything was clicking into place and if she got the job, she could be headed to Colorado in ten days.

CHAPTER SEVENTEEN

GINA WAS EVERYWHERE; she seemed to be in the very air that Jack breathed. The oppressive feeling of her presence in the house had him on edge. He didn't understand how their communication worked. He hadn't dreamed of her, felt anything from her for almost a week. But every second that he let his mind wander, he found himself reliving memories of Gina and Easton. He was going out of his mind knowing how close he'd been to his son just a few days ago. Danika was keeping a close eye on Janette and Easton, tracking her movements, and trying to find any evidence that could be used to get the police involved. It felt like they'd hit a brick wall and Jack was trying to climb up by his fingertips.

Jack put Hallie to bed and went to his room. It was Monday night, and instead of feeling better as each day passed, he felt more anxious. He knelt by his bed and prayed for guidance. There must be a way for him to get Easton back. After his prayer he slumped against the bed, resting his head on his knees. He thought again about calling the police to see if they could help, but then he remembered what

Vincent had said about evidence. The woman who had his son didn't have a record and she worked at a daycare. How much more innocent could a person get?

The whispers of Gina's presence filtered into the room. "Gina, I don't know what you want. I found Easton. I'm doing my best to get him back."

His chest felt heavy and he gasped for breath. Suddenly he was in the Camry with Gina. He heard the country music she loved to listen to, he knew instinctively that Easton was asleep in the back seat. She rolled down the window and let the cool breeze tousle her dark hair.

And then the collision—no warning, metal screeching, tires squealing as Gina braked, her head hitting the steering wheel hard. The smell of iron in his nose as it throbbed, blood pulsing. Just as he caught his breath and cleared his eyes, he felt the sensation of falling and could see the river rising up to meet them.

The car went in on the passenger side, the impact knocking the breath out of him again. Jack didn't know how it was happening but he was experiencing the crash from Gina's perspective. He could feel a sharp pain from her legs and looked down to see her broken leg pinned against the door, her foot caught under the dashboard.

Thirty seconds passed as Gina unbuckled her seatbelt and struggled to get her leg free. She turned back to the sound of Easton's cries. Panic bloomed in her chest and she released her seat so that it would lean all the way back. She had to push her back hard against the seat—every movement causing excruciating pain to rocket through her head, her nose, her leg.

"Easton, it's okay. Mommy's here."

Gina's seat finally fell back and bumped up against East-on's car seat. Gina twisted the top half of her body around and grabbed the bright red latch to release Easton's car seat. The latch released and she struggled to lift the car seat. It was too heavy. Easton weighed twenty pounds and the car seat probably weighed another five. "Someone help us," Gina cried out.

She felt the car tipping more on its side and she looked forward. The hood of the car was submerged in the water. With a ragged breath, she turned around and yanked on the car seat, wrenching her back, straining every muscle. She pulled the car seat forward onto her lap. The sound of the river was all around her and Easton was crying.

Gina leaned forward and kissed the soft skin of Easton's cheek. "I love you, buddy. I love you so much." Then she turned to her left, to the window, where she could see puffy clouds and blue sky. "Please, God. Save him!" She cried and pushed Easton's car seat out the window as water began flowing in. She kept hold of the car seat, balancing it on the side of the door as the car continued to sink in the river.

"Help! Please, someone save Easton!" Gina screamed as the water covered her legs, her chest. She wriggled sideways, the tendons in her leg stretching painfully as she held Easton's car seat on the side of the car. She found his little hand and felt his fingers clutching hers. She leaned as far out the window as she could, trying to keep her head above the water. Then there was a bump as the front end of the car dragged against the bottom of the river. For a moment, Gina thought they might be okay. Maybe they were close enough to the bank, where the river would be shallow. But then she felt the momentum as the back end of the car sunk into the water. She held onto Easton's car seat, keeping him above water, balanced on the side of her door. No matter how hard she pulled on her leg, it wouldn't come free from the mangled side of the car and only intensified her pain.

The water covered her face and she jerked forward, her head breaking from the water for a brief moment. The rushing river was relentless, but she kept her hand above water as the river drowned out Easton's cries. She opened her eyes. The dirty water stung and she blinked against the greenish hue. All she could see were the rays of sunlight flickering against the water and a dark object—Easton's car seat.

Every cell in her body cried for oxygen and still she held onto Easton. Her body convulsed, forcing her to open her mouth for a breath and she felt the water filling her lungs. Then darkness. No cries. No light. Gina was alone. In her mind, she cried, screamed for help, but no one came. After a time she fell asleep. When she awoke, she was on the bank of the Snake River next to her watery grave. Still alone, she looked for Easton.

Jack's vision cleared, his focus sharpening. The anguish he felt from Gina overpowered his senses and he cried out, "Gina, what should I do?"

Go and get Easton. Don't wait. Save our son.

The room felt cold. Gina was gone. It was hard to breathe. Jack kept feeling the choking sensation of water filling Gina's lungs. How many people could say they experienced death through another's eyes? It was torture. Jack's body was wracked with pain, and his anger flared at Janette. She must have been on the scene, she must have taken Easton. There was no other explanation.

Gina had saved her son, keeping him above the water and sacrificing herself. She was resourceful, so Jack thought there might have been a chance for her to get free, but with a mother's love, she had died saving Easton. Through reliving the experience, it was as if Gina had died all over again. Jack's eyes burned with fresh tears. He let them cascade down his cheeks, drip onto his hands, and soak his pants.

The emotion in Gina's memory had exhausted him, but at the same time he felt fueled with a hunger to get his son. Jack stood and rubbed his eyes. It was late, almost eleven o'clock, but he dialed Emily's number anyway.

"Em, I need your help."

"What's wrong?"

Jack swallowed and blurted out. "I have to get Easton back tomorrow."

"I don't think that's a good idea," Emily replied.

"It's the only idea I have. If you'll help me, I'll make sure that I take the blame if anything goes wrong." He heard a sigh.

"I'll help you. What's your plan?"

"I don't know yet," Jack said. "I have to call Danika first, but I can't wait any longer. Be ready at nine tomorrow. I'll pick you up."

"Jack?"

"Yeah?"

"Be careful."

Jack pursed his lips. "I will."

Jack hung up the phone and took two breaths before dialing Danika's number.

"Hey, Jack. Loneliness finally get the best of ya?" she answered in a husky voice.

"Yes, remember how you told me not to do anything rash?"

"Yeah, and I meant that."

"You said you liked adventure," Jack said. "If you're up for it, I'm going to kidnap my son tomorrow."

Danika swore. "Jack, you can't do that. We don't have solid evidence yet. Remember the DNA swab we're still trying to get?"

"I have to do this tomorrow. Are you in or not?"

Two beats of silence. "I'm in. Tell me your plan."

"That's where I need your help," Jack said. "I've been going over the reports of Janette's movements and I need a distraction."

"Even your body isn't worth going to jail for," Danika said.

Jack chuckled. "Nobody's going to jail."

"You will, Jack. Are you prepared for that?"

"Look, all I have to do is take Easton and get the DNA test in process. If I can keep him safe for six days, we'll have the results. Game over."

"You're crazy," Danika said.

"That's what everybody thinks and I don't care anymore," Jack replied.

Danika muttered something and he heard papers shuffling in the background. "Let's figure this out then. Hold on."

Jack gripped the phone and grabbed a notebook to write down ideas for the plan that had to work.

Helen seemed on edge the next morning when Jack dropped Hallie off. "Is anything the matter?"

She shook her head. "It's nothing."

"You can tell me about it," Jack prodded.

Helen kissed the top of Hallie's head. "Run, and get Grandma's slippers, will you?"

As soon as Hallie was out of earshot, Helen leaned forward. "I keep thinking about Gina. I know I have to accept that she's gone, but it still hurts." Helen adjusted her glasses.

Jack gripped her hands. "This time of year has been difficult for both of us. I think it has something to do with the harvest. You know how she loved it."

Helen nodded and her eyes brimmed with tears.

"It's okay to feel the grief." Jack decided to share some of the wisdom Dr. Radkin had given him. "It will always be a part of us, but once you feel it, let it go and keep moving forward."

Helen nodded. "You look better, Jack. Does Emily have something to do with that?"

Jack felt his face heat up. "Uh—well,"

"Hallie talks about her all the time lately. She's a good woman. I'm certain that Gina would want you to be happy."

Jack shook his head. "But it's so soon. I'm not sure what I'm feeling. It's confusing. I love Gina. I'm not over her."

"And you never will be. That's okay. When a heart breaks, it mends with room to hold more love, if you let it." Helen squeezed his arm.

Jack took a step back. "I'd better get going."

Helen smiled. "Don't worry. I won't be the meddling mother-in-law, but I just wanted to make sure you know that I don't think Gina would want you to be alone."

"Thank you." Jack waved and walked to his pickup.

He hesitated before opening the door and looked back toward the house. Hallie waved at him in the window and Jack blew her a kiss. Then he got in his pickup and headed toward the grocery store. While he drove, he mulled over Helen's words. Did Jack seem better because of Emily, or was it because he had found Easton? He shrugged. It was most likely a mixture of both things, but he didn't need all the answers right now. All he needed was Easton.

Jack pulled into the grocery store parking lot and found a space in the middle. He had instructed Emily to disguise herself, so when a dark-haired woman tapped on the passenger window, he jumped.

Emily laughed as she climbed into the pickup. "I did good, huh?"

Jack reached out and touched the black wig, his fingers brushing Emily's cheek. "Excellent."

Once they were on the freeway, she pulled off her wig and set it on the floor. Her hair was pulled back in a tight bun, the blonde strands slicked back against her head. She put her hands in her lap, clasping and unclasping them. Jack noticed Emily's hands trembling and covered them with his own. She intertwined her fingers with his and he felt his stomach flip. He glanced over and caught her staring at him.

"Jack, do you think this is going to work?"

"It will. Remember, we have an angel on our side."

Emily blinked, and took in a ragged breath. "I'm scared."

"Me, too. Hopefully it will keep us cautious. Danika was pretty ticked when I told her my plan, but she agreed to help."

Jack thought of the new car seat in the trunk and the small bag he'd packed with diapers and a few clothes that were hanging in Easton's closet. Brand new little boy clothes ready for him in the twelve month size, Gina hadn't even had a chance to cut the tags off yet.

"Easton's birthday is October fifteenth—only two weeks away. I keep thinking about how wonderful it will be to have my son back in time for that."

Emily squeezed his hand.

"I haven't told you all of my plan for a reason, Em." Jack watched dark clouds gathering on the horizon. "I don't want you implicated. No matter what, you can't tell the truth about today. I didn't even tell Danika your real name."

"Okay. I'll keep my lies close to the truth, and simple. Why would they think I was involved anyway?"

"Hallie has been talking about you a lot. Helen knows that you've been coming over to the house."

Emily blushed, and Jack smiled at how the tip of her pixie nose turned red.

"It's okay. Helen as much as told me today that she thinks Gina would want me to date you."

Emily's eyes widened. "She did?"

Jack realized his misstep. "I probably shouldn't have said that. I'm sorry. You've been so wonderful. It's helped Hallie a lot, and me too. I don't want to dishonor your friendship with Gina."

She tightened her hold on his hand. "I understand."

The tension inside the car increased, Jack struggled to find the words he needed to say. He'd opened the door on an important topic and he didn't want to mess up. How could he explain himself?

"Em?" He caressed her hand with his thumb.

She looked over at him. She appeared so vulnerable in that moment and Jack felt something in his heart that he'd been ignoring. He was attracted to Emily. Who wouldn't be? She was gorgeous, with her blonde hair, green eyes, and willowy figure. But there was something more. In his heart he couldn't ignore the way he felt about her sweet and caring personality. Her nature was a contrast to Gina's passionate temperament, but he could see how she held herself back as if afraid to enjoy life.

He cleared his throat. "I do care about you."

She released his hand and dropped her head, folding her arms tight. "Don't say it. I know it's too soon. It's probably too soon for me too."

Jack reached over and pulled her hand toward him, inter-lacing their fingers. The emotions were too fragile; he decided it was best to change the subject. "Thanks for coming with me today." He noted Emily shift and her shoulders relaxed slightly as he skipped over the subject they had just approached. "It's unreal—impossible to think that my son is alive and I'm going to hold him again."

"I hope so," she murmured.

Jack couldn't read her expression as she stared out the windshield. They were approaching the bridge crossing and the stratus clouds acted like a gray curtain across the sun. As they crossed the river, the air arced with electricity and he saw a flicker of lightning in the sky above them. He saw Emily tense as they started to cross the river. He didn't want to talk about the scene of Gina's accident. It was important to stay focused on getting Easton back.

"Rain would be perfect today if it'll hold off until we're on our way home." He looked over to the river, the force mercilessly moving forward.

Emily nodded. "It will make it harder for people to identify us."

They met up with Danika at a gas station just outside of Idaho Falls. She drove a rental, a nondescript black car with tinted windows. As they pulled alongside, she rolled down the window. "Ready to rumble?"

She wore tight jeans and a low cut shirt, the dark green shade contrasting against her red hair. Jack and Emily got in the back seat.

"I won't bite. You can sit up here," Danika said as she glanced over her shoulder and eyed Emily.

"I want to keep a low profile." He squeezed Emily's hand and then released it so he could put on his trucker hat. "This is my friend, Robin."

"Nice to meet you, *Robin*." Danika nodded and arched an eyebrow, as if she knew perfectly well that wasn't Emily's name.

"Thanks for doing this." Emily readjusted her wig and folded her hands in her lap.

"I should be keeping my face out of this mess," Danika said. "But we have to make this work, so I'll be wearing a wig too. The guy I hired insisted on two grand, so I hope you're good for it, Jack."

"You know I am." He thought of the extra money he'd earned in the past few weeks since he'd come back to life. It wasn't quite enough to cover everything, but the upcoming Hansen farms account would cover the difference.

"Okay, let's go over the plan one more time." Danika gripped the steering wheel. "We're hoping for a miracle, because, as I explained to Jack, Janette has altered her schedule in the last few days. She's been leaving the daycare early and taking Easton home in the stroller every day at two in the afternoon. He's usually asleep by the time she gets home and he goes down for a two hour nap."

"So we intercept before she gets home," Jack said.

Danika nodded. "My guy is going to trip and fall on the sidewalk at the halfway point. Jack, since you're the one who'll be taking the rap, you'll run up and grab the stroller—it's a jogging stroller, so you can run at top speed. Easton should be asleep and hopefully stay that way, so you won't have to worry about his crying and attracting attention from bystanders.

"After you take the stroller, my guy will be sure to trip Janette when she goes after you, and then I'll pull up in this car and see if they need help." Danika looked at them from the rearview mirror. "Robin, I'm taking you to another rental car. You'll park just around the corner and wait for Jack and Easton."

Jack covered Emily's hand with his. "It's going to be fine."

Danika tapped the steering wheel. "If anything goes wrong, we ditch the plan and call the police."

He felt Emily tense beside him. They both knew how important it was that the plan succeed. Although he didn't feel Gina's presence at the moment, he believed she was watching over them. *I'm coming Easton.* Nearly five months had passed since he had last held his son and he didn't want to waste one more day.

CHAPTER EIGHTEEN

THE DAYCARE HAD BEEN ESPECIALLY noisy and Janette felt her temples throbbing with the beginning of a headache. Maybe she could lie down for a nap while Andrew was asleep. The stroller glided along the sidewalks, his head lolling to one side, already drifting off. She made a right hand turn and was surprised to see a man walking down the sidewalk in front of her. The street was usually absent of pedestrians this time of day.

She admired his muscular build, wondering if he might be new in the neighborhood. She glanced down. Andrew was asleep. She looked back up in time to see the man stumble and fall to the ground. The impact made Janette cringe.

"Oh, dear. Are you all right?" She hurried forward. The man held his head on one side and moaned. Janette walked around the front of the stroller and stooped to help the man who cried out in pain as he tried to sit up. "Sir, maybe you should lie still for a minute."

He groaned and Janette knelt beside him. She heard a noise behind her and jerked her head to the right in time to see a dark-haired man grab her stroller and push it off the sidewalk at a dead run.

"Stop! That's my baby!" She jumped up and began running after the man—or at least that's what she had tried to do. Instead, she felt the rough concrete jarring the side of her face as she smacked the ground. Somehow her feet had tangled with the injured man's legs.

Janette heard the braking of a car and then a door open as she lifted herself off the ground to give chase to the man who'd taken Andrew. He was already half a block away, the stroller's wheels spinning rapidly to keep up with his sprint. As she stood, the world seemed to tilt, and she put her hands out to balance herself. A woman with dark blonde hair had jumped from her car and rushed toward Janette.

"What happened here?"

Janette blinked and looked past the woman. "Andrew! Help!"

The woman with blonde hair grabbed her arms. "Calm down. You look like you're going to pass out. Why don't you sit down and tell me what happened?"

"My baby!" Janette screamed and struggled to yank her arms free, but the woman's grip was like iron.

"What do you mean, your baby?" She asked and looked around. "Did you have something to do with this man's injury?"

Janette looked at the man and was surprised to see blood trickling from his head, staining the collar of his shirt. She hadn't noticed the blood before. "What? But I thought he— no, let me go! Someone took my baby!"

"Yeah, that guy took her baby." The man pointed in the direction of the kidnapper.

"He did? And then he attacked you?" the blonde-haired woman asked. "I'll call 911."

126

Janette ripped her arms free of the woman's grasp and sprinted after Andrew.

~

The adrenaline pumping through Jack's body was like nothing he'd ever felt before. With each step he pushed himself harder. He could see the top of Easton's dark hair in the stroller. He wanted to scoop him up and hold him close, but instead he put on another burst of speed and turned the corner to where Emily waited, the back door of the car open.

He heard screaming behind him, the pounding of his feet on the pavement, the wind whistling under the brim of his hat, blood pumping in his ears. He almost ran into the car with the stroller, jerking it to a stop at the last second. His hands shook as he undid the clasps keeping Easton in the stroller. He heard Janette scream behind him and he panicked. Danika must not have been able to detain her long.

The clip made a snapping sound and Easton was free. Jack pulled him out of the stroller and the baby's head lolled forward. His eyes fluttered open for a second and then he fell back asleep as Jack crouched and slid into the back seat, yanking the door shut.

"Go! Go! Go!" he yelled.

Emily's foot smashed down on the gas pedal and he heard the screeching of the tires as she made a sharp turn. He cradled Easton in his arms, protecting him against the fierce momentum of the car's movements. Jack glanced behind them, but he couldn't see Janette.

"Okay, Em. Slow down. We made it. Don't draw any attention to us now."

Emily turned to look at him with a triumphant grin. "We did it."

Jack nodded and kissed the top of Easton's head. He was holding his son. The love that radiated from his chest seemed to pull the pieces of his heart closer together. He kissed Easton's cheek and smelled the soft scent of baby shampoo in his hair. Gina had made everything possible. He said a silent prayer, thanking God for allowing one of His angels to rescue her son. Perhaps Gina would finally be at peace.

He buckled Easton into the new car seat, careful to connect the five point harness. Easton stirred again and sighed in his sleep. How would his son react when he awoke?

"He'll have forgotten you," Emily answered the question he hadn't vocalized. "I looked it up on the internet. After a month, most babies will react to parents as strangers, but they reconnect the memories within hours. But after four months...there's so much neural growth going on," Emily paused. "Some experts believe there is still a shadow of memory, but it takes more time to make the connections. Because babies are so resilient, they will build new connections within another month."

"So if Janette finds him..."

"He'll go to her," Emily's voice was just above a whisper.

Jack traced Easton's fingers, treasuring the feel of his soft baby skin. "This has to work."

CHAPTER NINETEEN

"MY BABY! Andrew! Please don't take him!" Janette screamed as she ran. Her lungs felt as if they would burst, but no matter how hard she pushed, she couldn't cut the distance between her and the man who had taken Andrew. He was a full block ahead of her.

She kept running, crying out as he turned a corner. Her feet gripped the pavement, making the same turn. "No!" she screamed as she watched the man pull Easton out of the stroller. Even after he got in the car and it sped away, Janette still ran after it. She saw the last three digits on the license plate as it turned another corner. "6Z4," Janette said to herself as she ran back to the stroller.

"No! No! No!" she cried as she fumbled in her diaper bag for her cell phone. Hopefully the other woman had already reported the kidnapping, but she wouldn't have had any details.

"911 What's your emergency?"

"My baby's been kidnapped," Janette said, and then she broke down, the sobs convulsing through her body.

~

When they arrived at the rendezvous point, Danika waited in the other rental car beside Jack's vehicle. They moved Easton as carefully as possible into his car. "Don't worry. My guy is going to return that rental. If Janette got the plate number, they'll be tracking down a fake I.D."

Easton woke up from all the movement and began fussing —his eyes searching for a familiar face among strangers.

"Shh, it's okay buddy. Daddy's here now." Jack took him out of the car seat and held him in his lap for a few minutes. "I can't believe that I'm holding my son." The adrenaline still had his heart racing, but his heavy breathing slowed as he held Easton close. The baby studied Jack's face for a moment, he frowned and then cried, his mouth opening to reveal two front teeth poking through his gum line. Jack felt his throat tighten when he thought of all that he'd missed—all that he might have missed if he hadn't listened to Gina.

Jack pulled out the DNA test kit and swabbed the inside of Easton's cheek. The baby tried to grab the test swab and smiled when Jack maneuvered his hand out of reach. Jack capped the evidence and dropped it into a manila envelope with another swab that carried a sample of his own DNA. He handed the envelope to Danika, not bothering to hide the way his hands shook.

"Don't worry," Danika said. "I'll overnight this and you'll have the results back within a week, five days if we're lucky."

"There's no way we can rush it?" Emily asked.

"You have to have a sample of the mother's DNA as well for that quick of a result," Jack replied. "Since we only have mine and Easton's it takes a bit longer—the test is slightly more complicated. But it could still come in less than a week."

The skin on Emily's forehead tightened with concern. "Let's hope that it's faster."

"Okay, let's go. Remember, low-profile. Don't take him outside." Danika pointed at Jack and then Easton. "I'll talk to you next week."

They parted ways. Emily agreed to drive Jack's car so that he could sit in the back next to Easton's car seat. Jack fed his son graham crackers and applesauce, and Easton stopped crying. Jack laughed when Easton tried to blow a raspberry on his own hand, smearing applesauce everywhere. Jack kept checking to be sure that he was awake, that everything was real and not a dream.

He leaned forward and put his hand on Emily's shoulder. "I know this was a risk for you—a huge risk. Thank you so much."

She put her left hand over his, patting it softly. "I wouldn't have missed this miracle. Thank you for letting me be part of it."

"So, are you okay to wait with Easton while I pick Hallie up?"

"Yes, but when are you going to tell Helen?"

"As soon as the test results get back. I don't want to risk anything right now. You and I know that this is Easton." He smiled at his son and tickled him under the chin. The baby giggled. "But other people might think I'm crazy."

Emily nodded. "You're right. You're going to have to keep Hallie home from school. Just say she's sick, throwing up, and all that stuff."

"That's true. There's so much to think of and this has happened so fast." Jack's mind was racing out of control with every detail he needed to keep under control for the next week.

"At least Easton is on his way home."

Emily's grip tightened on the steering wheel and Jack saw that they were almost to Blackfoot, to the bridge crossing. The clouds hung low and rain spattered the windshield. Jack remained quiet as they crossed the bridge. He held onto Easton's fingers and gazed out at the river as they sped past. Easton gnawed on the teething toy Jack had packed in the diaper bag, oblivious of the moment that seemed to suck the air from the car.

Easton's eyes were the same light blue color as Gina's, the dimple in his chin was identical to Jack's and as Jack stared at him, he could see parts of Gina and himself in their miracle baby.

"Janette must have pulled Easton from the river." Jack broke the silence.

"Or did she somehow take him before the accident?" Emily asked. "Do you think she caused the accident?"

That hadn't occurred to Jack, but he recalled the memory Gina had impressed upon him perfectly. The way she had pushed the car seat out the window of the car, keeping Easton above the river's suffocating force. "No, I think Janette must have been the first one on the scene. She saved Easton."

"And let Gina die?"

Jack swallowed. "I don't think so. The police told me that her leg was pinned against the door and the dashboard—the medical examiner told me it crushed part of the bones in her leg."

He heard Emily suck in a breath, and then she leaned forward, staring straight ahead. "No," she whispered.

Easton tried to lift his head and look behind him to Emily as if he could sense that she was in pain. Jack thought about how terrifying it had been to relive Gina's death from her perspective. He wanted to explain it all to Emily, but it sounded crazy to his own ears. How could she handle what he was still trying to figure out?

Emily sniffed, and Jack thought she might be crying.

"Em, are you okay? Do you need to pull over?"

She shook her head. "We'll be home in forty minutes. I can handle it."

She flipped on the radio and Jack figured that meant she didn't want to talk about it anymore. He tried to be understanding, to put himself in her shoes. Most people didn't know the details. They thought the car accident killed Gina or at least knocked her unconscious, so she died a less painful death in their minds. Jack had believed the same thing. Even when the coroner told him about the injuries in her leg, when the police reported that she wasn't wearing a seatbelt, Jack hadn't wanted to think about it. But he knew the painful truth now and it would have haunted him if he didn't know the significance of the details. Gina had saved her son. She had kept her wits about her and given Easton life all over again.

Jack ventured back into Gina's memory. Janette would have had to be right on the scene in order to save Easton. Jack had seen the wreckage, and the Camry had been about ten yards from the shore. The car seat would have slid off the car once Gina let go, the force of the current pulling it down to the bottom of the river. All the pieces snapped into place.

Janette must have rescued Easton and then kept him for herself. Even putting the car seat back into the river so it would look as if he had drowned. Jack's gut tightened with the familiar strands of anger, but he forced himself to relax. Easton babbled, and Jack turned his attention back to him. Janette had kidnapped his son, but she had saved him first. It was a strange turn of events.

He leaned forward and touched Emily's shoulder again.

"I'm sorry, Em. Let's not ruin today. I know that Gina is happy right now. I can feel it."

Emily relaxed against his touch. "It's just so sad. I hate that she's gone. I hate how that woman kept Easton from you all this time—that she caused more suffering for everyone."

"But that's over now. If it weren't for Janette, we wouldn't have Easton at all." Jack leaned over and kissed Easton, and the baby reached out to touch the stubble on Jack's chin. Jack growled and Easton squealed, and then gave a husky laugh. A feeling somewhere between crying and laughing expanded in Jack's chest. "That's my buddy E."

Emily stopped at her house to pick up her car so she could follow Jack home.

"Remember, park at the church. Don't follow me into the subdivision. I don't want anything connecting you to this."

Emily nodded and waved. It was almost six-thirty. Jack was thankful for the fading light as he approached his house and pulled into the garage. It wouldn't do to have his neighbors spot the baby in the back seat. He closed the garage and then pulled Easton out of his car seat. The baby clung to him and Jack kissed his cheek.

"I can't believe it's you."

He carried Easton into the house and a few minutes later Emily knocked on the front door. Jack let her in, his eyes scanning the road behind her for any sign of a witness, but the street was empty. He locked the door and stepped closer to Emily. Trails of mascara dotted her face and he could see a faint sheen of tears on her cheeks.

"Come and sit down. We'll let Easton get comfortable with you." He led her into the living room and sat down on the couch with the baby.

Emily sat down next to him. "Hello, Easton. It's good to see you again."

Easton stopped babbling and stared at Emily, tilting his head to one side. Jack sat the baby on Emily's lap and she smiled. Then she leaned forward and hugged Easton, pulling him into the crook of her neck.

"I'm so sorry you lost your mommy," her tear-filled voice wobbled.

Jack put his arm around Emily and pulled her close to him. She looked up at him and he could see the sorrow in her eyes.

"I didn't mean to upset you," he said.

Emily shook her head. "No, it's my fault." She let her head fall back against the couch. "It just hurts so much to think of Gina drowning—I mean, I knew that she drowned but I always thought she was unconscious—kind of a die-in-your sleep type of thing."

"I shouldn't have told you."

"Jack, you shouldn't have to carry this burden by yourself. It's terrible how Gina died." Emily wiped her eyes and Easton grabbed for her hand. "She saved Easton, didn't she?"

Jack nodded. "I'm pretty sure that she did. It all makes sense now, how the car seat made it out of the Camry and into the river."

"That helps a little." Emily frowned. "But I still miss her so much."

Jack pulled her closer, so that her head rested on his chest. "Me too."

Easton yanked on one of Emily's golden curls and giggled. She leaned forward and kissed his cheek, then tickled the side of his neck. He smiled so wide that Jack found himself smiling back. Emily turned to him.

"He's beautiful." She looked back at Easton and caressed his cheek with her fingers.

"He's a miracle," Jack said.

Emily nodded, the moisture in her eyes reflecting the overhead light. "I think he'll be okay while you go and get Hallie."

Jack felt close to Emily in that moment, with his arm still around her shoulders, the rise and fall of her breath steady. The color of her eyes looked to be a lighter green close up. Emily smiled at him and he realized he'd been staring. He gave her a one-armed hug.

"I'll be back in about fifteen minutes." Jack stood and then bent down and kissed the top of Easton's head. "There's some baby food in the pantry. Would you mind feeding him?"

"I'll keep him safe and we'll get his little tummy full." Emily hugged Easton, and he squirmed in her arms.

Jack hurried to pick Hallie up, doing his best to cover the nervousness he had being away from Easton even for a few minutes.

"I'll be happy to watch Hallie if you need some extra time this weekend," Helen offered.

Jack gave Helen a hug. "I appreciate it. I'll be sure to let you know."

He hurried out the door before Helen could suggest outright that he take Emily on a date. "Have you and Grandma been talking about Emily again?" he asked Hallie.

She grinned and bobbed her head up and down. "Grandma likes Emily a lot. I told her I love her and maybe when you love her too, she can be my mommy."

Jack raised his eyebrows. "Is that right?"

"Grandma said Emily is like her other daughter. Does that mean that Mom and Emily are sisters?"

Jack looked in the rearview mirror, watching Hallie chatter away and chuckled. "No, it just means that they were such good friends that Grandma knows her very well and loves her like she did Mommy."

"That's how I love her too."

Jack smiled. He thought about her words, the innocence held much truth behind it. He couldn't ignore the connection he felt to Emily either. He just didn't know what he should do about it.

"Hallie, I have a special surprise for you in the house," Jack said. He pushed the button to open the garage. "Emily is here and we found Easton."

"You found him!" she squealed. "Is he asleep like Mommy?"

"No, sweetheart. He's wide awake." Jack jumped out of the car and grabbed Hallie before she could dash in the house. "He might not remember you, so I need you to be careful. Remember the rules Mommy gave you about how we treat a baby."

Hallie sighed. "I know, careful, soft, and gentle."

Jack chuckled. Hallie had accepted that he found Easton without the slightest hesitation, like she'd been waiting for her dad to do what he'd promised. "C'mon, let's go see your brother."

Hallie raced into the living room and when she saw Easton sitting on Emily's lap, she skidded to a stop. "Easton, it's really you," she said. She reached out her fingers to Easton, who eyed her warily at first, then grinned when Hallie wiggled her fingers.

Hallie hugged Easton and then dropped her head onto Emily's lap, her body shaking with sobs. Jack rushed forward, lifting Hallie off the floor and pulling her onto the couch. He cradled her. "Shh, it's okay. Sweetheart, what's wrong?"

Emily touched his hand, tears spilling over her lashes. "It's a lot to take in. I think she doesn't know how to react." Emily patted Hallie's back. "I cried when I saw Easton too, but look at how happy he is."

Hallie lifted her head and wiped her hand across her nose and cheek. She stared at Easton. "I'm so glad he's not sleeping. Daddy, please don't let him go to sleep."

Jack looked at the concerned expression on Emily's face. It would be an adjustment for Hallie, but he hadn't anticipated her reaction. He turned Hallie so that he could look into her eyes.

"Sweetheart, when people told you that Mommy was sleeping, it's different than when you and I go to sleep at night. Remember how I told you that Mommy died? Mommy's body is sleeping so that her spirit can go and live with God. Her body will never wake up, but Mommy is awake in heaven. We just can't see her, but she sees us. You know that Mommy helped us to find Easton? She knew how sad we were and how much we missed him, so she helped us to get him back."

"But why did Easton go away?" Hallie asked.

Jack glanced at Emily, his mouth opening and closing as he tried to think of a response that wouldn't frighten Hallie more than she already was. Emily squeezed Jack's hand.

"Hallie," she said. "Your mommy died, but Easton didn't. He got lost when your mommy died and that's why we had to find him. He's going to fall asleep tonight and that's okay because in the morning, he'll wake up and still be here. Your family will be together again."

"Will you be here in the morning, Emily?" Hallie asked.

Emily smiled. "No, honey. I have to go and feed my fish. Remember how I told you about Mr. Rogers?"

Hallie nodded. "Will you come back tomorrow?"

Emily hesitated and Jack answered, "She can't come back for a few days because she has lots of work to do. But next week she's going to come back and finish painting your room, okay?"

"Okay," Hallie said. "And you can play with Easton too."

"I'm looking forward to it," Emily said.

"Hallie, hold Easton right here on the couch for a minute while I help Emily out," Jack said.

"Okay, I'm a good big sister," Hallie said as Jack put the baby on her lap. "Did you know I love you more than the sun, Easton?" she asked her brother.

Jack and Emily shared a smile as they walked toward the front door. He handed Emily an empty can of paint before she left the house. "Make sure you carry this out because you've been doing so much work on Hallie's room." He winked.

Emily nodded. She seemed hesitant to leave, but it was dangerous for her to be at the house, so Jack reluctantly opened the front door for her. He watched her walk down the steps and down the sidewalk and then he shut the door, eager to hold Easton again.

It had only been fifteen minutes since she'd left, but Jack called Emily. "I just wanted to make sure you got home all right and tell you thanks again for everything you did today."

"I'm so happy you trusted me enough to help."

"Ditto," Jack replied.

"If I walk from the church again, would it be okay if I came over on Saturday?"

"That's the other reason I called. I'm worried, Em. I don't know what's going to happen and a couple of my neighbors are pretty nosy. If they see you coming and going, I'm sure they'll be over with a plate of cookies, inviting themselves in to get the latest scoops. I can't risk it."

"You're probably right," Emily responded, the disappointment evident in her voice. "But you'll let me know if there's anything I can do to help you, right? I can even get groceries if you—"

"Emily, I don't want you to get hurt or in any kind of trouble. Don't come around until things are settled. In fact, I probably shouldn't be calling you either. If the police open an investigation, then they could come to you."

"But they won't. Everything's going to be okay now. You said it yourself. Gina helped us find Easton."

"I know, but it's smart to be cautious. Danika said that we could be in a lot of trouble until those DNA results come in, and even then we might have to go to court."

"That's ridiculous." Jack heard real anger in Emily's voice. "Easton is your son. That woman should be in jail, instead she's probably getting ready to kidnap someone else's baby."

"I know. Believe me, I'm just as angry as any father would be, but I care about you enough that I won't let you put yourself in danger more than you already have. There were probably witnesses. It might be only a matter of time until the police have a sketch of me circulating the news. Janette got a good look at me."

"Okay, you win," Emily grumbled. "I'll keep my distance."

"Get some work done. When this is all over, we'll go out for ice cream."

"Be careful, Jack."

"You too."

Jack hung up the phone and then adjusted the shades and curtains on his windows. He snuggled with Easton and Hallie, feeling like he was stealing time with his children. The thought bothered him. He'd done the right thing, hadn't he?

CHAPTER TWENTY

JANETTE'S EYES throbbed and her throat felt raw from crying. She sat in the Idaho Falls police department with a sketch artist and described the man who had taken Andrew. She ignored her conscience and the panic she felt as the police opened the investigation. They hadn't asked her for the birth certificates she'd made up yet, but they had asked for baby pictures. Thank goodness, she'd taken hundreds since May. She even had a little scrapbook made up for Andrew with pictures from his first year of life. She'd taken pictures from the Internet of newborns and used Photoshop to create the baby book.

As the sketch artist worked to bring the man's features to life, Janette felt her stomach tighten. How would they find him? And what would she do if they couldn't get Andrew back? It had already been six hours, she'd heard that the first twenty-four hours were crucial.

"Ms. Baker?"

Janette looked up and saw a burly Latino police officer.

"Yes?"

"I'm Officer Juarez. I'm going to help you find your baby."

~

Vincent flipped through the baby pictures again. It was past time for him to head home, but he felt uneasy, and he couldn't figure out why. There was something about the baby that bothered him. He rested his finger against the close up that they had put on the news. The Amber Alert was bringing in several tips, but none of them looked good so far. Half the force was out checking leads and the highway patrolmen were on full alert for the cars Janette had described.

He studied his notes. The kidnapping had been premeditated, he was sure of that. The blonde-haired woman and the injured man were definitely working with the man who'd taken the baby. And there was a getaway driver. That meant at least four people were involved in the kidnapping. His mind pinged with possible scenarios. The motive had to be powerful to involve such a high risk. As the net of suspicion spread, he was certain that they'd be able to find at least one of the people involved.

"Hey, Juarez." Gordon rapped on his door as he walked in. "We talked to the rental agencies. Seems the same guy rented cars from two different places today. Paid cash, used fake I.D. and info."

Vincent lifted up the glossy eight by ten of Andrew. "Does this baby look familiar to you?"

"Sir?"

"I mean, look at him for a minute. Has there been a news story recently with a baby that looks like this?"

Gordon took the picture and stared at it. "You know what they say about babies—they all look the same except to their parents."

Vincent shook his head. "I can't place it, but I swear I've seen this little guy before." He massaged his temples and flipped back through his notes. "I'll figure it out eventually." Vincent jotted down a few more notes, trying to decipher the pieces of the puzzle floating just beyond his consciousness that contained the answer to his question.

CHAPTER TWENTY-ONE

JACK WAS overjoyed and for the first few days he felt the same powerful emotion of love coming from Gina as he held his beautiful son. He held Easton and rocked him to sleep Friday night. "Gina, I can't believe it, but thank you for giving me back my son." Jack breathed in deeply. "I miss you," he whispered. He felt her then, her love for him, for Easton, for Hallie, and for Emily. He basked in the moment of peace and love, but then he felt Gina's pain—her raw anguish. He didn't understand the switch in emotions. Was it because their family would always be incomplete? Or maybe now that Easton was safe at home in his arms, Gina's mission was complete. Jack wondered what barriers kept them apart, what walls Gina had broken down in order to return her son to his father. He looked at his son, but his focus shifted and he saw again Gina's struggle to hold onto the car seat as the vehicle was overcome by the powerful waters of the Snake River. The pressure in Gina's lungs, her fingers loosening on the car seat as she lost consciousness for the last time.

"We'll be together again, Gina," Jack said. "I know I'll see you again someday." And Jack believed it. If God was merciful enough to let him find his son through his wife's assistance beyond the veil of death, then why wouldn't he allow them to be together in heaven?

Again, he felt a reassurance of joy and comfort from Gina, followed by anguish.

Easton isn't safe yet. Jack, keep him safe.

With that warning, Jack checked his calendar for the hundredth time. Danika had overnighted the DNA sample on Tuesday and was assured he'd receive results by the following Wednesday. The time period was too long. Helen was getting antsy to see him and Hallie, and Jack was running out of excuses. He decided it was time to move to the second phase of his plan. The car was already packed for an overnighter. The cabin in Lava Hot Springs had been in the family for two generations.

Even though he had promised himself he wouldn't involve Emily further, Jack called her on Saturday. As the phone rang, he thought about Gina and the impressions she continued to give him. She trusted Emily and for some reason thought she was integral to keeping Easton safe. Jack still felt afraid of the possibilities. He felt comfortable with Emily, like they'd been friends for a long time, but they were connected through Gina. What would happen when Gina's spirit wasn't there holding them together?

"Hello?" Emily answered. Jack heard the tension in her voice, and the question before she asked it.

"We're safe. Are you okay?"

"Yes. How are you doing?"

"Easton is amazing. Hallie is out of her mind crazy in love with him."

"But?"

Jack smiled at Emily's intuitiveness. "I felt Gina near again. She was happy, but I felt so much anguish from her, like Easton wasn't safe."

"You knew that was a possibility. I've heard the Amber Alert. It's all over the news. They put out a sketch of the abductor. It looks too much like you. How long do you think you have?"

"I don't know. I saw the sketch online. I'm in trouble if those DNA results don't get back in time."

"What are you going to do?" Emily's voice wobbled.

"I'm taking Easton and Hallie somewhere safe. I don't want you to worry and I don't want you to know where we're going."

"Are you sure?"

"Emily, there's a chance the police will question you. If they do, don't guess as to where we might be, okay?"

"Kiss Easton and Hallie for me."

"I'll talk to you when things are safe. I'm leaving my cell phone here so we can't be tracked."

"Jack, I'm worried. I wish I could go with you, help you somehow."

Jack felt the assuredness that Emily would be there for them if things didn't go as planned. "I know you would help us, but I'm hoping you won't have to."

"Please call when you can."

"I will."

Jack ended the call and for a moment he was tempted to call Emily back, to ask her to come with them, but that would be foolish. He didn't tell her the one important part of his plan—a failsafe—would be coming to her soon.

Jack had included an order with the DNA request for the results to be sent to both his house and Emily's. He worried what might happen if the police tracked Easton down. He had pictures of him, but Danika said it wouldn't be enough against a mother's claim to her child—even if the supposed mother was lying. If something happened, at least the results would be in the hands of someone who already knew the truth.

"Hallie, grab your extra blanket and stuffed animals. We're going on a sleepover."

CHAPTER TWENTY-TWO

VINCENT LOOKED through all the documents he'd requested from Janette. She was a head case, which was to be expected from someone who'd just had her baby kidnapped, but Vincent felt there might be a little bit more going on there.

He swiveled in his office chair and held out the file to Manning. "I'd like some more info on the mother. Can you find out if she's on any meds?"

Manning took the file. "Sure, do you want me to just ask her and see if she'll tell us?"

Vincent rubbed the stubble on his jaw. "Nah, I don't want to spook her."

"Do you think she had something to do with her baby's kidnapping?"

"I don't know, but I think we need to rule it out while we're checking into everything else."

"Okay, I'm on it." Manning tapped the file.

"If we need to, I'll open up a formal investigation on her, but I think we can find out what we need pretty easily. Obviously someone else did. They had to have been tailing her for a few weeks to get this all planned."

"I thought she was from out of state and hadn't lived here long. What do you think about the ex and his alibi?"

"That's the strange thing. He claims he doesn't know anything about a baby—that Janette couldn't get pregnant. He said it was one of the major reasons they divorced. He seemed authentic, as in he outright called me a liar when I said she had a son."

Manning lifted up his hands. "That does trip the alarm. What do you think is going on?"

"I'm not sure." Vincent swallowed. "I'm working on a couple theories."

"Well, I'll get back to you after I check Baker." Manning exited the office, whistling.

Vincent felt uneasy. This case had kept him up most of the night. Every time he looked at the picture of Andrew Baker, something niggled in the back of his mind. He toggled the mouse and his computer screen flickered to life. He scrolled through notes on his cases over the past six months. Ten minutes later, he clicked on the file for Bentley, Easton and Bentley, Gina, fatal accident, drowning.

He double-clicked on the folder for Easton and sucked in a breath when an image popped up on the screen. The dark-haired baby reminded him of Andrew. He zoomed in on the baby's face and then held the picture of Andrew Baker next to it.

"Hey, Manning," Vincent called out. "Come and take a look at this."

"Yo." Manning strode into the office. "What's up? Find something on Baker?"

"I have to do some more checking, but you'll think *I'm* crazy."

"How so?"

"Remember that accident last May in the Snake—the woman and her baby that drowned?"

Manning scratched the side of his head. "Uh, the one where they never found the bodies?"

"The woman was still in the car—her leg was crushed in by the door. They never found the baby's body."

"And how are these related?"

"Come here and take a look." Vincent clicked his mouse, and the screen filled with the chubby face of Easton Bentley. At the same time, Vincent lifted the photograph of Andrew Baker and held it next to the screen.

"That's freaky. They look like the same kid." Manning took a step back, rubbed his hand over his eyes and stared at the pictures. "What's going on, Juarez?"

Vincent shrugged. "I don't know. It kept bothering me, how I thought this kidnapped baby looked so familiar. I did some searching and found the connection in my mind at least, but it looks like you're seeing it too."

Manning nodded. "Look at that red mark by his eye." His finger touched the screen on Easton's face and then motioned to the photo. "My niece had one of those—called 'em a stork bite or something. It didn't go away 'til the kid was three years old."

"Here's what I think." Vincent scrolled through the details of the Bentley case until he came to the father's information. He pointed to the screen and then looked at Manning. "We need to drive down to Heyburn and give Jack Bentley a visit—see how he's doing."

Vincent leaned his elbows on his desk and stared at the picture again. He didn't tell Manning how broken Jack had looked when he'd delivered the baby blanket to his house—wasn't that only last week? Jack had called him frantic about seeing his son. He lowered his head into his hands. What if delivering that blanket had pushed Jack over the edge? Maybe he'd seen Andrew Baker and noted the similarities, then kidnapped him. It was a reach, but staring at the two boys, Vincent had to tell himself that they weren't the same child.

CHAPTER TWENTY-THREE

JACK SET the cruise control to seventy-eight miles per hour. He didn't want to attract any attention to himself. The sooner he could get off the freeway, the better. Lava Hot Springs was only one and a half hours away, but he hadn't been up to the cabin for over six months. He and Gina had planned a fun summer camping trip for late June, but of course, that was cancelled along with every other family event or tradition they'd planned or ever would plan.

He checked his rearview mirror and his heart swelled with emotion. Hallie was asleep, her head resting on the side of Easton's car seat, and it looked like he was finally asleep after crying for a good twenty minutes. Easton had never liked being strapped into his car seat for long periods of times, but his protests never got him out of the restraints. Easton sniffled in his sleep and Jack smiled. His beautiful children were a gift from God. If only God would help him keep them safe for a few days longer.

Before they left the house, he'd checked the internet for

news one last time and was rewarded with a pencil sketch of himself on the headline news.

"The police have no suspects. If you have any information on the whereabouts of this man, please contact the Idaho Falls police department."

Jack had turned off his computer and practically ran from the house. He had three days left. If he was careful, they could make it. But he didn't like the worry gnawing at his insides. There hadn't been time to contact a lawyer, but Danika assured him that there were always good ones to be found if things went south. The thought didn't comfort him at all.

Pacing by the phone did nothing but increase the roiling anxiety in Emily's stomach. She had watched the news and followed the kidnapping story on the internet. The sketch of Jack was easily recognizable to her, but she hoped that no one else would make the connection. Even if someone did, she doubted they would follow through on the connection. Everyone who knew Jack thought the world of him. That eased her worry slightly. At least until she thought of another connection that people might make. A probable headline ran through her mind: Grief-stricken father kidnaps baby that looks like his son.

Her fingers itched to call Jack, but he was already gone. The way he spoke, she figured he was probably headed to the family cabin in Lava. Gina talked about it as a fixer-upper that needed lots of love and more fixing. Emily smiled when she thought of Gina, then her mouth turned down. It had to work out, didn't it? For everything they had gone through to get Easton back, Emily prayed it would be enough to keep the family together.

The doorbell rang and Emily nearly cried out. A feeling of dread accompanied her to the front door and when she looked through the peephole, her heart thumped hard in her chest. Two policemen stood on her doorstep. Emily clenched her jaw, her mind racing to a hundred different possibilities.

Careful to avoid the creaky board in the entryway, she stepped back from the door and darted into the first bedroom. "Just a minute," she called out. Emily grabbed the paintbrush that she had placed inside a plastic bag yesterday after applying a coat of primer to the shelf she was painting for Hallie's room. She ripped open the bag and grabbed the end of the paintbrush, smearing paint on her fingers. Next, she picked up some rags and touched her cheek with her wet fingertips. She wiped her hands as she walked toward the door and pulled it open with a bright smile, that she let falter at the sight of the police. "Sorry to keep you waiting," she said. Her fingers curled around the paintbrush handle as she did her best to steady the expression on her face. One of the police officers was a large Latino with short black hair. His partner stood a head shorter with sandy blond hair. Emily didn't like the way his beady eyes assessed her.

"Hi, I'm Officer Juarez and this is Officer Manning. Would you mind if we came in for a minute to ask you a few questions?"

Emily furrowed her brow. "About what?" She kept her hand on the door, feet rooted to the spot in the doorway.

"It concerns Jack Bentley. We're trying to reach him, and we haven't been able to locate him. His mother-in-law, Helen Rasmussen, thought you might know where he is."

The heat crept into her face before she could stop it, but Emily thought quickly as to how she could cover the obvious revealing of her emotions. She cleared her throat and smiled. "I'm afraid I don't know where Jack is, but I can tell you that Helen is doing her best to play matchmaker." She paused. "You're aware that Jack lost his wife and son recently?"

The policemen nodded.

"Well, his wife and I were good friends. Helen worries about Jack and . . ." she trailed off, giving the police a meaningful look.

He nodded. "I understand, but Helen made it sound as if you two have been spending time together."

Emily held up the paintbrush. "I paint for a living. Gina started painting her daughter's bedroom before she died so that I could create a mural. I've been working on keeping my promise."

She saw something flicker in Juarez's eyes and for a moment she warred within herself as to whether she should let them come in. But nothing good could come of extending the conversation. This man was perceptive and Emily wouldn't be able to conceal her true feelings for Jack under closer scrutiny. She tipped her head and looked behind her.

"I'm in the middle of finishing a project. I left my paint can open and I really need to get this done by four. Is there anything else you needed?"

Juarez stared at her for a moment and Emily struggled not to squirm under his gaze.

"I hoped you'd be able to give us an idea as to Jack's whereabouts. When did you see him last?"

Emily squeezed the paintbrush and reminded herself to stay close to the truth. "Let's see, I dropped some paint by there on Tuesday, I think it was."

Both officers perked up. "Tuesday? What time?"

"Um, let me see. I was on my way back from prepping for

another job. It must have been around four?" She smiled. "I lose track of time, so don't quote me on that."

Officer Manning opened his mouth to ask another question, but Emily headed him off. "Look, I'm really sorry, but my paint is going to have a film on it by now. I really need to get back. Do you have a card or something? I have an appointment to work on Hallie's room Wednesday, so I'm sure Jack's around." She was talking too fast, but Emily needed to put some distance between her and the officers. She'd watched enough cop shows to know that she didn't have to answer their questions.

Juarez took a business card from his pocket. His fingers brushed hers as he handed it over. "If you hear anything from Jack, I'd appreciate it if you'd give me a call. If you think of where he might be, it's important that we get in contact with him. It concerns his son."

For a moment, Emily forgot to register surprise, then she dropped the paintbrush. "Crap," she muttered as it hit the tile floor of her entry way. She knelt and wiped up the spot of paint, at the same time looking up at the cops. "Did they find his—Easton's—body?" she asked, her lip trembling.

Juarez shook his head. "I'm afraid not, and I can't really discuss it. We're sorry to have disturbed you."

"Thanks for your help, Ms. Gray," Officer Manning said with a wave.

After she closed the door, Emily watched the two men through her peephole. They climbed into their patrol car and sat for a few minutes before driving off. She sat on the floor, her heart beating so hard it made her chest ache. Her body shook with fear. She replayed the conversation—each question—in her mind hoping that she hadn't given anything away. The business card was printed on a thick cardstock and she rubbed her thumb in a circle over the printed name of

County Sheriff Vincent Juarez. She was pretty certain he suspected she knew more than she was saying, but she hoped that he would think it was because she felt uncomfortable dating her best friend's husband months after her death. It even sounded bad to her; it would be a reasonable conclusion.

~

"I want a detail on her. She knows something." Vincent put the cruiser into drive.

"Really? What do you think she knows?" Manning popped the tab on a Dr. Pepper.

"Notice that she didn't ask why we wanted to find Jack?"

Manning nodded, tipping the can back and taking a long swig. "You think she was having an affair with him while her best friend was still alive?"

Vincent shrugged. "You never can tell with people anymore, but she definitely is doing more than painting his daughter's bedroom."

Manning chuckled. "Some guys have all the luck."

"As soon as the warrant comes through, we'll tag his phone. If he contacts her, we'll know."

"What about the call records? I bet we'll see her number pop up."

Vincent shook his head. "Won't work. She already explained that away. We'll need more to get her to squirm."

"But she was telling the truth about going over there Tuesday. Remember the neighbor across the street saw her go in the front door?"

"Let's swing back by that way." Vincent turned left at the next intersection. "Ask her if she noticed Ms. Gray carrying anything—like a can of paint."

Manning guzzled the rest of his soda and smashed the can

against the dashboard. "Once we can get into the house, we can see if she's really been painting."

"I'm not as concerned about that," Vincent said. "It's what she's leaving out in between."

"So when can we question the mother-in-law again? She seemed pretty nervous. Do you think she was holding back?"

Vincent crunched on a breath mint. "Possible. She definitely didn't know he had skipped town, but now that she's had time to think about it," he glanced at Manning, "she might have a few ideas as to where he would go if he wanted to get away from it all for a while."

CHAPTER TWENTY-FOUR

HALLIE SNUGGLED DEEPER into the covers with a sigh. Jack had told her that she could sleep in the big bed with him if she promised to go right to sleep. Easton was fast asleep in the crook of his arm. He had fussed when Jack tried putting him in the portable crib, so Jack had walked the floor with him and ended up in Great-Grandpa's rocking chair. It creaked every time he rocked back, but for some reason it comforted him.

He rested his cheek on Easton's head. The baby's soft, dark hair had grown past his ears. Gina would have insisted on a trim. Jack smiled. Easton seemed right at home with Hallie and his dad, but Jack wondered if he noticed Gina's absence. The way he looked around the room sometimes, made him wonder if Easton remembered his mother. Maybe it was wishful thinking, but Jack would do his best to make sure that Easton did have some memories of his mother, even if they had to be borrowed. The cabin was on the cool side, so Jack wrapped another blanket around Easton as he rocked him.

The foreboding sense of discomfort and worry hadn't gone away, and Jack didn't know what else he could do. If the police had made a connection to him, they'd be tracing his credit cards, cell phone, and be on the lookout for his car. The cabin was the safest place for his family. It was Sunday night. He only needed two more days. If he was lucky maybe the test results would come early on Tuesday. He'd find a way to call Emily tomorrow night and see if anything had come in the mail. He tucked a blanket around Easton and set him carefully in the crib, and then crawled into bed. As he listened to the sounds of his children breathing, Jack pushed back the feelings of unrest and drifted off to sleep.

"I told you, Trent and I divorced before he knew I was pregnant. Andrew isn't his."

"Who is the father?" Officer Juarez asked.

Janette looked down at her hands, splayed out on the table. "I don't know. I'm sorry. It sounds terrible. I'm not that kind of person, but for one night I was. I got drunk, but I don't regret it. Andrew is the best thing that ever happened to me. I thought I could make it work with Trent, but he was too far gone. So I packed up and left."

"Ms. Baker, we're working with the Feds now, so if there's anything you haven't told me before now, please do." Juarez tapped his yellow legal pad.

Janette felt like she'd been punched in the gut. Would the Feds have the authority to look closer into her medical history? If they found out about her stay in Blackfoot, the mental hospital would tell them that she didn't have a child. "Uh, there isn't anything relating to this case. My personal life isn't up for review just because my baby was kidnapped, is it?"

Juarez lifted an eyebrow. "We generally like to look at a detailed history so we can see if there is a pattern, some place where the kidnapper might have first noticed you."

"I'll think on that, but before Andrew was born," she paused and shook her head, "I don't like to go back to those times. He gave me a chance to start over." A tear slipped down her cheek and she rested her head on her arms.

"Don't worry about it." Juarez jotted something down with his black pen. "We'll do everything we can to get him back to you."

The sketch of the man who kidnapped Andrew Baker held too many similarities to Jack Bentley. Vincent tapped the page and compared it to Jack's photo. They still hadn't been able to contact Jack, and it had been two days. But they'd finally hit on what he felt would be a break in the case. After calling Helen again and pressuring her late Sunday night, she finally brought up that maybe Jack had gone to the family cabin in Lava Hot Springs. He felt bad for causing her stress but his gut told him that Jack was hiding out, possibly with Andrew.

Even as he prepared to notify a team to head out to Lava, little red flags kept popping up concerning Janette Baker. They'd looked back into her information and found some holes in her story. She kept insisting that her past was just that—past and she didn't want to go there again.

Four hours later, in the early light of Monday morning Officer Manning drove the pickup down the lane that led to the cabin. They stopped fifty yards away when Vincent motioned to the blue pickup parked outside.

"He's here." He pushed the button on his radio. "Suspect on location. Will approach on foot."

Manning cut the engine and they walked up the gravel path. They skirted around the pickup and Vincent peered into the back seat. His heart plummeted when he saw the base for a car seat. "The baby's here." He pointed at the evidence, and Manning stopped to take a look.

The cabin sported an old porch with several creaky boards that announced their arrival. They stood in the shadow of the doorway, outside of the front window's view. Vincent knocked three times and they listened for activity in the cabin.

He heard a young girl squeal and a man shush her, then tentative footsteps. Jack Bentley opened the door a crack. "Vincent? What are you doing here?"

"Jack, we have a warrant for your arrest in the kidnapping of Andrew Baker. I'm hoping that we're wrong."

Jack looked down at the ground and his shoulders fell. At the same time, they heard a baby cry out. Jack met Vincent's gaze—his eyes desperate. "Please," he spoke softly. "That woman—Janette Baker—she took Easton from the river the day Gina died. She stole my son and let all of us believe he was dead."

Vincent felt like the wind had been knocked out of him. Jack was a good guy, but obviously he'd reached the breaking point.

"May we come inside and see the baby?"

Jack held up his hands. "Please don't do this to Hallie. I'll come with you, but please don't take Easton from us again." He opened the door wider and jogged across the room, leaving the two officers standing there.

Manning tapped his cuffs. "What do you think?"

"If he'll come willingly, I'm okay with sparing the girl.

Wait until we get to the car to cuff him." Manning stepped inside and Vincent followed him.

The overhead light cast shadows along the walls of the cabin. Vincent walked toward a bedroom in back, almost bumping into Jack holding a baby boy. The baby clutched at Jack when he saw Vincent.

"Please don't upset him," Jack cried. "I know you think I'm crazy, but this is my son. I can prove it. I had a DNA test run and the results should be at my home by Tuesday, or Wednesday at the latest."

Vincent struggled to keep the surprise from registering on his face. He thought back to all the interactions he'd had with Jack. As if anticipating that train of thought, Jack turned the baby toward Vincent. "Deep down, you know I'm not crazy, even though I've had plenty of reasons to be. Look at him. Do you see the angel kiss on his forehead? I can show you pictures of his birth. This exact mark is there."

"Jack, you've got to know this looks bad for you," Vincent said. "Why didn't you come to me first with your suspicions?"

"I tried! You thought I was crazy."

"So you were calling about seeing Andrew?" Vincent shook his head.

"No, I was calling about Easton. I didn't call again because you said I needed proof. I knew you would look at me just like you are right now—thinking I'm overcome with grief and turned crazy. And then Janette would take off and I'd never have a chance to save Easton." Jack cuddled the baby. "I have videos of him. I know this is my son. Will you give me a chance to prove it to you?"

Manning stepped forward. "Just come with us and we'll get this all sorted out."

"What about Hallie?" Jack asked. "Can my mother-in-law come and get her?"

"She'll have to meet us at the station in Idaho Falls," Manning said.

"You're not giving Easton back to that woman, are you?" Jack asked. "You have to at least wait for the evidence."

"He'll be placed in protective services until we can figure out what's going on," Vincent said.

"Daddy, I'm scared." Hallie clutched Jack's leg, her eyes filling with tears.

Jack crouched down. "It's going to be okay. These police officers are my friends. They have to check on some things for Easton so he doesn't get lost again. Can you be brave for me?"

Hallie shook her head no. "I don't want to be brave anymore. I want Mommy."

Jack closed his eyes, squeezing them tight. When he opened them, the look in his eyes was like a punch to Vincent's gut.

"Hallie, I'll be brave for both of us. Let's take Easton and go for a ride in Vincent's police car." Jack handed the baby to Vincent, and Andrew—or was it really Easton—immediately started crying. Jack's chin trembled as he put his hands behind his back.

CHAPTER TWENTY-FIVE

WHEN THEY ARRIVED at the station, Jack forced a smile for Hallie. "I don't want you to be scared, okay? We're going to get everything figured out so that we can bring Easton home."

"Where are you going Daddy?"

"I have to talk to the police, to help them know that we found Easton."

Hallie started crying when a young woman took her hand and led her away from Jack. Another officer carried Easton, who squirmed and cried out. Jack felt as if his heart was being ripped from his chest. If only they would listen to him. He did his best to keep his face neutral so that Hallie and Easton wouldn't be more frightened than they already were. A familiar anger crowded out his fear and Jack clenched his fingers tight. He wanted to punch the wall; instead he imagined himself doing so and the effects it would have on the cops listening to him.

They would call Janette and have her come down and identify Easton. What would she think if she saw Hallie?

Gina's memory of her drowning had made it clear to Jack

that Janette was probably the first on the scene of the accident. She stole his son and if he didn't do something fast, she
would do so again. As soon as Hallie and Easton were tucked
quietly in some back room, Jack turned to Vincent. "I need to
make a phone call now. I have a friend who can bring Helen
to pick up the kids."

"We'll keep Hallie here until six. Can Helen get here by
then?" Vincent asked.

Jack noted how Vincent hadn't argued with him outright
about Easton; he'd just left off mentioning him. He clenched
his jaw and looked at the clock. It was almost three, plenty of
time for Helen to get here *if* he could reach Emily.

Jack called and had to leave a message on Emily's phone.
"Em, this is Jack. I've been arrested for kidnapping. I had the
DNA results sent to your house as well as mine. If they've
come, bring them to the Idaho Falls police department. I
need you to drive Helen up here so that she can stay with
Hallie. Please hurry. Oh, and I need a lawyer. Call Danika if
you need help finding someone."

He hung up the phone and walked back toward the inter-
rogation room with the officer. Emily was probably screening
all of her phone calls. Most likely, she'd heard the message,
but what he didn't know was how she and his mother-in-law
could help him get out of police custody and back home with
Easton.

Emily cursed herself for stepping outside to clean out paint
trays. She had missed Jack's call by about thirty seconds.
Emily didn't dare call Helen; she'd have to tell her face to face
and hope that Helen could move quickly after hearing the
terrible news. She changed out of her grimy paint clothes and

into a clean pair of jeans and a pink sweater. Then she dashed out to the mailbox, but the mail hadn't arrived yet. Her mail carrier usually delivered after four. Emily decided that she would pick Helen up and then stop back at the house on their way to Idaho Falls. It had been a smart move for Jack to have the results sent to her as well, but if they didn't come today—Emily cringed—what would happen to Easton? They would surely press charges on Jack and start proceedings to close the case.

On her way to Helen's, Emily called the police department and let them know that she and Helen were on their way to pick up the kids. After she ended the call, she made a split decision and stopped by Jack's house to check his mailbox. Examining the postmark date, Emily was certain that his mail for the day had arrived, but there were no letters with the information they needed. She swallowed back the disappointment and tucked the mail back into the box.

She walked around the side of the house and stood on tiptoes at the gate. She reached her hand over the fence and lifted the spring action closure on the gate. It swung open and she darted through the fence that enclosed the back yard. Then she let herself in through the side garage door. Jack had mentioned that he kept it unlocked most of the time. Emily hoped that she'd be able to get into the house through the garage. She turned the knob and was rewarded with the swish of the door opening across the hardwood floor.

The house was quiet and Emily felt a pang of loneliness for Jack. He had tried his best to get his son back, even hiding out from the police, but now it all depended on the results of the DNA test. If there was enough doubt, the police might look into this other bizarre scenario where Janette was the kidnapper and Jack and Easton were the victims.

Emily walked into Jack's office and grabbed the manila

folder resting against his computer. She flipped it open and saw the pictures of Easton from eight months and the pictures Jack had taken at the park. There was no way that someone could discount the similarities. She tucked the folder under her arm and headed for the door.

As she passed the coat closet, she stopped and opened it. She pulled out a jacket for Hallie just in case she didn't have one. Then she rummaged around until she found a jacket that said twelve months on the tag. She bit her lip to keep the tears at bay as she thought of Easton's chubby arms in the little jacket. A camouflage print hoodie was on the floor of the coat closet, so Emily picked it up as well. She tried thinking positive—that the DNA test results would be waiting in her mailbox, that Jack would be released tonight. But a nagging worry ate at her insides as she returned to her car and placed the jackets in the trunk.

When Helen answered the door, Emily thought about trying to smile, but she didn't have the energy. "Helen, let's sit down for just a minute. I need to talk to you and it's not good news."

Emily clutched Helen's hand and relayed the details of Jack's suspicions that Easton was still alive.

"Oh, dear. Did Jack really take that woman's baby?" Helen's face went ashen and Emily realized that this scene was probably a replay of when she first heard the news that her daughter and grandson had drowned. Her mind spun around the web of words to choose from that would cause the least pain and worry.

Emily pulled out the manila folder and decided to let the pictures say what she couldn't. Helen gasped. "It's Easton!" She held the most recent picture closer, glancing back to his baby picture. She traced the red mark above his right eye. "His little angel kiss."

"Helen, this is Easton." Emily pointed at the picture and pivoted toward Helen. "Jack saw this woman and a baby at the park and took pictures. He hired a private investigator and had her followed. He believes that Andrew Baker is actually Easton Bentley and that Janette saved him from the river, but took him for herself."

Helen covered her hand with her mouth and shook her head. Tears ran along the wrinkles on her cheeks.

"It is Easton. I held him. Jack had a DNA test done and we're just waiting for the results. He had hoped that they would get back in time, before the police figured out it was him."

Helen rubbed her hands on her slacks. "So they've arrested Jack, haven't they?"

"Yes, and I need you to hurry and get your things together so we can head up to Idaho Falls to pick up Hallie. I'll explain more on the way. Do you trust me?"

Helen stopped and made eye contact with Emily, and then she nodded. "If you think it's Easton, if you believe Jack, then so do I."

Emily smiled. "I know we're going to get Easton back, but I'm worried about how many obstacles we're going to have to climb to get him."

"I'll be ready in five minutes," Helen said.

Emily watched her jump into action. She grabbed some homemade bran muffins and apples and put them inside a cloth bag. Then she pulled on a light jacket and added a couple water bottles to the bag. Helen grabbed one of the stuffed bunnies from her couch. "I'm ready."

"I'm going to drive by my house. Jack had the DNA results sent to my house as well as his. I already checked his mail and it wasn't there so I'm afraid they won't come until tomorrow."

"Couldn't he have put a special rush on it?" Helen asked.

"He checked into it, but without the mother's DNA, the testing place couldn't move any faster. I think he paid extra to get the results within six days."

"So, you're saying that Jack has been arrested even though the evidence is on its way in the mail?" Helen leaned her head back. "Won't they even give him a chance to prove himself?"

Emily shook her head. "That's what I keep hoping for. But I'm so glad that you don't think he's crazy. Jack told me that was what most people would say, so it would make it harder for the police to take him seriously."

"I've watched Jack. I know it's been hard on him—terrible —but I've never worried that he was losing it. He is such a good father. He loves Hallie so much." Helen put her fingers to her mouth as if to steady the trembling that hinted at more tears to come.

The mailbox stood just as Emily had left it, not hinting to any promises inside as she approached her house. She jumped out and opened the mailbox, finding a couple bills and a magazine. "No," she whispered. With heavy steps, she retreated to her car, where Helen waited expectantly. Emily shook her head. "It didn't come."

"That's all right, dear," Helen responded. "We'll just call a lawyer."

Emily almost laughed at how practical Helen sounded, as if it wouldn't be difficult at all to find someone to help Jack.

"My second cousin has a daughter who works as an assistant in a law firm in Pocatello. I'll call her and see if she has any suggestions."

Helen pulled out her cell phone and after clicking for several minutes, finally located the phone number she needed. Emily watched her from the fuzzy edges of numbness which crowded her brain as she attempted to sift through everything that had happened and the things that would happen if they didn't do something. She half-listened to Helen's conversation as she drove, while the other part of her mind filtered through possibilities.

If Janette got Easton back, Emily was certain they'd never see him again.

CHAPTER TWENTY-SIX

"I'm sorry, Jack. But you know we need evidence to support your claims," Vincent spoke, his deep voice emphasizing each word. "I wish there was something I could do. I really am sorry. Manning will escort you to holding."

"Will I be able to get out on bail?" Jack asked.

"Not until we've finished pressing all charges and the judge has reviewed our case. Then bail will be set, but because you've already orchestrated a rather elaborate kidnapping, it will probably be pretty high."

"Isn't there anything you can do to help me? Vincent, you know I'm not crazy. Look at Easton. It's him."

Vincent frowned. "You know I can't say anything. It's not what I think. It's what the evidence says."

"Like hell it is!" Jack shouted. "You didn't have to arrest me today. You could've waited until the test results got back. You could do something now if you wanted to. If you let that crazy woman take Easton home without a DNA test, it'll be your department under investigation for aiding and abetting a kidnapper."

Vincent blew out a breath, and lowered his head. He motioned to Manning. "Get him down to holding."

Jack stood as Manning approached. "If either of you had the courage, you would do the right thing and help me get the evidence I need to keep my son from that psycho who stole him in the first place!"

"I'll advise you to quit talking now before you make things worse, Jack." Vincent folded his arms and gave him a steely glare.

Jack had pushed it too far. Once again, he'd let his anger get the better of him, but how could any father sit there while plausible information fell on deaf ears? He winced as Manning handcuffed him, pulling his arms back sharply. He remembered how Gina used to tell him, "Hold your tongue. Bite if off if need be, but don't say something you'll regret."

And now he'd gotten the cops on the defensive, so they wouldn't listen to him. Listening. That's the other thing Gina always lectured him about—to be quiet and listen. He'd definitely developed an art for that over the past four months, but where was she now? He felt like crying out for her, asking her what he should do, but all he could do was walk down the hallway with a police officer. His feet clomped against the linoleum tiles, echoing against the scuffed walls and the row of doors they passed. He kept his eyes hooded against the false brightness of the fluorescent lights

Jack made eye contact with each of the three men in holding, letting his anger bubble to the surface again. He didn't want trouble, but he'd heard plenty of stories about what could happen to you if you turned your back on a cell mate. A white trash special sat in the corner, high on something, singing to himself. He had his legs folded against himself and he rocked slightly back and forth as Jack entered the cell.

A short Latino dressed in a suit and tie sat against the far right wall. He met Jack's stare and nodded. The kid in the left corner must have been barely eighteen. He reeked of alcohol, so Jack sat next to the cell door, closer to the suit and tie.

The door slammed shut and Jack felt like he was in the middle of a bad prison show on TV. Everything had seemed to go perfectly, but now it was all falling apart. One more day.

Jack recalled what Danika had said about there always being good lawyers when you needed them and he shook his head. Vincent told him he'd have a little time to come up with someone or else the courts would appoint someone. Jack kept hoping that Emily would show up with the test results and the nightmare would end.

The white trash special started banging on the bars in time to his discordant melody. Jack tried to block out the sound. His thoughts turned to Gina, willing her to talk to him, to give him some hint. But there was nothing. Maybe it was a good sign she wasn't haunting him again. Maybe it meant that Easton was safe, that the charges would be dropped and Jack would be released. A sharp pain encompassed his heart when he thought of how just hours before he had rocked Easton to sleep. The baby was cuddly, just as he had always been, and when Jack sang to him Easton had softly patted Jack's shoulder.

Jack opened his eyes and looked around. The clanging of the bars continued. *C'mon, Emily. Where are you?*

It only took Janette an hour to pack her suitcases with what she would need to go into hiding. If the police didn't find Easton soon, she'd leave a note saying she was looking herself. They were getting too close. Janette figured it was only a matter of time before someone broke confidentiality and alerted them to her stay at the mental hospital. She started packing a suitcase for Easton. She would take it with her in case she found him or if the police did. Either way she would have to run.

Her phone rang and Janette screamed when she recognized the number from the police department. "Did you find him?" she shouted into the phone.

"This is Officer Manning. We've found your son, and we need you to come down to the station for questioning and identification."

"I'm leaving now. I'll be there in ten minutes." Janette grabbed her purse and headed for the door. She tried not to speed on the way to the station, but then decided it was worth the risk. When she arrived and was told that Andrew was at the hospital for a special check-up, it was all she could do to keep the panic from crushing her. Officer Manning and Officer Juarez led her to a small room with blue plastic chairs and a folding table.

"It will be just fine," Officer Manning told her as he sat down. "This is standard procedure in a case like this. I know you want to see the baby right away, but for his safety we've put him with social services until we can get everything straightened out."

"What is there to straighten out?" Janette demanded. "You found my son and the man who took him, right?"

"We've arrested the man who kidnapped Andrew," Juarez said. "But there are a few problems. The man insists that Andrew is someone else, that the baby is his son."

"What?"

"I know it sounds crazy," Juarez replied, "but this man is a good guy. He's had a pretty rough time of it. His wife was killed in a car accident last May. The car went into the Snake River and his baby son was inside. The wife drowned, but they never found the baby." Juarez looked like he had to struggle for the words. "He has pictures of his son. They look a lot like Andrew." Juarez touched his forehead. "The baby even has a little red mark like Andrew."

Janette sank into the chair beneath her. There was no way that God could be so unjust. It was His will that she find Andrew, so why would God try to take him away from her now? It was impossible. How could someone find her in a city of nearly sixty-thousand people? She drew in a ragged breath. Her eyes snapped back into focus when she saw Juarez squatting in front of her.

"Ma'am, are you okay?"

She reached out and grasped his hands. Juarez stumbled into a kneeling position.

"You're not going to let me take Andrew home, are you?" Her eyes darted back and forth as the hysteria worked its way to the surface. "Please, don't tell me that you believe him?"

"You'll be able to see your baby soon. We're just going to ask you a few questions and see if we can't get this cleared up. Jack is insisting on a DNA test to prove that you are Andrew's mother."

Janette gasped. "Can he do that?"

"That is still to be seen, but because we have an open investigation, you won't be able to take Andrew home today," Juarez said.

Janette dry-heaved and bolted from her chair, heading for the nearest bathroom. Her purse banged against the door as she entered and dashed into the first open stall. She threw up and watched the swirling waters in the toilet as her own eyes filled with tears. It couldn't be possible.

She should have been more careful. The man—Jack Bentley—had found her. Janette knew his name from the accident reports on the news. All this time, he must have been looking for his son. He must be wealthy or powerful to have the resources to search for his son for so long. She briefly considered whether she should just flee from the precinct before the police could investigate into her past further, but then she thought of her sweet little Andrew. She loved him so much!

Andrew loved her too. He had started babbling about a month ago and Janette had cried when he first said, "Ma,ma,ma."

Being a mother was the most wonderful thing in the world. She wouldn't let anyone steal her dreams again. Trent had tried to stomp on her dreams. He told her to be reasonable, to deal with the loss, get over it, and get on with life. He'd even gone so far as to tell her that some people weren't meant to have children because they had something unique to offer the world. He was so frustrated when she didn't agree with him. He absolutely wouldn't consider adoption.

Andrew was her only chance. She was his mother now and a baby needed a mother. It wasn't as important that he have a father. She knew that, because her own father was never around. If that man claimed Andrew, her sweet baby would sit in daycare with some woman who was trying to watch six other kids. He'd be with someone who didn't care what time it was when he took his first step or what day of the week it was when he first tried banana squash. Janette stood and washed her face in the sink, her resolve building like so many drops of water pushing against a great dam.

She fished in her purse and took two extra blue pills. Calmness would be her defense. The lies, the accusations—they wouldn't faze her. Andrew was her baby and if they couldn't see that, she would make them. She loved him.

A woman entered the bathroom carrying a box of juice.

"Are you okay? You're Janette Baker, right? Would you like to lie down for a few minutes?"

Janette gripped the edge of the sink. "I'll be fine. It's all been so overwhelming. I'd like to see my son now."

The woman nodded. "Follow me."

For half a moment, Janette thought she would take her directly to Andrew, but she followed her down a hallway and back to the same stuffy room where Juarez sat next to another officer. They were going to continue questioning her. She willed herself to relax, inhaling slowly through her nose.

"I want to see Andrew. He's my son. I want to be sure he's okay."

Juarez studied her and Janette could see the questions behind his eyes. She could imagine the things that he'd been told by Jack, Andrew's biological father, but *she* was Andrew's mother now. She had been preparing for this moment all of her life, because all she ever wanted was to be a mother. If these men thought they could take it away from her with a few questions and some swab with DNA, they had no idea who they were dealing with.

"He's mine. You have no right to keep him from me. I demand to see my son!"

Juarez stood and took two steps toward Janette. "You'll be able to see Andrew as soon as we get the information we need to press charges against Jack Bentley. You do want to see the kidnapper brought to justice, right?"

Janette lost her train of thought, momentarily stunned by the apparent change in Juarez's behavior. Maybe it was the paranoia taking over when she thought he'd looked at her suspiciously. Her meds would kick in soon. "Will it take long?" her voice sounded much smaller with Juarez standing next to her.

"First, we need to swab your cheek for the DNA test. Are

you in agreement with this?" Manning stood and Janette could see the test kit in his hand.

She had no choice but to comply. She nodded. Her mind raced through her options, but there were none that wouldn't cause more problems. Manning pulled out the swab and held it in front of Janette. She opened her mouth and he rubbed it along the inside of her cheek. Something so simple would be the means of taking Andrew away from her if she didn't take action.

"Okay, I'll take this for processing," Manning said. "We'll utilize the resources we have, but it could still be forty-eight hours before we get results."

"Have a seat, Janette." Juarez indicated the chair in front of him.

Janette pulled out the heavy wooden chair. It scraped along the floor as if a piece of gravel were stuck under one of the legs. She lifted it slightly and the scraping noise ceased. When she sat down, her foot found the pebble that had been under the chair. Strange that something so small could cause such a disturbance.

"There are a few gaps in your history that I'd like you to fill in for me." Juarez opened a manila file folder. He ran his index finger down a few lines, and then stopped. "I'm working back from the present because it's most likely to help us find the evidence we need."

"I don't understand why I need to answer any more questions. You have my son. You've arrested the man who kidnapped him." She leaned back and folded her arms, the chair creaking with her movement.

Juarez lifted his head slowly and met her gaze. She saw the flicker of a question in his eyes again, that subtle hinting that he didn't fully trust her. He was a good policeman and he would do his job. That was a problem for Janette.

He cleared his throat. "Put yourself in my position. I have to make sure there are no mistakes made. When we press charges, it's a serious thing. So if there's anything I can do to make this move along faster, I will, but I need your cooperation."

"I can't sit here any longer. I have to see Andrew. I'll answer whatever questions you want later." Janette stood and slung her purse over her shoulder. "I would appreciate your cooperation."

Juarez flinched, but if she hadn't been looking for it Janette would have missed the reaction. She waited for him to stand.

"Are you sure you can't stay for just a few more minutes? It would really help us with this case?" Juarez asked.

Janette swallowed. "After I make sure that Andrew is okay, you can ask me all the questions you want." She swiveled on her heel and left the room.

CHAPTER TWENTY-SEVEN

THE IDAHO FALLS POLICE DEPARTMENT had several trees out front, their branches swaying in the gentle breeze. Emily thought of the tree she had painted for Hallie and hoped that the little girl was okay. Helen opened her door as soon as Emily put the car in park. They hurried into the station, Emily's heartbeat increasing with each step forward.

The building was alive with energy. Emily saw three police officers cross the waiting area as she entered. Helen approached the front desk, adjusting her cloth bag higher on her shoulder. The receptionist looked up, and offered the barest of smiles. Her curly brown hair was shoulder length and she sported a pair of dark-framed glasses. Emily noted the wrinkles around her eyes. She looked serious. Emily wondered how much strain the job put on the woman.

"We're here to pick up Hallie Bentley," Helen told the receptionist.

"Yes, you must be the grandma. I need to see your driver's license."

Helen handed it over. The woman studied the license and

handed it back. "I'll call and have them bring her out." She picked up the phone and relayed the information.

Emily waited until she was done talking to lean forward. "And we'd like to visit Jack Bentley, please."

The woman lifted a thin brow and her right nostril flared. "I'll have to check if booking is done with him. You can have a seat right over there."

"Oh, uh—okay," Emily stammered. Her lungs felt like they were shrinking. She looked down at the brown rug until the straight grid lines blurred. She felt Helen squeeze her arm.

"It's okay, dear. He'll be okay," she murmured. "He'll be so relieved that we've come to get Hallie. He's such a good father."

Emily pulled an envelope out of her purse and slid it across the desk. "I also brought these photos for evidence. They belong to Jack and they are pictures of Easton that prove the identity of his baby."

The secretary hesitated and then took the envelope. "I'll make sure these get to the right people."

Emily walked back toward Helen, hoping she'd done the right thing. She sat on the hard vinyl couch. The cushions made a whooshing noise when Helen sat beside her. The tears kept gathering in Emily's eyes, no matter how rapidly she blinked. A few escaped and trickled down her jaw line. She wiped at her eyes, looking past the large potted plant toward the hallway where she expected Hallie to be escorted.

In a few moments, she was rewarded with a squeal and bouncing pigtails as Hallie launched herself toward her grandma.

"I colored a picture, Grandma," Hallie said. "Did you come to see it?"

Emily looked up at the female officer who smiled down at

Hallie. She held out a piece of paper. "Here you go. She's such a sweetheart."

"Grandma, I hugged Easton when he cried. He really wants Daddy and me, but he has to have a sleepover here first in case he wants to be a policeman when he grows up." Hallie giggled. "Isn't that funny?"

Helen nodded. Emily could see how hard it was for her to smile. How difficult it must be for her to know that her grandson was in this building, and she couldn't see him. But maybe it wasn't impossible. Emily stood next to the officer and spoke in a low voice. "Can Helen see her grandson for a minute?"

"I'm afraid the answer is probably no on that one. I can check, but officially, Social Services has him under their care while we investigate this case. He was taken to the hospital for a routine checkup."

"If you don't mind checking, I'd appreciate it," Emily answered. "I don't know if you've heard all the details, but Helen thought Easton was dead until two hours ago."

The woman nodded. "And because it's still under investigation, we don't want to confuse the baby or give her false hope."

Emily swallowed another round of defeat. "I understand." She chewed on her bottom lip. "We'd really like to talk to Jack though. Could you help us with that?"

"Sure. Let me see if Juarez will allow it." She pushed her radio. "Juarez, Jack's mom and girlfriend are here to see him. Is that okay?"

With a start, Emily realized that Juarez was the same officer who had questioned her earlier. She remembered the lies she'd told him, and although she felt guilty, it wasn't the time to come clean. Jack had told her he didn't want her held responsible for anything, so she'd have to do her best to act as surprised as Helen.

"Come this way. Juarez said they just finished booking Jack, so we can arrange a visit."

They followed the officer down the hall. He swung the door open and Emily's stomach rolled when she caught sight of Jack dressed in an orange jumpsuit. Even though she knew he'd been arrested, she had hoped they hadn't booked him for the crimes yet.

Jack looked like every ounce of energy had been slugged out of him. He sat up, his eyes seeking hers, straying to her hands and back to her face. He was looking for the test results. Emily shook her head.

"It didn't come." Her voice sounded weak and small in the concrete room.

Jack nodded, and then did his best to straighten up and smile when Hallie bolted through the door.

"Daddy, I missed you! Easton missed you too, but that police lady looked at him and he cried." She held her arms out and furrowed her brow. "Another lady wants Easton and he might go with her. Why Daddy?"

"Because Easton is a baby and babies don't know when people are bad. Sometimes people act nice to trick kids. Remember how we talked about strangers?"

Emily watched him clench his fist tight and then release his fingers one by one, pushing his hand down his pant leg. "Helen, I'm sorry about all this. I did what I had to."

"I know, Jack. You don't have to explain to me. Gina would be proud."

Jack hung his head. "Not if I can't get him back."

"Keep your chin up. You didn't get this far to give up. I have a lawyer coming to help you."

"Really?" Jack looked up. "Who?"

"A friend of a second cousin. He'll be here by eight tonight but I'm hoping these people will come to their senses before then." Helen sat in the chair next to Jack. "I can't believe Easton is here and I can't even hold him."

"They won't let you see him?"

"No, I already asked." Emily sat on the other side of Jack. "I didn't know Helen overheard me."

Helen gave her a wan smile. "I had prepared myself for that answer considering the charges they've brought against Jack."

"I didn't think this through as well as I thought," Jack murmured.

"Don't beat yourself up." Emily took his hand and squeezed it gently. "This is so much better than the alternative. You didn't want to risk spooking Janette and making her run."

"Daddy, when can we go home?" Hallie asked.

Jack hugged Hallie and kissed the top of her head. "You get to sleep at Grandma's tonight."

"Yahoo!" Hallie cheered. She slid off Jack's lap and took Helen's hand. "Let's go, Grandma."

Helen stood. "That's probably a good idea. I'll take Hallie to the bathroom first. You take a minute, Emily."

Jack rose and gave Helen a hug. "Thank you for everything."

"I'll keep praying," she said. "Don't forget we have our own angel up there. That has to count for something."

Jack smiled and Emily felt the weight of those words, the things Helen didn't know about how her angel daughter had led them to this very point. After Helen left with Hallie, Jack sat back down and turned to Emily.

"How are you, really?"

Emily nodded and swallowed past the constricting fear in

her throat. "I'm okay. That sheriff—Juarez and his partner came and questioned me."

Jack pressed his lips together and tilted his head toward the window. The slight shake of his head was almost imperceptible. Emily nodded, catching his warning that they might be overheard.

"I had no idea where you were, Jack. But I brought some photos of Easton to give to Juarez. They can't ignore the evidence that proves he is your son."

Jack rubbed a hand across his face. "If only the evidence were here."

"I'm sorry that the test results weren't there yet, but don't you think they'll come tomorrow?"

"I think so."

"I thought about calling the post office and asking if there was a way to pick up my mail early. I figure it's worth a shot," Emily said.

"That's actually a good idea," Jack replied. "I just worry about Janette. She's a loaded gun and Vincent isn't taking me seriously—he thinks she's harmless."

"Why doesn't he believe you?"

"I think part of him wants to believe, but Janette has been a good mom. There aren't any signs of neglect or abuse and I'm the one who kidnapped him so everyone has tunnel vision where I'm concerned."

Emily's lips twitched as she tried to think what was safe to say. The words blurred and she found herself squeezing Jack's hand tighter. He reached out his other hand and grasped her shoulder. "Hey, it's gonna be okay," he whispered.

"But will it? I can't imagine how you're feeling, Jack, but it's tearing me up."

Jack pulled her into an embrace. "I'm sorry, Em." She felt his breath by her ear and a tingling sensation traveled down her spine. "Call Danika. Get the info from her. Her number is on my cell phone in my third desk drawer. But don't take any risks. I need you safe."

Warmth spread through her chest and she had the sudden urge to kiss Jack. He was so kind, sitting there in his jumpsuit telling her not to take risks. Some people were accusing him of acting out of desperation and grief. Emily knew his every action was from love. That thought kicked her heart up a few notches. She loved him. The thought struck her that she'd been doing her best to deny her feelings out of respect to Gina when maybe she should have been accepting them for the same reason.

Emily hugged Jack, breathing in the cool scent of his cologne. He leaned back, his hand lingering on her cheek. "Thank you."

She nodded, not trusting her voice. When she stood, Jack held onto her hand. "You're a good woman, Emily Gray."

"And you're a good man, Jack Bentley." She smiled and walked out of the room.

When the door clicked into place, Emily resolved that she would do whatever she could to help Jack get his family back together. He'd told her not to take risks, but that was exactly what she was prepared to do.

CHAPTER TWENTY-EIGHT

THE INVESTIGATION into Janette had finally brought up something worth taking a look at. Vincent stared at the note about a possible mental history file. It could be the reason Janette had resisted more questions into her past. If she had problems with mental stability, he understood that she would feel threatened when they started digging for more information.

The file couldn't help them until they got a warrant to read it, but the anonymous tip telling him to look for such a thing did cast a new light on Janette. Whoever had called in the tip mentioned that Janette may have been in Blackfoot as recently as May. The source of the tip was most likely someone in Jack's inner circle, but they must be good to have found dirt so quickly. Unless they'd already been looking. Jack hadn't mentioned anything about a private investigator, but the more Vincent thought about the case, the more convinced he was that Jack had worked with an expert to pull this off.

Vincent shivered as a cold chill moved down his back. He flipped to Jack's file and his finger rested on the date, May fourteenth. Then he looked at the scene of the accident in relation to the Idaho State mental hospital. Less than five miles separated the locations.

He thought of Jack's explanation, his insistence that Janette had kidnapped Easton. Even though Vincent had wanted to believe Jack, he couldn't, but the tip had him looking at Janette in a different light. What if she wasn't all that she claimed to be?

He'd questioned Janette and picked up on a level of tenseness as she told him about her past. At the time, he'd disregarded his suspicious nature explaining to himself that the woman was beyond frazzled with the kidnapping of her child. But now, looking at it from a new angle, he recognized the breaks in her story, the pauses in their conversation, how she'd considered some of her answers while others sounded almost rehearsed.

There was more to her than she'd let on. Tomorrow morning he would ask her outright about the mental hospital and see her reaction.

Janette looked down at her feet, closed her eyes, and took a deep breath. She thought of her love for Andrew. The fear taking up residence in every bone of her body would not help her. She couldn't let them take him away. She could be stronger than the fear. For Andrew. Everything she had planned was for Andrew, to give him the kind of life he deserved with a loving mother. A baby needs a mother and if she didn't act, they would take him from her.

An image of the swirling waters of the Snake River flooded her mind. His tiny cries, the cold water. *I saved him. He's mine.* Janette trusted God's will; she just needed to exercise more faith and do her part to keep the blessing God had given her safe.

She lifted her head slowly and opened her eyes. Social Services was taking care of Andrew, but Janette had been granted permission to see him. She threatened a lawsuit against the police department and Manning had been the one to nudge Juarez into letting her visit Andrew this morning. Juarez agreed on the condition that Janette would come and answer more of his questions once she'd seen Andrew. Now she was here and nothing would stand in her way. She'd filled out more paperwork and answered more questions, but Andrew was on the other side of the door.

"Please remember all of the instructions and follow them carefully or you'll be removed from the room," the stern woman said as she held open the door.

Rolling her shoulders back, she entered the playroom. There was a young woman with her back turned, picking up toys. Andrew played next to her.

He stood next to a wooden box with wires extending from it in big loops. Each colored wire had several wooden beads on it and Andrew slid them from one end to the other.

"There's my baby," Janette cooed.

Andrew smiled and held his hands out to Janette. She scooped him up and cuddled him.

"Oh, hello." The woman turned around. "He's a darling little boy. My name's Teresa."

"Thanks for watching him." Janette sniffed, and then checked Andrew's diaper. "His diaper is dirty. How long has he been sitting in his own poop?"

The young woman's cheeks reddened. "It must've just happened. He's been so happy. I haven't smelled anything."

Luckily, the woman didn't argue because Andrew's diaper was clean. Janette reminded herself that she was in charge of the future. She narrowed her eyes. "I'll go and change him."

"No, you can't leave with him. I have direct orders to keep him under supervision." Teresa stepped forward. "You can change him over there." She pointed to a changing table.

Janette took a step back and frowned. "Let me see your diapers."

Teresa fumbled with the latch on the cupboard door and pulled out a diaper. "Here, we have wipes and everything you need on the table."

Janette glared at Teresa. "That is a size three. Andrew needs size four and he gets bad diaper rash if he uses anything other than Huggies." She turned to the door, lifting Andrew higher on her hip.

"I'm sorry, but you have to stay in this room." Teresa was in front of Janette before she could react, her finger reaching toward a buzzer by the window. Andrew tensed and dug into Janette's shoulders as he clung to her.

Janette hesitated, reminding herself of the careful plans she had laid out. This was the only situation she couldn't plan exactly to the minute. *God will help me*, she thought. She relaxed her hold on Andrew. "Look, you're scaring him. If you don't let me go and change my baby, I'll have every examiner in the state down here."

Teresa pointed at the baby. "Put Andrew down. If you want to use your diapers go out to your vehicle and get them."

Janette's shoulders slumped. "You're right. I should have thought of that. I'm sorry. This is all so terrible." She carefully set Andrew on the floor where he began to whimper. "Maybe I should wait a moment since he's upset."

Teresa watched her with a furrowed brow, and then dropped her hand to her side. She walked back to the cupboard and bent down. "I'm sure we have a size four in here. We might even have some Huggies."

Janette saw her opportunity and took it. She grabbed the wooden box, the beads jiggling slightly as she lifted it in the air. Teresa turned just as Janette brought it crashing down on her head. Her scream was muffled against the carpet as Janette hit her again and again. The skin broke on Teresa's forehead and Janette stopped when she saw blood trickling down her temple. She dropped the wooden toy, scooped up Andrew and opened the door. With a shaky breath, she walked across the hard flooring on the balls of her feet, making only the slightest noise from her running shoes.

Andrew laid his head on her shoulder as she approached the main entrance to the building. Janette's brain screamed for oxygen and she sucked in a breath, alerting her that she'd been holding it. As she stepped from the hallway, two police officers and a young teenage girl came through the front doors. The girl was screaming. Andrew burrowed his head deeper into Janette's shoulder. She put her arm around him and took advantage of the diversion. By the time she hit the front doors, she was almost running. She heard someone else shout and she pushed through the doors, sprinting to her car. More shouting, but Janette didn't look back. She didn't know if the yelling was because of the girl or her, but she couldn't spare even a second to look.

Her car was unlocked with the key in the ignition as she'd left it. She slid in, locked the doors, and started the engine. Andrew cried out as she set him in the passenger seat.

"I'm sorry, baby. Mommy has to save you." She peeled out from the parking space with a direct shot to the street in front of her. There was more yelling, this time, she was certain it was directed at her. She only needed to make two right turns and Andrew would be safe. They'd never find her or her baby.

As she made the first right turn, Andrew rolled forward, bumping his chin on the cup holder. He started crying at the same time Janette heard a siren wail behind her. "It's okay, Andrew. We're almost safe."

She sped down the block and careened around the second right turn, noting the flashing lights in her rearview mirror. "Almost there," she cried. Her heart pounded so fast, that her chest hurt. Andrew cried louder and she felt her nerves tightening with the pressure. She pushed down on the gas pedal. Her careful planning would save them. She roared straight ahead to the cul-de-sac and jumped the curb to drive down a little dirt road next to a two story home.

Tree branches scraped against her car as she edged her way around the large oak tree that shaded the road. Rocks pinged at the underside of her car as she drove through a grove of trees and exited onto a street five blocks south of the cul-de-sac. She could still hear the siren, but it sounded farther away. She hoped that meant her plan had worked. The cops should have come up to the cul-de-sac and been momentarily confused as to where she went. The side road was not obvious to everyone. Janette only knew it was there because she had taken the short cut a few times with Andrew in the stroller after going to the library.

She only needed a two-minute lead to put the final part of her plan into action. The streets were quiet in this neighborhood. Janette eased behind a vacant home and parked next to a silver Honda. The rental car was packed and ready to go, with Andrew's car seat strapped in the back seat.

"Hush, my sweet baby. Everything is going to be all right

now," she crooned to him as she pulled him carefully from the car.

His lip looked a bit swollen and he whimpered, clutching at her sleeves as she leaned into the back seat of the Honda. "Mommy has to buckle you in so we can drive safe. Here's a cracker for you."

Janette grabbed a graham cracker from the tote beside the car seat. Andrew cried as she buckled him in, but then he started gnawing on the cracker. With a sigh of relief, Janette slid into the driver's seat. She put on the blonde wig that had been sitting on the passenger seat and a pair of sunglasses. Then she pulled around the side of the house and onto the street. She had just reached the stop sign when she heard sirens. They were faster than she thought. Sweat ran down her sides as she watched the police cruiser speed past her. As soon as it was clear, she pulled onto the street and drove as fast as she dared away from the freeway.

They would find her car within ten minutes and block off the freeway entrance as soon as they saw the tire tracks next to her car. But Janette had thought of everything this time. Evidence was what they wanted, so that was what she left them. Plane tickets to Mexico with a flight boarding out of Idaho Falls within the hour. But she and Andrew weren't heading south. They would take the back roads and head north, where she planned to leave the car and take a bus. She had even tossed her cell phone into the back seat of a frazzled-looking mom's blue minivan while the woman was loading up groceries and kids. If they tracked the phone, they wouldn't find Janette and Andrew.

"It'll be hard to start over, Andrew. But we can do this. We'll have to think of a new name for you, but we have some time." Janette smiled at Andrew's feet kicking in the back seat. She handed him another cracker and faced the white lines of the road. She had found the perfect place to hide while she arranged for new birth certificates and an identity change for herself. In one week, they would be across the border in Canada—a country so vast, that no one, not even Jack Bentley, would ever find his son again. Her son. Andrew was her son, and they would always be together.

CHAPTER TWENTY-NINE

TUESDAY MORNING ABOUT NINE-THIRTY, Jack was escorted from his cell to meet with Vincent. He hadn't slept much and his mouth felt like he'd gargled with sand. The hopelessness sat in his gut like a bowling ball, pulling him toward the ground. Part of him wanted to curl up and close his eyes, while the other half warred with the constant anger simmering beneath despair. He didn't make eye contact with Vincent when he reached the room.

"I have some bad news." Vincent's voice sounded weak, laced with anxiety.

Jack snapped his head up, wondering what he was missing. Vincent's head was down, his lips pursed. Jack could hear his own ragged breaths. The air felt heavy—with anger, sadness, and something else Jack couldn't comprehend. Vincent swallowed and Jack watched his Adam's apple flex up and down his throat.

"Just after eight this morning, Janette attacked the woman with Social Services who was watching Easton. She took him."

Jack tensed. His head felt like something had just exploded inside and he couldn't hear what Vincent was saying. He fell against the wall, covering his face, jamming his ears against the truth. Janette had taken his son. Again. As he slid to the floor, he realized that Vincent had called his baby Easton when he told Jack what had happened.

"Jack, we'll get him back." Vincent crouched in front of Jack and put a hand on his arm. "Stay with me, man. You can still help us here."

It felt like Jack was swallowing gravel, but he managed to whisper, "So you believe me now?"

Vincent lifted his hands, and then let them fall to the table. "I don't know what to believe, but I will tell you that there is a warrant for her arrest. Teresa's in the emergency room getting stitched up."

Jack stood slowly. "She's desperate because she stole Easton. I know you can see it. You have to let me out of here now."

"I'm already working on it. I contacted the county attorney and once she fills out the papers, we'll release you."

Jack pushed his hands through his hair. "In the meantime, Janette is going to flee the country with my son."

"We've got everyone on this. She had a flight booked to Mexico that she didn't take. Either she didn't make it in time or it was to throw us off her trail. We're working on tracking her cell phone, though."

"I can't believe this," Jack cried. "I had Easton and you took him away from me. I told you this would happen."

"You have every right to be angry at me. I'm sorry," Vincent said. "We made the wrong call."

"You let this happen!" Jack pounded the table. Easton was gone and there wasn't anything Jack could do, still locked up, trapped, and letting Gina down with every minute that passed. He sucked in a breath. "How soon do you think I'll be out of here?"

"Probably by three."

"Three?" Jack's anger burned like a desert brush fire. "That's six hours from now. I need to be out there looking for Easton."

"I know. Look, if there's any way I can speed things up I will. Why don't you call someone and arrange for them to come pick you up?"

"Okay." Emily would help him. Hallie was safe with Helen. He needed to calm himself down before he called Emily. She would be just as upset as he felt.

Vincent led him to a phone and Jack dialed Emily's cell. She answered on the first ring. "Hello?"

"This is Jack."

"Jack? I'm heading up there now."

"You are?"

"Yes, I called the station twenty minutes ago and told them I have the test results. I was able to get them from the post office early and Jack, they're positive! We have the proof. You'll be able to take Easton home with you."

Jack groaned.

"What? What is it?"

"Emily, will you pull over to the side of the road for a minute? I have something important to tell you."

"Uh—okay. Just a second."

He waited, forming the words in his head, grateful that Emily trusted him enough to pull over.

"Jack, you're scaring me. What is it?"

He took a breath. "Janette took Easton from Social Services. She attacked the woman watching him."

He heard Emily gasp and then cry out. "No. She's not going to get away with this. The police will find her, right?"

"They've already lost her trail," Jack muttered. Everything around him seemed faded and muted, as if it couldn't be real. "They're trying to track her cell phone now. She had a flight booked to Mexico, but she wasn't on it."

"No! I—oh, Jack, no!" Emily cried.

"I know." Jack breathed in and out and shook his head. He couldn't give up now. He thought of Gina and all she had done to help him find Easton. There must still be some way to save his son. "They've got everyone working on this with a check-point on the freeway, but there are so many back roads. I'm betting that's the route she took."

"It's exactly what you were worried might happen," Emily's voice shook.

"The good news is that Vincent believes me now and he already talked to the prosecuting attorney. They're filling out paperwork so that they can release me. Those test results will just be another slap in their face."

"Oh, Jack. I'm so sorry."

"I'm glad you're coming," he replied.

"I'll be there in an hour."

"Emily, be careful."

"I will."

Jack hung up the phone. Vincent was standing just outside the door, watching, and shifted his stance.

Jack's eyes strayed to the clock on the wall. Just after ten. Janette had already been on the run for two hours. She could be in another state.

Could Jason Edwards help him? Jack probably should have called Jason when he was first arrested, but he never dreamed that things would turn out this way. He was supposed to get the DNA test and take Easton home. Jack turned to Vincent. "I have a friend who is an FBI agent in Utah. Can I call him?"

"I'm afraid not, but if you'll give me his name, I can alert him to your case," Vincent answered. "The feds are assisting on this case, but they haven't called in agents from other states at this point."

"Okay, his name is Jason Edwards. Please tell him that I would appreciate his help."

Vincent nodded.

"What version of the story will you share with him? Janette's or mine?"

"Jack," Vincent narrowed his eyes. "I'll give him a call, okay?"

There wasn't anything else Jack could do. Jason might not even be able to help him at this point, but at least he could be made aware of the crazy circumstances. Jack grimaced when he thought of how Jason had warned him not to do anything crazy.

After Jack was escorted back to his cell, he knelt by the bed and rested his head against the hard mattress. "Please, God. Help me save my son. Please don't let Easton be lost from me again. If Gina can help me, please let her." He repeated the phrase, his chest tightening as he begged for a miracle.

The cell block held silence. It wrapped Jack tightly in its grip. He heard nothing. Felt nothing. With every passing minute, his son was farther away from him, out of his reach, out of his control. Even though he could see the solid concrete wall in front of him, he felt as if the world were crumbling. The silence mocked him, scorned his weak faith.

He thought of the first time he'd seen Gina standing on the bank of the river and he clenched his jaw, his teeth grating against each other. He hadn't listened to her at first. He hadn't believed her because he didn't believe himself. Even though he'd listened afterward, maybe Gina had tried to warn him or help him before but she couldn't get through his stubborn head.

Jack punched the mattress again and again, dust motes circling in the dim light. His legs tingled from kneeling for so long. He unfolded them, stretching his feet in front of him. He sat on the cold floor with the walls pressing in on him.

Please, he repeated again in his mind. Jack struggled to breathe evenly as he prayed into the silence.

The swath of blue sky in front of her grew smaller as dark clouds encroached from either side. Emily loved autumn time in Idaho. Blue skies, bright sun, and a crisp breeze scattered leaves and dirt in the air. Gina loved autumn too. The desert sagebrush lining the freeway, robust in its natural climate looked less parched than usual. When she'd left Heyburn, the skies had promised a glorious fall day, but now an hour from Idaho Falls, she could see the storm brewing.

She rolled down her window and felt the cool rush of air prickle her skin. The electricity in the air was palpable. It had been storming the day Gina died. Maybe this was God's way of showing his displeasure that His angel in heaven was still afflicted by the evil actions of others. Wherever she was, Gina was sad. Emily could imagine her filling a rain cloud with her tears over her family, especially her miracle baby Easton.

Emily's mind spun with scenarios involving Janette and Easton. Each one made her feel more terrible about the situation. Once she arrived, Jack would want to hunt down Janette and he probably wouldn't want Emily to come along for safety reasons. That gave her motivation to wrack her brain to find her angle—the one that would convince him he couldn't go without her. Following Jack's instructions, she'd stopped by his house and picked up his phone in order to contact Danika. She'd also done her best to think of anything that would help them in their search. After driving for another twenty minutes, she thought of something that might help and she had made an important phone call.

She checked her cell phone. Still nothing from Danika. When Danika had found details about Janette's mental history, she'd widened her search to see if there were other details that might motivate the police to look deeper into the case. Emily told Danika of her suspicions and Danika thought she was brilliant. She had promised to call as soon as she could with the information. Almost thirty minutes later, the phone vibrated in her lap and Emily pushed the Bluetooth in her ear to answer.

"Hello?"

"It's Danika, and you were right."

"Thank goodness," Emily said.

"Janette's sister used to live just across the border near Glacier National Park. She has to be heading there for help; maybe someone she has a good connection with there. I'll let you relay the information to the cops. They could still charge me for something and I agree with Jack that it's not worth it at this point."

"I'll take care of it. But where is her sister now?"

"It looks like she's back east, in Maine, but I can't be sure," Danika said.

"Jack said they were tracing her cell phone, so maybe they're onto her by now."

"I doubt that she would be that stupid."

"What do you mean?"

"If she was smart enough to break Easton out of protective custody, she won't have her cell phone with her," Danika answered. "I bet she's planted it somewhere and they're following a dead end."

"Wow. I hadn't thought of that."

"I'm worried about what else we haven't thought of, but this is a good lead."

"Thanks for getting back to me so fast."

"Good work," Danika said. "Take care of Jack. He wasn't interested in me, but you seem more like his type."

"Oh—thanks," Emily said.

She ended the call and gripped the steering wheel. Blowing out a breath, she pushed down on the gas pedal. She was minutes away from reaching Jack, and with this information they could be on the right track to intercept Janette and save Easton. She whipped into the police station and ran toward the entrance, gripping the manila envelope with the test results that had come hours too late. She bypassed the grumpy receptionist and went straight to the first officer she saw.

"Officer Manning, I've brought the positive DNA test results." She shoved the envelope at him. "I'm hoping it will move things along to get Jack out."

Manning raised his eyebrows, and then opened the envelope. He pulled out the paper and squinted, then shook his head. "This is such a mess."

"But why? I thought this would help," Emily said.

"It will. I just was thinking it's too late."

"No, it's right on time. Please take me to Jack."

"The D.A. has already been informed and his paperwork should be done."

Emily held up her hand. "I know you guys can pull strings. Considering the evidence you're holding and the liabilities stacking up against this department, I suggest you pull them."

Manning's face hardened, and then he turned and strode

down the hall. Emily didn't wait for an invitation. She followed close at his heels. Manning rapped on a door with two fingers and then turned the knob.

"Lady's here demanding to see Jack. She brought the test results."

Emily leaned forward. "*Positive* test results." She made eye contact with Vincent. "I came to pick up Jack. Manning said things are in process, but something needs to be done now."

Vincent stood. "I'm surprised you could get away from so much painting, Ms. Gray."

Emily caught the veiled accusation. Vincent knew she was involved and that was fine as long as he would act to release Jack. She folded her arms. "There's never a good time to deal with emergencies, is there? Especially when it concerns a man who tried to save his son from a psycho and almost succeeded until the police got involved."

She wasn't winning points with the officers, but the information Danika had relayed to her was boiling under the surface. "Did you know Janette Baker was suicidal and did a stint at Blackfoot just before she took Easton from the scene of the accident? And that she's on medication for more than one problem?"

Vincent stiffened. "That information is classified, but yes we discovered that."

"Just a little too late, right?" Emily retorted.

"Look, let's not do this," Manning said. "Emotions are high. We'll bring Jack to room five and you can wait with him until the release order comes through. His lawyer is working with the D.A."

Emily lifted her chin. There wasn't much she could do, but at least she'd gotten her point across. "One more thing. I've done a lot of checking and found that Janette had a sister that lived just over the border in Canada. I think there's a good chance she's traveling in that direction."

"Well, her cell phone and credit card say otherwise," Vincent replied. "But we'll look into it."

"Thank you." Emily followed Manning past several more doors until he opened one on his right. "Wait here. I'll have Jack up within ten minutes."

It was excruciating waiting and watching the clock when each minute took Janette another mile closer to escape. Emily stared at the cheap table, her fingers tracing lines in the patterns of the fake wood grain. They would need a miracle to find Easton. She closed her eyes and began praying that they hadn't used too many miracles already.

CHAPTER THIRTY

THE CELL DOOR squeaked and woke Jack. He rubbed the side of his face where he'd fallen asleep leaning against the mattress.

"Are you doing okay?" Vincent asked as he entered the room.

"Yeah," Jack's voice sounded raspy and he coughed. His legs were stiff as he moved slowly to a sitting position on the cot. He looked up at Vincent and that's when he noticed the bag with Jack Bentley written on the side.

"Your girlfriend's a spitfire." Vincent handed Jack the bag which contained his clothes.

Jack tensed. "Emily?"

"That's her. Spent the last ten minutes chewing us up and down for not having you out of here already."

Jack smiled. He would've never described Emily as a spitfire. She was quiet, pensive even, always seemed to be mulling something over, thinking carefully before she acted. But then Jack remembered the stories Gina would tell of her best friend, how the two free-spirits roamed the campus of Idaho

State University looking for a challenge. Emily's divorce had taken a lot out of her; she'd even pulled away from Gina. It had surprised Gina and worried her, but she'd given Emily some space and time to sort things out. If Emily's fire was coming back that was definitely something to smile about.

"She's not my girlfriend—she's a close friend of our family."

"Whatever," Vincent shrugged. "She brought the DNA test results, which were positive."

"So does that speed things up then? You're letting me out, right?" Jack motioned to the clothes in the bag.

"A little. I'll have you dressed and ready to go so as soon as the paperwork goes through you can go home."

"Thank you."

Vincent leaned against the door. "That is where you should go—home. I know you want to look for Easton, but let us do our job. We found him once, we'll find him again."

Jack nodded and began unlacing his shoes. Vincent stood there for a moment as if waiting for Jack to agree verbally. Then he walked away. Jack listened to Vincent's footsteps echo down the hall. If he had any idea where to start looking, he would. Making promises to the police wasn't something he needed to be worried about.

His clothes were wrinkled, but it felt good to get out of the orange jumpsuit. Jack adjusted his watch and waited. Vincent had said that he'd probably be out by three. It was one-thirty. The cell felt cold and still, and even though Jack listened for Gina, she wasn't there.

Manning returned about twenty minutes later. "You can wait with Ms. Gray. I put in another call to the D.A. and faxed over the test results. They'll be calling me back in about ten minutes."

Jack walked in the room and he saw Emily's face brighten

when she scanned his clothes. She jumped up and gave him a hug.

"Are they letting you out now?"

"Probably in about ten minutes." Jack held her close. "Thanks for coming and bringing those results."

"I just wish it would have been sooner," Emily murmured. She stepped out of the embrace and they sat in a couple of metal folding chairs. Emily handed Jack his cell phone. "I'm glad you thought to have me bring this."

"Me, too. Thanks, Em. I really owe you," Jack said. "Vincent told me they have some good leads. He also told me you wanted to hurry things up."

Emily grimaced. "I think I offended Vincent and Manning, but I was so angry. They were trying to make it sound as if they have things under control when they don't even know what direction Janette is headed."

"No one does," Jack said.

"I think I do."

Jack leaned forward. "You do?"

"Danika has been helping me. I had a hunch and we followed through on it. Turns out Janette has a half-sister. She used to live just over the border in Canada. We couldn't locate her, but I think that's where Janette is headed."

"Do the police know this?"

"Yes, I had to write it all down on one of their reports, but they kept saying they had things under control." Emily shrugged. "I've already traced the main roads that she would take using Google maps. I searched the back roads too."

"Wait a minute," Jack grabbed Emily's hand. "Are you saying that you're planning on helping me find Easton?"

"I'm saying that if they weren't going to let you out, I was ready to start looking on my own."

"Vincent was right. You are a spit-fire."

"Huh?"

Jack laughed. "Never mind. Let's wait to talk about our plans until I'm out of here. Vincent pretty much warned me off going to look for Easton. I think he figures I've been enough trouble."

Manning opened the door. "The order just came through. You're free to go. I'll take you through."

Jack followed with Emily close behind. He had to keep reminding himself not to hold his breath. It suddenly seemed too good to be true that things were shifting in his favor.

"I'm sorry about all this," Vincent said as he fell into step with them in the main hallway. "I want you to know that we have the Feds working this case with us and we're putting everything we can into finding Easton and Janette."

Jack nodded. "Let's just hope that someone sees her. Did you get a hold of Jason?"

"Not yet, but I've left messages." Vincent clapped him on the back. "I'll call you if I hear anything."

"Thanks," Jack said. "I'll expect a call soon."

Emily didn't say anything more until they were both in the car. "Are you hungry? I thought we could grab something on the way out of town. You in the mood for anything?"

"I'm starving," Jack said. "Anything will do."

As she pulled out of the station, Jack saw her looking behind at the cop cars lined up.

"Don't worry. They can't arrest us for looking for Easton. We're not doing anything illegal."

"Yet," Emily said.

Jack raised his eyebrows. "Well, I guess you'd better fill me in on your plan."

Emily smiled. "I'll let you know when I figure the rest of it out. In the meantime I have supplies in the trunk—food, water, a change of clothes from your house. I even grabbed your tennis shoes."

"You weren't kidding when you said you were prepared." Jack leaned forward as they pulled into the Wendy's parking lot. "Do you mind if we just eat while we drive? I don't want to waste any more time."

"I think that's the best idea anyway. Some people might still think you're a wanted man," Emily said.

They ordered hamburgers from the Wendy's drive-thru with a large order of fries and a Frosty. Jack leaned back into the seat; it felt like his body was one big coil of stress. For this moment, he decided to concentrate on his food and try to release some of the tension he was carrying.

After Emily pulled back onto the highway, she scooped up a heap of the chocolate ice cream and flipped the spoon over just before she put it in her mouth. She used her knee to keep the steering wheel straight as she scooped up another bite.

"Gina used to eat her ice cream that same way," Jack said.

Emily smiled. "We both did. We used to make midnight Frosty runs." She swallowed. "It doesn't taste the same without Gina."

"I know what you mean. My pastor told me that I have to search and find the new normal in my life. Not forgetting Gina, but moving to a new place where everything doesn't hurt so much."

Emily nodded. "I've struggled with so many memories, but that's what I'm trying to tell myself—that's it's okay to remember the good times without the hurt. Gina wouldn't want me to be sad."

"It's nice talking to someone who really understands," Jack said. He took a bite of his hamburger and chewed slowly. "Lots of guys just tell me it's something I'll have to step back from, heal, and move on."

"People just don't know what to say."

"But you do," Jack said.

"Sometimes." Emily smiled. "Jump onto the maps app on my cell and pull up the searches I did to help us find Janette."

Jack tapped on her phone until he found a saved location labeled *Janette*.

"Janette's sister lived near Vancouver in British Columbia, so she'll be heading to Washington. But I don't think she'll be taking the I-90. She couldn't get on the freeway outside of Idaho Falls, so Danika and I figured she would have taken one of the old highways across the state and she'll jump on the I-84 around Boise." "If we take Highway 20 now, I think we can cut off over an hour of her lead time."

Jack traced the lines of freeway with his finger. "You've put a lot of thought into this."

"But?" Emily turned her head so she could look in his eyes.

"I'm just worried if we set out after her, do we really expect that we can find her and get Easton?"

Emily took a fry and swirled it in her Frosty. "There must be something that we're missing. She can't drive all night, but she wouldn't want to stay in a motel—too obvious."

"Maybe Danika can help us," Jack said.

"She told me she'd keep looking and she'd let us know if she found something," Emily replied.

"Do you want me to drive for a while?" Jack asked.

"Why don't you close your eyes for a few minutes? We can trade in a couple hours."

Jack nodded. He was tired, but he wasn't sure if he'd be able to sleep with all the nervous energy coursing through his body. He closed his eyes, determined to try so that they could keep driving through the night. Images of Easton, Gina, and

Janette clouded his mind, but finally he felt sleep overtake him.

Jack saw a cabin as if he were approaching by car. He was dreaming, but it didn't feel like a dream. He felt like he was on the edge of consciousness, but he needed to pay attention to the dream before he woke up. Two enormous blue spruce trees flanked the entrance way as he came around a bend in the road. He saw a little sign out front that said 'For Sale' with an arrow that pointed down a lane. He stopped by the mailbox on the side of the road. The name was Charlesworth, though it was missing the 'R' and the 'T' letters, Jack could see where the stickers had peeled due to the weather. He turned to look at the cabin for any type of a house number when he felt his focus being pulled toward the rent sign. A ten-digit phone number written in black marker stood out from the white background of the flimsy plastic sign. The number grew closer until it seemed as if he were standing right in front of the sign.

He heard a noise from behind him, almost like someone turning a key in a lock. Jack started to turn his head, but he couldn't. *Jack. Easton is here. Save him.* He recognized Gina's voice. The phone number loomed before him, and then he heard a door opening and shutting. Jack awoke with a start.

Jack sat upright, rubbing his forehead with his palm.

"Are you okay?" Emily studied him with a worried expression.

Jack looked from side to side until he saw a pen stashed between the seats. "I had a dream. The number. I need to remember the number."

Emily grabbed a small notebook and handed it to him. Jack took it and closed his eyes, remembering the sign with the number written in black. That phone number was important. The Idaho area code was easy to remember; he focused on the prefix and the last four numbers with all his concentration. Gripping the pen, he opened his eyes and wrote the number down, checking it with his memory and hoping that it was right. "I dreamed that Gina took me to a cabin and showed me this phone number on the sign. I think I should call the number and see where it is. Does that sound nuts?"

Emily smiled. "Nothing would surprise me at this point."

Jack grinned and punched the number into his cell phone. A realtor answered the call and Jack asked him about a cabin that might be for sale.

"The one in Mountain Home?" the man asked.

Jack's heart jumped into his throat. "I saw some pictures online but I'm away from my computer and I can't remember all the details. Are there two large spruce trees by the lane?"

"Yep, that'd be the one. Little lane goes down to the cabin with two bedrooms."

"Is it available for rent or only for sale?"

"Funny you should ask that. We just decided to rent it last week and we have a tenant that popped up out of nowhere. She'll only be staying a week though, if you're interested."

"I am," Jack could barely get the words out. "I'll be in the area and I'd love to drive by and take a look. Is it easy to find?"

"Easy enough, but let me give you a few pointers."

By the time Jack got off the phone, he had the address and directions to get to the cabin. Adrenaline was spiking his blood again and making it hard for him to sit still in the car. He grabbed Emily's hand. "The cabin is in Mountain Home. It'll be available for rent next week. He just got a tenant for the week."

"Do you think it's Janette?"

"It has to be her. I'll bet she's planning on staying there

until the search loses some steam. Then she'll continue on to her main destination, which is probably Canada."

Emily nibbled on her bottom lip. "Are you going to call Vincent and tell him?"

Jack looked down at his hands. He wasn't sure what to do. Vincent had told him to go home. Jack had no proof that Janette was hiding in the cabin in Mountain Home. "I can't really explain to Vincent that my dead wife told me where Easton is."

"Then don't tell him that. Tell him you hired a P.I. and you got some good intel on a location."

"How about this? Let's head for Mountain Home. We got Easton once on our own, we can do it again. I'll call the police when we're close."

"I don't know," Emily replied. "Isn't it better to have more help at least on the way?"

"After what happened, I can't take the chance that someone will mess this up again." Jack pulled up a map on his phone, squinting at the lines crisscrossing the terrain near Boise that led to Mountain Home. "Since we're this far, it's best to head for Mountain Home. We'll jump off the freeway there. There's a highway that goes right into Mountain Home. The man gave me directions to the cabin."

Emily covered her mouth and Jack could hear the shaky breath she sucked in through her nose.

"Em, it's gonna be okay."

She dropped her hands. "I don't know. What if we mess this up? What if Janette has a gun?"

"I trust Gina. She told me to go and save Easton." Jack put his hand on Emily's arm. "I doubted her before and I was lucky that she kept coming back, but I think if I don't take this chance, it may be the last."

"It's like she's connected to Easton somehow."

"Or the Snake River."

"Huh?"

"I was just thinking how whenever Easton has been close to the river, Gina has contacted me. It might not be right, but I think her spirit's trapped there until she can find peace."

Emily shivered.

"Don't be scared," Jack said. "It sounds like some kind of weird ghost story, but here," he touched his chest, "it's right. I can feel how much she loves us. She's here to save Easton."

"And once you find Easton..." A question hung on the end of Emily's words as she trailed off.

"I think she'll finally be at rest."

"Then let's go and get Easton." Emily tapped the steering wheel.

Jack could see that she was getting tired so he offered to drive and they switched seats near Wendell. "We should be there in about two hours, depending on how slow-going the highway is into Mountain Home. Why don't you get some sleep?"

"Thanks. I think I will." Emily closed her eyes for a moment and then Jack felt her staring at him. "My heart keeps beating faster. I'm so nervous."

"Me, too. But I keep trying to tell myself that it won't help Easton if I'm a nervous wreck."

Emily chuckled. "You're right. I'll try to tell myself the same thing."

The night was dark with no moon, and the normally bright northern stars were covered with clouds. Jack had driven through a handful of raindrops, but the storm seemed to be hovering, threatening but not taking action yet. The highway into Mountain Home was quiet, and Jack squinted into the distance as he attempted to gauge the distance until the turnoff to the cabin.

His gut tightened when he thought of the possibility that he was wrong. He had placed full faith in Gina's guidance and the impressions he'd received from the dream. Clenching the steering wheel, he continued driving into the darkness.

Emily moved and stretched beside him and he heard her seat click back into the upright position.

"Feel better?"

"Some. How are you holding up?"

"I think my stomach is about to turn inside out. I had a bad thought a minute ago about what we'd do if Janette and Easton aren't at this cabin."

"She's there," Emily reached over and patted Jack's leg. "We're only about twenty minutes away now, right?"

"I guess it's time to call the cops. Will you dial for me?" Jack motioned to his cell phone sitting in the console. "It's in my call history."

Emily scrolled through as Jack placed his Bluetooth in his ear.

"This is Vincent. Jack, we don't have any new leads at this point, I'm sorry."

"Well I do have a lead and I want you to follow up on it as quickly as you can."

"I'm listening."

"There's a cabin that is for rent in Mountain Home. I think Janette took Easton there to hide out."

"And how did you come by this information?" Vincent's voice sounded tired.

"It's a tip I got from my P.I., but Vincent, I need you to trust me on this one. I wasn't wrong before."

Two beats of silence and then Vincent spoke, "Give me the info."

Jack relayed the phone number from memory and told Vincent the address. "If you call the guy and tell him you're the police, he might give up info on who the renter is, but I bet she gave him a fake name."

"That's probably right," Vincent replied. "Jack?"

"Yes?"

"You're not heading there, are you?"

"Not at this moment, but I will be."

"Good. Stay put. I'll call over to their county sheriff and have him go and take a look."

"I don't think that's the best idea." Jack's blood pumped harder in his ears. "She'll just take off again. We don't know anything about her, except that she's crazy and willing to attack people to keep my son."

"Well, I can't call out the cavalry on some tip that has no backing."

Jack took a breath, forcing himself to sound calm. "Let me know what you find out."

"Will do."

Jack ended the call and cursed. "He said he'd send over a sheriff to check things out."

"Just like you thought," Emily said. "It's a good thing we have a plan."

It was after ten o'clock by the time they reached the heart of Mountain Home. It had taken longer than they'd hoped to get there, but the cloak of darkness would help now. Jack turned off the highway and headed down a quiet road. He switched off his lights as soon as he saw the lane that led to the cabin. Jack drove slowly, turning off the road and wincing as the gravel crunched under the tires. The cabin was exactly like the one he'd seen in the dream. Jack shivered and pulled the car sideways across the lane leading up to the cabin. If Janette tried to escape, she'd have to find an alternate way to the road. The lane was flanked by pines and bushes. Jack hoped that there wasn't a rear entrance he didn't know about.

"Don't shut the door," Jack told Emily as he switched off the interior lights. "See if you can push on it until it clicks into place, otherwise just leave it open." The forest was alive with the noises familiar to Jack from camping with his family. The crickets were raising a deafening chorus and as Jack took a couple steps away from the car, he hoped they would help cover his approach. Emily came up beside him and grasped his hand, her fingers trembling.

"We're going to have to move slowly and watch our step."

He saw a dull beam at his feet. Emily had switched on a flashlight, but she had it on a dim setting that just barely showed the road in front of them. She flicked it off.

"I brought it just in case. It might be a good idea to check the path."

Jack couldn't see the front of the cabin clearly from where he stood. "As long as you don't use it in view of the house, I think we'll be okay."

The light came back on and Emily made a broad sweep of the ground in front of them. Jack saw several roots tangled along the road. He squeezed Emily's hand. "Let's go. Remember, once we get close enough to the house, we'll split up. You find a back way in. I'll go through the front in case she has a weapon."

"I'm scared, Jack," Emily whispered.

"This is going to work," Jack said.

Emily squeezed his hand in return and they continued their slow approach to the cabin. Jack's ears were tuned to every sound, and to him it sounded like they were making an incredible amount of noise with the pine needles crackling underfoot and an occasional twig snapping. He tried to walk more on the balls of his feet, but he couldn't avoid the undergrowth scattered in front of him. He was banking on the element of surprise. If Janette was asleep and he could break into the house, it should all be over in a matter of minutes.

CHAPTER THIRTY-ONE

ANDREW HAD BEEN VERY fussy all evening and nothing Janette did seemed to console him. She rocked him and he'd fall asleep for a few minutes, then cry out and start thrashing again.

"I'm sorry, my sweet baby," she crooned to the child. "You're probably worried someone is going to take you away again. Nightmares, maybe?" she murmured half to herself. "Don't worry. No one will take you away from your mama again."

She sat in the dark of the front room with the window slightly ajar. Thousands of night noises competed with each other, the chirp of the crickets against the croaking of the frog. The noise soothed Janette though. After the adrenaline rush of escaping with Andrew, she had felt weak and exhausted. That was probably part of the reason he wasn't sleeping well. He'd taken a late nap with Janette right after they arrived at the cabin.

The clock on the stove in the kitchen glowed a bluish-green and Janette squinted to see the numbers: 10:37pm. She'd rock Andrew for a bit longer and see if he would settle down enough to sleep in the bed with her. She was just dozing off, her head lolling to the side, when Janette noticed something that brought her fully awake.

The crickets' symphony had decreased and though she could still hear the forest noises in the background, it was eerily quiet outside the front window. Janette's heart jumped in her chest as she sat up, careful not to disturb Andrew. Slowly, she rose to her feet and took a step nearer the window.

The night was cold, but that was to be expected for late fall in the mountains. She probably should have shut the window earlier. Andrew's blanket hung loosely around him, so she tucked in the edges and cradled him closer to her body. She stood, her ears tuned to the night noises and in her quiet space she heard the tune change yet again. Janette stood as close to the window as she could without touching it, holding Andrew tightly, and peered into the darkness. Something was out there.

Perhaps it was a deer, and in that case Janette was sure she wouldn't be able to spot it, but she continued scanning the yard anyway. Her shoulders started to ache from the tense position she held Andrew. Exhaling slowly, Janette relaxed her shoulders and took a step away from the window. At the same moment, she saw a flicker of light and her skin crawled with fear.

She inhaled sharply, her gasp amplified in the silence of the cabin. Not something. *Someone* was out there. She stepped back, biting her lip in fear. They had found her.

Even as her mind whirled through the impossibility, she moved to action. Andrew was finally asleep. Janette hoped that he would stay in a deep slumber so they could make their escape. She had prepared for the possibility of being found, but never did she really think that she'd need to escape in the dead of night. She eased Andrew into his car seat, holding her breath as she buckled him in. The baby remained asleep, and Janette tucked a blanket around him.

Her suitcase stood by the door and with frantic movements she grabbed the diaper bag and stuffed Andrew's toys inside. She grabbed the suitcase and diaper bag and hurried out to the car. She'd parked behind the cabin so that it would appear vacant to onlookers. Her heart rate spiked as she popped the trunk and tossed her luggage inside. She opened the back door and ran back inside to get Andrew.

Jack and Emily were about thirty yards from the house when he heard an interruption in the background noise. Emily froze, so she had heard it too.

"What was that?" she whispered.

Jack pressed on her hand and they both kept silent, straining for another sound. He looked toward the cabin, but it remained dark. A soft plop of moisture fell on Jack's face and he looked up at the sky, ominous and deep black. He felt two more drops and then a jagged burst of lightning streaked across the sky. His head snapped forward. He stared at the house and another bolt of lightning lit the sky. In the split-second illumination, he saw movement. Then he heard the sound of a car door shut seconds before thunder rumbled around the cabin.

"It's Janette! She must have seen us!" Jack cried. "We have to stop her." He took off running toward the cabin.

"Be careful," Emily called out. "She might have a gun."

He sprinted around the side of the cabin at the same time

he heard the engine start up on the car parked near the back door.

"Stop!" he screamed. But the car was already moving forward, just out of his reach. Janette gunned the engine and shot around the front of the house.

"No!" Jack yelled as he ran after the car.

Janette increased her speed as she drove up the lane and Jack saw her flick the headlights on bright.

"Emily, watch out," Jack hollered into the darkness. He kept running, anticipating the screeching brakes that were sure to come. When Janette stopped in front of their car that was blocking the lane, Jack would reach her and save Easton.

He put on another burst of speed, running over the uneven terrain. There was no time to look for tree roots or rocks; he kept his impact as low as possible, springing with each step toward Janette's car.

A high-pitched sound of screeching metal echoed through the night as lightning flashed through the sky again.

"No," Jack said. "Emily hurry!"

Janette had hit Emily's car. Jack rounded the bend and saw red taillights and for a second, he thought the impact had stopped Janette. But then he heard the roar of her engine and more screeching metal as Janette's vehicle pushed against Emily's car.

The tires spun out on the gravel and Jack reached the rear of the car. He saw the whites of Janette's eyes as she looked behind her.

"Stop!" Jack screamed. He pounded on the window and heard Janette cry out. The tires spun again. She was gunning the engine. The car seat was snapped into the back seat and Jack caught a glimpse of Easton. Jack leaned forward to pound on the window again, when suddenly the car jerked backwards.

Janette had put it in reverse and Jack barely missed getting run over as she spun out. He looked to where Emily was on the other side of the lane and saw her jump out of the way.

Jack held his hands up and took a step forward. Janette looked right at him, honked the horn, and put the car in drive.

He dove to the side just before her car plowed into the back end of Emily's pushing it aside. The pine tree branches scraped against Janette's car and Jack screamed as he collided with a sharp branch. The limb punctured his side with a sting that made his vision swirl. Sucking in a pain-filled breath, he struggled to stand and stumble after the taillights.

"No! No! Stop!" He felt like his heart had been slammed into a brick wall. His knees buckled and he fell to the ground. Warm fluid oozed down his side, blood from where the tree branch had punctured the skin on his back. "Please, God. Stop her," he whispered, the pain radiating down his leg.

Lightning flashed through the clouds, followed by a sharp crack of thunder. The rain came down in earnest, pelting Jack and turning the hard dirt into a wash of mud and pine needles. A siren overpowered the sound of the storm. Jack lifted his head, looking toward the road. He glanced at his watch—it had been over thirty minutes since he'd called Vincent. It had to be the county sheriff coming to check the cabin.

"Thank you," Jack cried, lifting his face heavenward. The rain cascaded down his face and Jack heard the siren recede into the distance. If he was giving chase to Janette, she wouldn't get away this time.

He turned to find Emily in the darkness and saw the interior light of her car. Emily sat in the driver seat and the engine turned over smoothly. Jack limped to the car as Emily began backing it out of the trees. She had the driver's side window down and was craning her neck to find the road.

"Em, I'll guide you out," he called.

She gave him a thumbs up and followed his hand signals. The rear end of the car on the passenger side was badly dented, but the tire wasn't damaged. Jack was impressed that Emily still had her wits about her enough to consider driving her wrecked car. She had to make a six-point turn to ease out of the pine trees and back onto the lane. Jack jumped in the car.

"I heard the siren. I thought we should try to go after her, just in case." Emily glanced over at him as she pulled onto the road. "Are you hurt?"

"I fell into the trees. It's not too bad." He winced as he put his seatbelt on.

"Doesn't sound good," Emily said.

Jack reached his hand inside his jacket and felt the warm, sticky substance of his blood. It wasn't gushing, so he took shallow breaths and tried to relax against the seat, wrapping his jacket tighter around his middle. Emily reached the main highway.

"Which way should I turn?"

"Left. I think she'd head for the freeway, but she won't get far if that cop calls in reinforcements."

"Maybe she'll pull over."

"No, she knows we're onto her," Jack answered. "What I can't figure out is how in the world she knew we were out there."

Emily shook her head. "It's freaky. Almost like she was up watching in case someone came."

"She got out of there fast. I thought for sure I could catch her."

"She's psycho. I can't believe she ran into my car. I hope Easton's okay."

"He was in his car seat. I saw him."

"Why didn't her air bags inflate?"

"She didn't hit your car with enough speed to activate them." Jack squinted through the windshield wipers' fast-paced pattern. "You're going to have to go faster. I'll call Vincent and let him know what's happening."

"He's going to be ticked."

"I don't care." Jack held his phone up to his ear, listening to it ring, repeating a silent prayer for Easton.

CHAPTER THIRTY-TWO

WHEN JANETTE PULLED out onto the highway, she smiled. "See, I told you I'd keep you safe," she said to Andrew. He cried out in the back seat, the jarring impact when she'd ran into the car had awoken him, but Janette hoped that the motion of the smooth freeway driving soon to come would lull him back to sleep.

It had been Jack Bentley, she was sure of that, but how did he find her? The man just didn't know when to quit. Maybe God would strike him with one of the lightning bolts shooting across the sky. Andrew was *her* son.

Her heart pounded in her neck and she reminded herself that she needed to calm down. She reached into her purse to grab her meds, and swerved to the right. She jerked the steering wheel back and continued feeling with her hand for the pill bottle. Blue lights flashed behind her and Janette cried out, "No!" She looked in her rearview mirror and saw the cop car gaining on her, lights flashing blue, then red. She almost blacked out from the panic, but shook her head violently and jammed her foot on the gas pedal. The highway would meet up with the freeway in less than five miles. If she could just keep ahead of him, maybe she could still escape.

"Sorry, Andrew. Mommy has to drive really fast." She gripped the steering wheel with both hands, the pill bottle forgotten in the bottom of her purse. Fear for Andrew eclipsed every other emotion. She had to be careful so he wouldn't be hurt, but she couldn't let the police catch up with her. Leaning forward, she pressed the gas pedal to the floor and watched as the speedometer ticked up to one hundred miles per hour. Her dashboard shook and something clattered inside, probably from the impact with the other car.

The highway was deserted, but the rain pouring down made the high-speed chase akin to suicide. For a moment, Janette considered pulling over and trying to explain to the officer that someone wanted to kidnap her baby. But Jack Bentley probably wasn't far behind the police. He was probably calling in favors from Officer Juarez and Officer Manning. No one would believe her. The only choice was to run—drive as fast as possible. She covered the five miles quickly and skidded under the bridge.

The rain started to let up, and her windshield wipers didn't have to click at top speed anymore. The police car was still right behind her, its sirens blaring. Andrew wailed from the back seat and Janette couldn't do anything to comfort him. All of her energy had to be focused on the wet blackness of the road. The highway began to curve to the north. Janette knew she should slow down, but if she did the police car might try to force her off the road. It would only be a matter of time before his reinforcements joined in the chase.

She decided the safest route would be to stay on the highway. Uncertain as to where it led, Janette kept driving, looking for options to escape. Lightning flashed across the sky and then plummeted down toward its target and Janette gasped.

She was driving alongside the Snake River. Shaking off the fear, she reminded herself that the river had always been on her side; it had brought Andrew and her together. God had saved her by the river—had given her another chance at life.

The lightning came in vibrant bursts, illuminating the massive body of water. Thunder boomed around her. Janette eased her foot off the gas pedal as she rounded a sharp curve going nearly one hundred miles per hour. She looked forward and saw a bridge. Lightning flashed again and Janette screamed. A woman stood in the middle of the road, her yellow blouse like a warning, the rain drenching her tan capris. The woman's black hair whipped around her face. Janette slammed on her brakes and honked, but the woman didn't move. Her eyes seemed to pierce Janette's soul. Janette jerked the car to the left to avoid the woman. The tires squealed and Janette felt the car lose control. She kept pumping the brakes, but the car went over the embankment and crashed into a tree.

The airbags deployed and Janette felt the rush of wind before the impact knocked her unconscious.

CHAPTER THIRTY-THREE

"I DON'T KNOW if I should drive any faster. We might hydroplane," Emily said.

Jack grunted. "Yeah, don't go over seventy-five. We'll catch up to them when she goes through Grandview." They'd been driving for twenty minutes already though, and he couldn't see another vehicle. He rolled down his window and heard the faint sound of the siren. "We must be heading in the right direction."

"That siren means he's still chasing her though," Emily replied. "I hope she doesn't do something dangerous." She tightened her grip on the steering wheel and continued driving. They saw a sign indicating that the little town of Grandview was ahead. Two miles later, she straightened and pointed out the window. "I can see the cop car."

Jack recognized the blue and red flashing lights in front of them. The rain blurred the surroundings and it was still too dark to see anything but taillights as they approached.

"Just pull up behind the police cruiser," Jack said. "I can't see Janette's car."

"Jack, the river." Emily pulled off the side of the road and they both jumped from the car. Jack could hear shouting as he ran toward the river. Janette's car hung off the edge of the road precariously, dangling above the river. Panic overtook his senses as he struggled to climb over sagebrush.

"Sir, you need to stay back," a police officer called from beside Janette's car. "This car could go over any second."

"My son is in the backseat!" Jack screamed. He pushed his way closer to the car, ignoring the officer. Metal screeched and the car slid downward a few more feet onto the river-bank. Part of the car edged into the river. "No!"

The police officer had climbed down into the water and was using a Slim Jim to break into the driver's side door. He popped the door open just as Jack reached the back door.

"You can't take my baby," Janette screamed.

She launched herself from the car at the police officer. He toppled back into the water, surprised by her sudden move-ments. The interior light from the car gave off enough light that Jack could see blood on the side of her face and head. She scrambled over the police officer and headed for Jack. The car slid a few more feet down the steep embankment and into the water. Easton's screams were like nothing Jack had ever heard. His baby was reliving a nightmare. Jack opened the door and started to reach inside.

"Get away from my baby," Janette screamed and clawed at his back.

Jack turned and punched Janette, aiming at the injury on her head. He'd never hit a woman, but he hardly considered her human. His fist connected with her skull with a sickening jolt. She cried out and fell back into the water.

"Easton is my son and if you don't stop, this car is going to go under and he'll die," Jack yelled at Janette.

He leaned into the back seat and grabbed the car seat,

pushing in the red locking mechanism to release it from the base. Easton's eyes widened and he continued crying as Jack pulled him from the car. The water was up past Jack's knees and the swift current tugged at him. He looked back and saw the police officer struggling to stand, holding his head. Emily had her arm around him, helping him out of the water. The bank was littered with large boulders; he must have hit his head in the scuffle with Janette.

Jack lifted the car seat higher and tested his footing as he waded back through the water. He could hear Janette coughing and spluttering behind him. The riverbank was only about ten yards away. Emily helped the officer to the ground and then turned toward Jack.

"It's okay, buddy," Jack tried to make his voice sound soothing as he gripped the car seat. Easton continued to wail.

"Jack, watch out!" Emily screamed.

Jack turned as Janette grabbed for the car seat, stumbling through the water. "Andrew is my son. Give him to me!" she screamed. She grabbed Jack's hair and yanked his head back. He brought his right arm back with a snap and felt his elbow hit her squarely in the neck. She released her grip.

The river bottom was mossy and slick, Jack's feet slid out from under him as he dodged Janette's attacks. He fell to his knees, reaching out with his left hand to try to brace himself. His head went under the water and he came up coughing. The edge of the car seat dipped into the icy water, but Jack maintained a tight grip on the handle. If he couldn't get away from Janette, she'd end up drowning Easton. The sound of thrashing in the water surrounded him. He dug his feet into the mud and pushed himself back up to a standing position.

There was a huge splash and Emily's dark form passed him.

"You're crazy!" Emily screamed. She dove for Janette and both of the women went underwater.

Jack sloshed forward and stumbled over the rocks with Easton to find a patch of dry weeds to set the car seat on. His heart hammered against his rib cage as he gripped the car seat and looked toward the river where Emily had diverted Janette's attention. As Jack approached, the police officer rose. "Help is on the way...you should—" the policeman slumped to the ground, holding his head. Jack noted the blood running down the side of the officer's neck.

Jack heard the shrieking of twisted metal and turned around. The river washed over Janette's car pulling it sideways. Emily and Janette were still in the water. It looked like Emily was struggling to put distance between her and the psychotic woman, reaching for the shore. Janette screamed and thrashed in the water, pushing Emily's head under.

Jack held Easton and looked to the river, then back to the police officer. His gut twisted. He didn't want to leave Easton, but he couldn't stand by and watch Emily drown. He carefully sat the car seat next to the police officer. "It's going to be okay, buddy. I promise."

He'd already lost one woman he loved to this river, and he couldn't bear to think of losing Emily. A siren blasted through the noise of the river and Jack saw an ambulance approaching. Sucking in a breath, Jack took several steps toward the dark forms of the two women.

"Stop! Get off me!" Emily screamed.

Jack plunged into the river. He resurfaced, gasping for air as the frigid waters attacked every nerve. He kicked forward with a crawl stroke until he was right next to Emily. He saw the problem. Janette had a handful of Emily's hair and was trying to drag her under the water. Emily spluttered and kicked, her arms flailing as she tried to loosen Janette's grip.

Jack swam against the current and grabbed Janette's arm. He twisted it until she cried out and let go of Emily's hair. He released her arm and she went under the water.

"Em, swim back and stay with Easton." Jack yelled as he struggled to keep his head above water. Janette was frantic and she would drown if Jack didn't try to help her. The water temperature was probably only sixty degrees. His body shook as his core temperature dropped. For a moment, he wavered, thinking that he would let Janette fend for herself. He watched her resurface and begin kicking toward the east side of the river.

"Janette," Jack called. "You won't make it across. You've been in the water too long."

She didn't respond and as he began swimming toward her, he lost sight of her. He paused and treaded water for a minute, which was futile because the force of the current was too strong. His energy was nearly spent. He couldn't see Janette in the darkness and he wasn't going to risk his life for a kidnapper who had just attempted to drown Emily.

He sucked in a breath, readying himself to swim toward the shore when he heard a splash and felt his head jerk back as arms encircled his neck. The water covered his head and Janette pushed to hold him under. He felt a moment of panic, but reminded himself that he had plenty of air. The cold water was his biggest enemy. His mind slowed. In order to save himself, he would have to do the opposite of what Janette expected. So with a burst of adrenaline, he used the momentum of her pushing force and let himself be carried downward with the current.

Jack touched bottom and kicked off hard, jolting her in the process. As he broke the surface, he turned and grabbed hold of Janette's hair with both of his hands. She screamed and released her stranglehold. Before she could grab hold of him again, Jack dove and grabbed Janette's legs, kicking hard with the current. If he could pull her close enough to the shoreline, she might have a chance of surviving. They were in the middle of the river and because of the mountain terrain, this part of the river would probably have shallow parts and rapids frothing through jagged boulders.

He had no idea how the course of the river ran in this part of the mountains; it was incredible that he hadn't smacked up against a rock already. It was time to get out of the water. Janette kicked and struggled against his hold. His arm burned as he clenched her legs. She thrashed and he could hear her cough behind him. Her head was still above water, but he couldn't hold on much longer. Then one of her shoes slipped free, releasing her foot at the same time. She kicked him hard in the side and he let her go. He saw stars as the pain from his previous injury coupled with her kick overtook him. Jack sucked in another breath and pushed away from Janette. He didn't look back; instead he swam as hard as he could with the current toward the river's edge.

The Snake River was as powerful as any time he remembered swimming in his youth. The cold water and unrelenting current pushed him forward as he dug in with arching strokes pulling himself to the shore, the pain in his side screaming with every stroke. His knee knocked against a rock, the pain shooting through the numbness of his leg. Pulling himself up, he stumbled over the smooth rocks toward the shore. It was still raining and the bank of the river was slippery. His feet stuck in the mud, but he kept pushing forward away from the water and into the underbrush.

He collapsed next to a gnarled sagebrush and took huge gulps of air, wondering how much of the river he'd swallowed. More sirens pierced the dark night and Jack turned his head to see the flashing of blue and red through the sheet of rain.

Pushing himself upright, he looked out toward the river, squinting. Visibility was so poor he couldn't hope to locate Janette. He had tried to save her and almost drowned himself.

The cold felt as if it had layered his bones with ice. His joints felt stiff and painful as needles of pain perforated the numbing chill. Droplets of rain mixed with the river water dripping from his hair into his eyes. He tugged at his wet jacket, peeling off the heavy layer. A searing pain raked up his side. Wincing, he touched his side and felt warmth among the wet. His wound still bled and he wondered how much blood he'd lost or what kind of infection he might get from the dirty river.

The rock next to him provided support as he stood and looked upriver toward the wreckage and flashing lights. The river had carried him at least a quarter of a mile. He needed to get back to Easton and Emily, but the thought of trekking along the riverbank seemed impossible. Through the darkness and the cold rain, he could hear someone calling.

"Over here," Jack yelled. "I need help over here."

The flashlight's beam bounced through the trees until it settled on Jack and he held his hand up against the glare.

"Is my baby okay?"

"Yes, sir. He's just fine. They were drying him off and getting him warmed up. We hoped to find you before they took him to the hospital. The lady said you would freak otherwise."

Jack smiled. Thank goodness for Emily. The officer handed him a wool blanket and Jack draped it over his shoulders. "There's a woman. She's still in the river." His teeth chattered as he spoke.

"Yes, we're doing our best to locate her," the officer replied. "Can you walk?"

"I think so. I have a cut on my side. It's been bleeding, but I don't think it's too bad."

"Let's have a look." The officer knelt beside him and shined the light on Jack who motioned to his side.

"Hmm, it looks messy. Let's get you to the road. The ambulance can pick you up."

Jack nodded and the officer radioed to the paramedics to meet him. He helped Jack up, and they hobbled through the underbrush. Thoughts of Easton and Emily helped Jack focus on putting one foot in front of the other as his teeth chattered and his side ached. He wondered about Gina—did she know that Easton was safe now? He wasn't certain about their connection but she had always seemed to know in the past where Easton was and if he was in danger. Jack felt a sudden desire to have her near, to feel her spirit again and the love that flowed from her when she shared her memories. The pain in his side was eclipsed by the aching scars over his heart. Gina was gone—he had almost come to terms with that when he first saw her standing by the Snake River.

For the past few weeks, it almost seemed as if she was part of his life again. The times were fleeting and it wasn't like he'd had a full conversation with her, but Gina had been there. It hurt to think that she might be gone again. The rational side of him reasoned that now Easton was safe, Gina would travel to that other sphere where spirits were supposed to rest in peace. But the selfish side of him wanted her near, hoped that he'd have a chance to feel her presence again. His mind suddenly filled with images of Emily—laughing, crying, smiling, and holding Easton on the couch in his home.

Jack shook his head, but he could clearly see Emily in his mind because she was a part of his life now. He did love her, not like he loved Gina, but as he trudged forward he knew why Gina had communicated with Emily too. His sweet wife, ever unselfish, wanted them to be happy. Jack remembered something his pastor had told him, "The heart's capacity to love is unmeasured. You will always love Gina and that is right and good, but it is also good to share your love with another. Don't feel guilt when your heart is ready to love another good woman. Gina will never be replaced. Love can't be replaced; it can only be added to."

The brush was thick in parts and Jack leaned against the officer to keep from stumbling. He saw the ambulance lights just before he heard someone call his name.

"Jack!" Emily cried and ran toward him.

He heard the crunching of leaves underfoot and the silence of the river behind them. When Emily saw how he leaned against the officer, she stopped.

"You're hurt."

He continued stumbling forward and saw a dark line of scratches across her face swathed in the garish emergency lights. Her right arm was bandaged and she held it still by her side.

"It looks like you are too."

She put a hand to her cheek and shook her head. "It doesn't matter. Easton's safe. He's okay now. Come and see."

She held out her hand and Jack took it. Ignoring the pain in his side, he increased his pace toward the ambulance doors. Just inside the doors, a young paramedic, held Easton. The baby was wrapped snug in a blanket and his face was peaceful, his eyes half-closed.

Jack looked at Emily and stepped forward, pulling her into an embrace. He held her and felt his body trembling as the tears fell like rain.

They rode to the hospital where Jack was treated for shock and received seventeen stitches for the gash on his side. Emily had long scratches on her arms and face from Janette trying to drown her, but otherwise she had escaped without injury. Easton was perfect. He gulped down a bottle and some crackers that one of the nurses helped to feed him.

Jack held his son and looked into his blue eyes. He saw some of Gina and he hugged Easton tighter. "I won't ever let you go," he whispered. "And I won't let you forget how much your mommy loves you."

CHAPTER THIRTY-FOUR

SEARCH AND RESCUE found Janette the next day. Her foot was caught up in a tree root near the riverbank about two miles downstream. They figured she had drowned and the current had pushed her forward until she got tangled in the roots.

It was a relief. Jack could admit that much to himself as he stood on his back patio next to Emily. Hallie and Easton played in a pile of leaves under the maple tree happily unaware of all that had happened in the past few days. Janette had attacked the police officer, Emily, and Jack. She had also attacked the woman at Social Services when she'd kidnapped Easton. So many people had been hurt by Janette. But even without all that, she deserved to die for stealing Easton while his own mother succumbed to a watery grave. When Jack told Emily that, she shook her head.

"It's a strange sort of justice and it's awful to say, but at least we know we're safe from her." Emily looped her arms through his and leaned against him. "It will be hard, but I want to forgive her—I think we both should so that we can let her go."

Jack swallowed back his first response—how could he ever forgive Janette? But then he watched Easton smile and try to put a leaf in his mouth. He had his son again. Jack breathed out and nodded. "Janette did save Easton. I don't think she could have saved Gina—the way her leg was trapped inside the car, but she didn't try either." Jack stared out at the horizon. "At least I have my son again; for that I did try to save Janette." His fingers grazed the scratches on Emily's cheek. "But I don't want to think about her anymore. I'm ready to get on with my life, with my family."

Emily smiled. "Me too."

Jack hugged Emily, feeling more alive than he had in months. He took her hand and they joined Hallie and Easton in the leaves, giggling, and breathing in the crisp fall air. There was peace, but Jack still searched for a sense of Gina. He'd felt no impressions from her that day and he wondered if rescuing Easton signified the end of their communication. It was bittersweet, and Jack didn't know how to sort out his feelings. He was incredibly grateful to hold his son again, and at the same time he missed Gina with a renewed loss. And then there was Emily. He turned and caught her watching him with a concerned expression. He smiled and she reached out and caressed his cheek. The bond between them was growing stronger, and even though Jack hadn't said it yet, he loved Emily. He opened his mouth to test the words at the same time Hallie tossed a handful of leaves in his face.

They ended up in a leaf war with everyone laughing. Jack allowed himself to soak in the moment. His life was changing again and he welcomed the new days ahead.

Later that day his phone rang and Jack smiled when he saw Jason Edwards' name and number.

"Don't say it," Jack said instead of saying hello.

"What? I told you not to do anything crazy, so you went and kidnapped your own son." Jason chuckled.

"I told you not to say it," Jack repeated, but he laughed.

"You had me going there, but I'm so glad to hear that you're okay—that Easton's okay." Jason paused and his voice sounded lower when he continued, "I'm so sorry that I couldn't help you."

"Don't be sorry. If I had waited any longer, it would have been too late. The police found out that she was in the process of selling her home and moving out of state. Everything had to line up perfectly for me to find Easton." Jack thought of Gina—the truth was that she had guided him every step along the way. Without her help, Easton would be lost forever.

"Man, it's quite the story. I'm looking forward to taking some time off next summer so we can go boating. What do you say?"

"I think that sounds like a great idea," Jack said. "Let's keep life normal until then, okay?"

"Stay out of trouble and enjoy those kids," Jason said.

"I want to say the same thing for you, but I know that's not an option. You're a magnet for trouble."

Jason snorted. "It comes with the job. You sound happy, Jack. It's great to hear."

"Thank you. I am happy. I'll always miss Gina, but things feel better now." Jack didn't mention Emily, there would be plenty of time to talk about dating later. Maybe he'd get more intel on Jason's dating situation then. "Talk to you later."

Jack ended the call and smiled to himself. Life had changed, but there were more changes ahead and he was actually looking forward to them.

CHAPTER THIRTY-FIVE

EMILY STARED at the door until the grain of the wood blurred together. She lifted her hand to knock and still hesitated, taking another deep breath. She'd only been able to stay away from Jack for three days. It had been painful and he'd called her every day. Part of her wanted to believe that it would be okay to love him, to let him love her, but then she thought about what people would say and she felt nervous and uncertain.

Once they had returned home and Helen was able to reconnect with her grandson, Jack had invited Emily over for dinner. She declined saying that she had a lot of work to catch up on and still didn't feel very good. Jack's house had been swarming with reporters. When the story went national, he'd called Emily to tell her he was turning his phone off, but he still wanted her to come to dinner. She declined again, citing the problems that the press might cause when she showed up at his house. Jack said that didn't matter, and he called again the next day. He had asked her every day for the past three days.

She had tried to give Jack a little space to reconnect with Easton and Hallie together and to test the divide between them. But there hadn't been a divide. She'd felt the pull to him stronger than ever and because Gina had always looked out for her, Emily had accepted Jack's invitation for dinner that evening. But then her courage failed her again and doubts seeped in. What would Carrie think? She'd always been a good friend to her and Gina. Would she think that Gina's best friend had betrayed her trust so quickly?

Searching within herself, Emily pulled up the memories of that first dream she'd had—where Gina had visited her and told her what needed to be done.

"Help him find Easton and be a family again. Please."

And here she was, standing on Jack's step, studying his front door. She'd driven past the house to make sure the reporters were gone before circling the block and parking her car. Hopefully the news had had its fill of Gina's tragic death and the miraculous recovery of her son. Thinking about Gina brought a smile to Emily's face, even though it was bitter-sweet. The fire she carried within her couldn't be extinguished, even beyond the grave. Emily did love Jack and maybe he cared for her too, but her fears were that he might fold under the same kinds of pressure and accusation from friends and family that she was envisioning.

Find your courage, Emily, she whispered to herself. Then she remembered the catch-phrase Gina recited all through college. *Who cares what anyone else thinks? Be your bold self!*

Emily rolled her shoulders back and knocked on the door three times. She heard Hallie run through the front room and a second later her face smashed up against the window. Emily heard a squeal and smiled in spite of the anxiety twisting its way through her system.

The doorknob clicked and turned, and Emily faced Jack.

"Hi. Wow, you're pretty early for dinner, but we'll have you." He stepped aside to let her enter and Emily followed him inside.

"I want to finish Hallie's room—that's all," she murmured. Her heart felt heavy, like a river rock half submerged in the mossy undergrowth. Times were uncertain and she didn't want to pressure Jack, no matter how she felt.

Jack's brow furrowed. "What do you mean, that's all?" He took a step closer to her, placing his hands on her arms. "You've been avoiding me."

Emily started to shake her head, but stopped. "I know how hard it's been. We've both been under so much stress and now things have changed. You have Easton back. Your family can be together—but Gina is gone and you're still in pain."

"Em." He leaned forward. "It's okay—we're okay."

His words filled her heart with warmth and she took a deep breath, breaking free of the dark waters trying to cover her soul.

Jack looked into her eyes. "You're right. Everything has been crazy hard. I lost my wife, my best friend, and I'll always miss her, but there's something I should have said before now." He swallowed and Emily pressed her teeth into her bottom lip, waiting for him to say the words that would evaporate the last shred of courage she had gathered.

"Gina wants us to be together. I don't know how to explain it, but when I think about her and honoring her memory, I know she wouldn't want me to let something so good pass by. She loved being a mother. She wouldn't want her children to be raised without one. And she loved you. She always went on and on about what a good friend you were— the salt of the earth."

"Oh, Jack." Emily put her head on his chest as he embraced her. She felt him kiss the top of her head, and she smiled, soaking in the words. It would be okay. Her best friend had always looked out for her. Death hadn't stopped that. "Maybe it's too soon?"

"It's not too soon for you, Emily. You deserve happiness." He leaned toward her, cupping her face in his hands. A hundred emotions passed through her eyes just before he closed the distance between them. Her lips softened against his and she wrapped her arms around him, her fingers threading through his hair. He broke the kiss and their eyes met, then Emily smiled and he kissed her again, softly, his intent clear.

"I love you," Emily whispered.

"I love you, too."

Jack tilted his head and covered her mouth with his. She answered his kiss with all the emotion that pulsed through her as the worry and insecurity of her feelings for him melted away. He had said the words she needed to hear. It showed that he was aware of her yearning to be a mother. She had confided in Gina many times after her divorce how she felt like her life was a failure—that nothing would ever go right. Gina had told her, "You're a good person. Things aren't good right now, but one day you're going to wake up and look around and see that happiness you want. I know it will happen for you."

"It won't," Emily had argued. "Things never turn out right for me."

"Well, then. I'll just have to give God a hand."

They had both laughed at the time, but that was exactly what Gina had done. Emily leaned back and smiled at Jack.

"She made everything right," Emily whispered. "Just like she promised she would."

Jack nodded. "She did."

~

It took a full week to finish Hallie's room with all the other work Emily had to complete for clients. She had dinner every day with Jack, Hallie, and Easton and worked afterward on Hallie's room. Emily felt the importance of the project every time she walked through the door. The dreams Gina had put into it helped fuel her imagination as she extended her creative energy into the very walls of the room. Every brushstroke was to honor Gina and her love for her family and friends.

Easton took his first steps only ten days after Jack rescued him from Janette and the Snake River. Emily was there to see those steps because Easton walked back and forth between her and Jack with Hallie cheering on. The milestone brought feelings that couldn't be ignored, so she and Jack embraced them and talked about how excited Gina would have been to see her healthy baby boy growing and learning.

"It's so nice to be able to talk to you about Gina," Jack said later that night as they cuddled on the couch. "For so long, I felt like I couldn't speak of her. I could see it made people uncomfortable."

"I think it's because they don't want you to hurt more and they think talking about someone who died only reminds you of your loss and pain." Emily interlaced her fingers with his and leaned against his shoulder. "I understand now because I've been able to talk with you—how much it helps to talk about Gina, not avoid her."

"Exactly. It tears me up inside that she couldn't be here today to see Easton's first steps, but that doesn't mean I never want to talk about her again." Jack sighed. "It's been hardest on Gina's mom. Helen cries every time I say anything about Gina, but she told me it's because she sees such a great loss for our family having to go on without Gina. I just wish I could help Helen."

"You are helping her," Emily said. "She told me so when we drove to break you out of jail."

Jack chuckled and Emily felt him relax a bit more beside her.

"She told me that tending Hallie every once in a while had kept her going. And even though seeing you hurting was hard, it helped her too."

"Thanks for sharing that," Jack said.

"Thanks for listening to me," Emily answered. "And for loving me."

Jack turned his head and she could see the warmth in his eyes. "I do love you."

Emily arranged to finish the room on a Wednesday when Jack made his commute to Idaho Falls. He brought the kids home at seven when Emily had just folded up the last drop cloth. She closed the door and stood in the hallway.

She heard Jack come in through the garage and walk across the kitchen with Hallie in tow. Easton babbled to his daddy and Emily smiled as they came around the corner. Jack smiled when he saw her and lifted an eyebrow.

"It's finished," Emily whispered.

"She'll be so excited," Jack said. He leaned toward Emily and kissed her lightly. "It's nice having you here."

Emily barely had time to register the implications of what Jack had just said before Hallie bumped into him as she headed for her room.

"Emily, you're here! Is my room done?"

"It is. Would you like to see it?"

"Yes! Yes!" Hallie bounced in place.

"Put your hands over your eyes. No peeking."

She waited until Hallie's small hands were pressed tight against her face, and then she opened the door. Emily heard Jack's intake of breath as they walked into the room and the anticipation was practically buzzing off Hallie. Easton struggled to get down and Jack released him, holding onto his hand as they walked inside.

"Okay, you can uncover your eyes now," Emily said.

Hallie moved her hands and squealed. "My room! It's so pretty." She climbed onto her bed and reached up to touch the leaf hanging from the tree with a tiny silver chrysalis.

"That's a chrysalis." Emily pointed to the leaf. "Look over here and you'll see the caterpillar. It weaves a special cocoon around itself and then turns into a butterfly."

Hallie spotted the multi-colored butterfly soaring beneath the clouds and clapped her hands. "It's going to the rainbow."

The arch of the rainbow touched some of the clouds Jack had helped her paint. Emily smiled as she watched Hallie absorbing all the tiny details she'd included. Someday, she'd tell her about the golden halo on the edge of one of the clouds. Emily's eyes traced the swirl of cloud where she'd painted Gina's name. It was a bittersweet moment, one that had come full circle with so much more than Emily ever imagined. She thought back to that first day when she had called Jack and offered to finish painting Hallie's room. It had changed her life. That was Gina's gift to her. "You have quite a talent," Jack said. He put his arm around her and kissed her temple. "I'm so grateful you wanted to share it with us."

Emily covered his hand with hers. "Thanks for giving me the chance."

Easton toddled into the room carrying a stuffed kitty. He stopped and looked at Hallie bouncing on her bed. With a giggle, he plopped the kitty onto her bed and began pulling himself up.

"Uh-oh, looks like we have some monkeys jumping on the bed," Jack said in a sing-song voice. He released Emily and reached out for Hallie. She giggled and dodged out of his way. Easton followed, laughing. Jack pulled them both toward him and they collapsed on the bed squealing as Jack tickled them.

Emily watched them and felt as if her heart would burst. She looked around the room and back at the family she hoped to be adopted into. What a difference a few years made. Jack sat up and grabbed her hand, pulling her toward the pile of monkeys jumbled on the bed.

"It's nice to laugh again," he said.

Emily nodded and then laughed until she squealed while Jack and Hallie tickled her and Easton slobbered her with kisses.

CHAPTER 36~ EPILOGUE

JACK PUSHED Easton in the stroller through the cemetery while Hallie skipped alongside Emily. He'd only visited Gina's grave a couple times before. It had been too painful to stare at the concrete slab with death dates of his wife and son. Today would be different. The November chill seeped in through his coat and he tugged it tighter around him.

With Emily beside him, he felt stronger. Next week he would invite Helen to come along and he hoped soon after to ask Emily if she would be his wife. The thought sent a pulse of electricity through him and he wondered again at the miracles that had come to pass in his life over the past few months.

The ache for Gina had been replaced with an amazing gratitude for the gift she'd given him. Saving Easton had saved him from despair. There would always be some hurt, a part of his heart that would never fully heal from the loss of his wife, but Jack accepted that and let it be a part of him. Like a soldier with a limp, he could compensate and carry on, making life better for those around him.

His throat tightened as they approached the corner where Gina was buried. The stroller slowed in the grass as the thick green lawn grabbed at the tires. Easton kicked his feet happily and leaned over the front of the stroller, taking in his surroundings. Emily tugged on Hallie's hand and stopped walking, waiting for Jack to catch up.

"You ready?" she asked, and Jack could hear all the questions bundled into those two words. He nodded and pushed forward, toward the mottled gray headstone flanked by two circular holes for flowers. The pink roses in the bottom of the stroller filled his nose with their sweet scent as he pulled them from the cellophane and approached the grave.

He stood in front of the headstone and studied the words as he held the roses close to his chest. The headstone had been repaired. Easton's name and dates had been filled in and the granite was smoothed over. No longer would a bystander gasp at the tragedy of a mother and her son dying on the same day. The birth and death dates of Gina were there along with an extra inscription, Jack had ordered:

Gina Rasmussen Bentley
Loving Mother, Guardian Angel
Thank you for bringing back our son

Jack knelt and fitted the roses carefully in the holes on either side of the headstone. Emily poured water from the jug he'd stowed in the stroller and adjusted a few of the flowers. He stood, brushing off his pants and took a slow breath inward, reading the etchings on the granite again. The change marked the fork in the road his life had veered towards. Because of Gina, he had taken the path to the right and Emily stood next to him.

Emily squeezed his hand and rested her head on his shoulder. Jack looked at her and at his children close by her side. His eyes drifted to the headstone and then to the large ash tree just beyond the grave. He stiffened, his eyes straining in the grayish November light.

Gina stood next to the tree. She wore a white dress that shimmered in the sunlight. Her dark hair looked soft, draped over her shoulders and her face was so beautiful. She was radiant. The light in her blue eyes seemed to fill Jack with warmth. His focus sharpened and he felt his face crease in smiles. She smiled and Jack struggled not to blink, keeping his eyes on her.

Gina lifted her hand and blew a kiss toward Hallie and Easton, and then to him. She waved and with a smile walked behind the tree. For a moment, Jack wanted to run after her, to beg for one more chance to hold her in his arms, but she was gone. He focused on the love he felt in the circle of people around him. Gina was finally at peace. His arm tightened around Emily and he allowed the warmth of rightness to flow through him.

"Thank you, Gina," he whispered.

Emily looked up at him, smiled and then her gaze shifted to the headstone. She nodded and reached forward to pat Easton's head.

Easton wriggled in his stroller and babbled, "Mama, mama, mama."

Jack wasn't sure, but he thought his son was looking at the tree just before he turned and smiled at Emily.

THE END

SNEAK PEEK OF SILVER CASCADE
SECRETS

2014 RONE Award Winner for Best Romance Anthology of
the Year

Crown Heart for Excellence Awarded Book —IND'TALE
MAGAZINE
From the Amazon #1 Bestselling series in *New Release* for
Clean Romance

"Again!" a little girl squealed as she brushed leaves off her
pants.

I smiled and continued digging in the flower bed, planting
tulip bulbs. Silver maple trees lined the sidewalks of Silver
Cascade Park, where I worked five days a week as caretaker.
My nails were bad because I didn't like gloves, and I had
perpetual dirt stains on my knees, but it was my dream job.

I watched the girl sail into the pile of leaves and seconds
later run to a man screaming, "Again! Again!"

As I wondered if they were father and daughter, a woman
approached and hugged the girl. The man put his arm around

her in a side hug, and they talked for a few minutes before the woman left with the little girl.

Hmm, didn't seem like a divorced couple, but then my people-watching skills had proven that there was always more than meets the eye. The man sauntered down the sidewalk. I thought I heard him humming something. Carpenter jeans with a good fit were a weakness of mine, and his retreating form was straining my eyes, so I put some muscle back into the flower bed and grabbed another handful of tulip bulbs.

A few minutes later, a light wind picked up several leaves and sent them skittering across the sidewalk. The points of the maple leaves made a distinct sound, signaling that autumn had taken root in Boise, Idaho. I watched the leaves swirl and ignored thoughts of raking and leaf blowing.

I saw someone out of the corner of my eye and noticed that the man had come back and was on his hands and knees, searching through the grass. His carpenter jeans had a dark wash, which complimented his olive-toned skin. He appeared to be in his late twenties, maybe a few years older than my twenty-five years. I approached him, kicking a few leaves up as I walked.

"Not to ask the obvious, but did you lose something?"

He looked up. "Yeah, my keys."

"I'm Jillian Warren, Silver Cascade Park caretaker and finder of many sets of lost keys. Would you like some help?"

He stood and brushed his hands on his pants then held out his hand. "Travis Banner. I'd love some help, because it helps to have keys if you want to drive home."

With a laugh, I shook his hand then knelt in the grass and began combing through the leaves. I stole a few glances in his direction. With dark hair and stubble along his jawline, he reminded me of Hook on my favorite TV show, *Once Upon a*

Time, minus the sexy accent. "I saw you playing with that little girl. Is she your daughter?"

"My niece. I'm not married, but I like playing favorite uncle."

"It looked like you were definitely in the running."

Hook, or Travis, looked even better with that info, and I had to remind myself I was searching for keys, not a date.

"Four-year-olds are pretty easy to please." He nodded toward the flower bed I'd been digging in. "So do you like your job? The park is beautiful, by the way."

"Thanks. I do enjoy working here. I graduated in landscape architecture, and this seemed like a great stepping stone into the field. My grandma was a bit underwhelmed— not many bragging rights— but I really do like it more than I thought I would." I ducked my head, embarrassed at all the information I'd just given a stranger. Well, I knew his name, so he wasn't a complete stranger.

Travis met my gaze, picking up on my admission. "It's okay to love your job, even if it's different from what everyone else expects. I'm a diesel-engine mechanic. My white-collar dad definitely didn't approve of me donning the blue collar, but I love what I do and hope to have my own shop one day."

My hands stilled in the leaves, and I looked at Travis. He had dark-brown eyes unlike Hook, so surely he couldn't be an evil villain. "It's so nice to talk to someone who understands."

He paused, brushing a hand across the stubble on his chin. "I was thinking the same thing."

My heart felt jittery, and a rush of heat came to my cheeks. "Um, don't laugh, but I'm going to use my favorite trick to try to find your keys."

He raised his eyebrows. "I can't make any promises. I might laugh."

I shrugged. "Fair enough." Glancing behind me, I saw the remains of the leaf pile Travis had been tossing his niece into. The leaves crunched under my feet as I walked to the pile; I kicked some of the leaves then backed up a few paces. Travis was hot, so it was worth embarrassing myself to find his keys. I lay flat on my belly and squinted at the millions of blades of grass and crumbled leaves scattered in the distance. A few strands had come loose from the knot of hair I'd fixed earlier, so I tucked them behind my ear. I heard Travis chuckle but ignored him and continued using the Warren Secret Spy Method, angling my head so my view skimmed along the ground.

Leaves crunched beside me, and I looked over to see Travis mimicking my pose. He winked at me. "I know this trick. My brother and I used to do it to find stray marbles in the gravel."

"Most kids know it, but most adults have forgotten."

"Or maybe they have more pride than we do."

I giggled and rolled over in the leaves, moving to a different vantage point. The sun chose that moment to break through the mass of cumulus clouds scattered across the sky. The leaves turned from red to golden, and I caught a glint of metal about ten feet in front of me.

"Aha!" I shouted and jumped up, keeping my eyes trained on the sparkle I'd seen. When I picked them up, the keys jingled together. "Found 'em." I dangled the keys triumphantly as Travis approached.

"Thanks, Jillian." Travis held out his palm, and I dropped the keys into it. "You're amazing." His tone was light, but I chose to find a deeper meaning in his words.

"Glad to be of service."

"I really appreciate you helping me out." Travis pocketed his keys. "There's this great café a couple of blocks down.

They serve the best Mexican hot chocolate. Could I treat you to some?"

"I love The Sugar Cube. Let me just finish up with these bulbs."

"Ah, so you know the place. Let me help. I owe you big time." Travis followed me to the flower bed and plopped a tulip bulb into one of the holes I'd dug.

"Thanks." I examined his work with a nod. "I'm impressed you knew which way to plant the bulb. My brother doesn't know anything about flowers."

"I may be a bachelor, but my mother had a prized flower garden, and she taught me a few things." Travis pointed at my fingernails. "Her hands always looked like that in the fall— mine, too. She's been gone for almost ten years, but for a while, I had my own bulb garden in her honor."

I had started to curl my fingers inward at his attention, but the affection in his voice made me proud to show my work-worn hands. I patted the earth down around the new plantings. "Really? What was her favorite flower?"

"Daffodils. She must have had a dozen varieties. I always liked these little miniature ones she used to plant around the tulips." He got a faraway look in his eyes as he grabbed a handful of bulbs. "How about you?"

"Hyacinths. I'll be planting a pink variety tomorrow that I think smells a little like heaven."

As he reached for the last tulip bulb, his hand brushed mine. He liked the dirt under my fingernails. I almost laughed at the thought. Too many dates with business men, lawyers, and would-be doctors had me feeling ashamed of my chipped nails. Travis was different. We'd just had a conversation about varieties of flower bulbs. He was handsome and looking better by the minute.

We stood and brushed the dirt from our clothes. "Thanks

for the help. I usually don't work this late, but I got a little carried away with this flowerbed."

"I'm sure it'll be beautiful. I'm glad you were still here." His smile widened. "I have to say, I'm kind of glad I lost my keys."

The blush tinting my cheeks had me feeling like a school girl, so I hurriedly gathered my tools and tossed them in the back of the Gator— my golf cart on steroids. I loved driving it around the park.

"Can I give you a ride to The Sugar Cube?" he asked.

I looked at my dirt-smudged jeans and wrinkled my nose at the dark smear of mud on my t-shirt. "I'm kind of a mess."

"I think you look cute." He motioned to his right knee. "And look; I have a matching stain."

My resistance melted when he proudly showed off his grass stain. "Okay, let's go." I stowed my tools and followed Travis to his car.

*Continue reading *Silver Cascade Secrets* and find out more about the Silver Cascade Suspense series at www. rachellechristensen.com

ACKNOWLEDGMENTS

Thank you to the incredibly talented team of creatives who helped bring this book to life. Steven Novak's cover design is stellar. Thank you to Tyler H. for providing the cover photo and sharing your talents. My editor, Nancy Felt, helped me finesse the words to bring you this story. I am so grateful for all of my beta readers: Patrick and Necia Jolley, Cathy Jeppsen, Tim Jolley, Amy Koster, Nina Johns, Cami Checketts, and several other friends who read snippets of this story.

This story might have just stayed an idea if not for my wonderful mother, Andrea Jolley. She helped me brainstorm the entire novel while painting the top floor of our home several years ago.

A huge thanks to Dave Wolverton for excellent advice on pacing and key elements with my plot at one of his fantastic writing camps. I followed his advice and changed the title, as well as a few other details that made the story much stronger.

Every novel requires a lot of research, and this one was no exception. Thank you to a couple excellent police officers, Jeff McEwan and Jeremy Leonard, who did a wonderful job of fielding my questions. Thank you for your patience with me, for sharing your expertise, and for serving our country.

Thank you to Mick Austin for information on the high-tech potato cellars just down the road from my house. Steve and Barb Bodily gave me information and ideas on traveling to Idaho Falls and brought up excellent points that grounded fiction in reality.

I am so lucky to have such a brilliant circle of writing friends who inspire me every day. Thank you for giving me feedback, answering questions, and offering support. You know who you are.

A special thank you to my family—my children and stepchildren and my best friend and husband, Tyler—you are my deepest inspiration. Thank you for supporting me in this writing journey and for cheering me on.

I'm grateful to God for the blessings and talents He has given me, for opening so many doors when all I saw was a wall, for helping me climb higher, hold tighter, and keep working toward my dreams.

And thank you to each of my readers. I write because I love to read and nothing delights me more than to talk books with someone who loves words on a page as much as I do. Thank you!

ABOUT THE AUTHOR

Photo by Erin Summerill

Rachelle writes mystery/suspense, clean romance, and women's fiction. She is the mother of a large family and she solves the case of the missing shoe on a daily basis. She enjoys raising chickens, laughing with her family, and traveling with her husband. She graduated cum laude from Utah State University with a degree in psychology and a minor in music.

Rachelle is the award-winning author of over twenty books, including *The Soldier's Bride (a Kindle Scout Selection)*, the Rone award winner for mystery, *River Whispers, Diamond Rings*

Are Deadly Things, Hawaiian Masquerade, and *the Echo Ridge Romance series.* Her novella, "Silver Cascade Secrets," was included in the Rone Award–winning *Timeless Romance Anthology, Fall Collection.*

Join Rachelle's VIP mailing list to learn more about upcoming books and get your free book at www.rachellechristensen.com.

Free Book!

Thrills *for the* Heart

FOR A LIMITED TIME

Sign up for Rachelle's
VIP Mailing List
to get your *FREE* book.

★ ★ ★ ★ ★

Get started here:
www.rachellechristensen.com

www.ingramcontent.com/pod-product-compliance
Lightning Source LLC
Chambersburg PA
CBHW021001120726
47905CB00009B/2793